WHEN HE TAKES

A DARK MAFIA ROMANCE

FALLEN GOD

GABRIELLE SANDS

To everyone afraid to leave an old version of themselves behind: Do it. Reinvent yourself. You might discover you are more vast and complex than you ever imagined.

CHAPTER 1

"Midway upon the journey of our life,
I found myself within a forest dark,
For the straightforward pathway had been lost."

- The Divine Comedy, *Dante*

BLAKE

In the first few hours of December twenty-eighth, we pull into the far end of a parking lot outside a small Las Vegas chapel. It's the kind of place where people get hitched after they drink enough to think getting married to a stranger is a good idea.

The door to the chapel opens, and a couple comes tumbling out, the woman's fingers getting tangled in the man's hair as they exchange a vigorous kiss. She giggles and leans against a wall while he devours her neck. A few long seconds pass with them feeling each other up before they manage to pour themselves into a waiting cab. I watch them drive off, feeling more sober than I've ever been in my entire life.

We're next.

I'm about to start my year by marrying the man sitting beside to me. Not that I want to. Not that it's my choice.

"Blake. Listen to me," my kidnapper says. My captor.

Not Rowan Miller, the man I fell for, but Nero De Luca, the man I don't know.

"I'm going to step out of the car and come around to your side." His voice is low and steady. It infuriates me how he can sound so calm while he's destroying my life. "Don't run, and don't try to fight me."

At first, I tried to run each time we stopped at a red light, but I can't do that anymore. Not since Nero attached my wrist to the door handle with a zip tie.

But he'll have to cut the zip tie off to get me inside the chapel. Which means this will be my best chance to try again.

I look out the window, searching for anyone who might be able to help me.

I've never been to Vegas. As far as I can tell, we're nowhere near the famous strip with the hotels and casinos.

This area is desolate. Run-down. The only other business that's still open at this hour is the porn shop on the other side of the four-lane highway.

Euphoria Emporium. That might be my best bet.

"And if I do?" I ask while keeping my eyes on the shop.

"You'll get yourself hurt."

"You mean, *you'll* hurt me."

2

"I have no intention of hurting you, Blake."

My hands turn to fists in my lap. "But you will, if you have to."

Rowan Miller was a lie.

And this man? A liar.

I can't believe that before I found out who he really was, I was going to tell him I loved him.

In love with a criminal, just like my mom.

I spent my whole life determined to be nothing like her, and then I went and did it anyway. I fell for a man who's no better than my father.

Nero betrayed me, but I betrayed myself. *Again*. I was cautious, until I wasn't, and then I was so invested in proving Brett wrong about him, that I refused to acknowledge the signs that something was amiss.

How could I be so stupid? I just can't help it, can I?

"I know you're hurt and upset, but we have to do this," Nero says. "We don't have a choice."

"*You* have a choice. *You* can let me go."

"I can't. This is the only way I can keep you safe. I've already explained that to you."

"You haven't explained shit. You just said that if I'm your wife, I'll be protected. I don't understand what that means, Nero. Protected by who? Maybe if you want me to go along with your plan, you should start by telling me the full extent of it, instead of saying I'm better off not knowing."

Nero lets out a heavy sigh, his jaw clenched tight. "All right," he answers gruffly. "I'll tell you."

I look at him. He turns off the truck and darkness wraps around him like an old lover. Shadows dance across the tense expression on his face.

He's terrifying. How did I not see it earlier? How did I kiss those lips and not realize they belonged to a killer?

There's something wrong with me. There has to be.

His gaze lifts to meet mine, and my heart breaks all over again. When I stare into those hazel eyes, I still see a hint of the man I thought I loved.

I have to remind myself that Rowan was never real.

Why couldn't he have just stayed out of my life and let me leave Darkwater Hollow like I wanted to?

I wish I could go to sleep and wake up in a different reality, one where he never drove me home in the middle of a blizzard, never convinced me to fake date him, and never told me all those things that made me feel like I was special to him.

It was all a lie.

Nero drums his fingertips against the wheel, thinking, calculating. At least that's how it comes across, and it raises my guard. I asked for an explanation, but I'm hesitant to believe anything that comes out of his mouth.

"When we arrive in New York, I'll go and see my old boss, Rafaele. Once he knows I have a wife, he'll take you under his protection."

New York.

Nero De Luca's old playground. That's where he ran from so that he wouldn't be killed by a rival mob family.

I swallow past the tightness in my throat. "Why would he do that?"

"Because that's law. *Our* law. And despite what happened with me, Rafe won't break it."

He makes his old boss sound like someone noble, but these people are mobsters. How can I ever be safe if I'm surrounded by mobsters?

"And what about you?" I demand.

"What about me?"

"What will happen to you? Don't you also need protection?"

A muscle in his jaw ticks. Seconds pass, but he doesn't answer.

Dreads slithers through my veins. "You told me earlier that the other family, the Ferraros, wanted to kill you. That's why you pretended you were dead. So why would you go back to the city that you ran from? Won't they find you there?"

"Maybe they will."

"I don't understand." What am I missing here? It sounds like he's saying we're going to New York for my benefit, despite the risk to his own life.

"We can't outrun the men that are after me," Nero says quietly, his gaze on the chapel. "Not now that they know I'm still alive. They'll find us eventually, and then they'll kill us both. It's better for me to just give myself to them to do as they see fit. At least you'll be safe."

Yeah, right. I refuse to believe that. He is not capable of a sacrifice like that. Surely not for my sake. He wasn't even capable of letting me leave Darkwater because of his own selfish desires.

He's lying to me again. Whatever his real plan is, he's not telling it to me.

I've been numb for hours, but now that numbness is replaced with something that burns like gasoline.

"Just leave me here. I'll go to California and stay with Del."

He shakes his head. "The Iron Raptors will be looking for you too, and the first thing they'll do is check if you're staying with any of your friends or family."

My stomach drops. "You're saying... Are you saying I may have put Del in danger?"

"If you're not there, they won't do anything to her. But if you are, you'll bring them straight to her doorstep."

No. That can't be right.

Desperation and anger claw their way up my lungs. "I didn't kill those guys. *You* did."

He rakes his fingers through his hair. "I know, but that doesn't matter. They'll want us both dead."

"Won't they track us back to New York then?" I ask, searching for any flaw in his logic that could give me a way out of this nightmare.

"They might. But they won't do anything to you if they know you're protected by Rafaele Messero. The Messero family is far too powerful for the Iron Raptors to provoke."

I want to scream in frustration.

"We have to do this, Blake. Let's go." He reaches for me, but I jerk away, plastering myself to the door. I don't want him to touch me.

"Don't," I snap.

Something pained flashes inside his gaze. "I need to cut the zip tie. May I?"

I glare at him for a long moment and then give a terse nod. He leans over again and quickly snaps the tie with the tip of his pocketknife.

"If you don't come willingly, I will have to carry you inside," he warns.

"I'd like to see you try."

My weak attempt at bravado doesn't seem to affect him. "I could do it easily, and you know it."

As much as I hate to admit it, he's right. Physically, I don't stand a chance against Nero. I can't fight him off. I can't outrun him. The only thing I can do is beg him to let me go or try to reason with him, but I already tried both, and I'm still here.

I push a dirty strand of hair behind my ear. "The officiant won't marry us without my consent."

"The officiant will do whatever I tell him to do when he sees my gun."

The tiny balloon of hope I still had inside of me deflates.

With one last lingering look at me, he gets out of the truck. I track his movements as he walks around to my side and opens the door.

A cold desert wind blows in, whipping my hair against my face. My lips are cracked, and my skin is dry. The bruises Uncle Lyle left on me pulse with dull pain, but they're the least of my problems.

Nero offers me his hand to help me out of the truck. I ignore it.

My Converses land on the pavement with a dull thud, but my knees are so achy from sitting inside the car for all those hours, they buckle beneath me.

Nero catches me, wrapping his palms around my waist. "Careful."

I suck in a breath. He's standing close to me, his brow furrowed in concern, and when his gaze snags on the bruises on my face, it darkens.

"After we're done here, we'll stop by a Walgreens to get more ice. I want a doctor to take a look at you, but that'll have to wait until New York."

My attention is fully zoomed in on his touch. "Let go of me."

His lips press into a firm line. He drops his hands and glances away from me, his throat bobbing on a swallow.

There has to be another way. Another option. If I can just get whoever's working in that porn shop to call the cops, Nero will have to leave me behind and run. He can't risk getting caught. He'd go to prison for the rest of his life. The cops will protect me from the Iron Raptors. They have to.

This might be my last chance.

I knee him in the groin and run.

"*Fuck*," he huffs.

My shoes pound against the cement.

Faster, faster!

The neon sign above the shop is my beacon, and I race toward it, my breaths coming out in harsh puffs—

"Ungh!" I trip on a pothole and tumble to the ground. Pain explodes through my right knee.

I push myself up, my palms scraping against the rough pavement. My heart thunders in my chest as I try to scramble to my feet, but a strong hand grips my arm and yanks me up.

"Goddamn it, Blake. What was that?"

His face looms in front of me. Humiliation and despair prickle over my cheeks. He didn't even need to chase me. I barely made it twenty feet.

"Your knee's bleeding," he says roughly, angrily. "Why would you do that? What were you hoping to accomplish? Did you really think whoever's in that shop would be a match for me?"

"The police," I whisper.

He looks at me like I've lost my mind. "You were going to call the police?"

When I nod, he barks a humorless laugh. "You'd be signing your own death warrant. They'd ship you right back to Missouri and let the local PD handle the case. Do you think the Iron Raptors don't have at least a few of those cops in their pocket? You'd be dead within a week."

He doesn't seem to expect a response, which might be for the best, because I've got nothing. If even the cops can't help me, then...I guess I'm marrying him.

Nero pulls me back to the car, lifts me onto the passenger seat, and rummages inside the glove compartment for tissues.

I stare at the dark sky above him as he dabs at the scrape and will myself not to cry.

It turns out, Nero's right. The officiant does exactly what he's told, casting only a mildly concerned look at the bruises on my face and the tear in my jeans. There's no need for threats —Nero's tone inspires complete obedience. It's the tone of a man you'd be an idiot to defy.

It's the tone of a killer.

And of my new husband.

The cheap silver ring on my finger burns almost as much as my knee as we drive toward a Walgreens. In the parking lot, he leaves me alone inside the truck, secured with a zip tie again. He didn't need to bother. The hopelessness of my situation has finally sunk in. I have no documents, no money, no phone. I'm exhausted. My body is this close to giving out.

Nevada isn't far from California, and from here, I could probably hitchhike my way to Del, but I won't risk putting her on the Iron Raptors' radar. I won't be responsible for another person getting killed because of me.

A searing pain spreads through my chest.

Sam didn't need to die. He could have left through the back and saved himself when Uncle Lyle showed up at the house. He *should* have saved himself.

Instead, he fought. Fought to protect me, to buy me time, even though we both knew the odds were stacked against us. His bravery cost him his life, and the guilt I carry weighs heavier than any chain Nero could bind me with.

Maybe I should be angry at Sam—Sandro—for lying to me the entire time too. But there's no anger when I think of him. Only sorrow. The kind that leaves a permanent scar that won't ever fade.

The passenger door opens. Nero frees me from the door handle and drops two plastic bags at my feet. "Got us some food and water."

I take him in. He's tense, like a coiled spring. There are dark bags under his eyes. We drove straight from the motel where he found me to Vegas, stopping only twice to use the bathroom and get some food. I slept for a few hours here and there, but he's been up for at least two days.

I don't know how he's still functioning.

A tinge of concern for him appears in the back of my head, and it makes me so angry that I bite down on my tongue hard enough to make it bleed.

What is wrong with me? I shouldn't care if he lives or dies given what I know about him now.

And yet you do.

He takes a bottle of water out of one of the plastic bags. "Turn this way and scoot to the edge of your seat. I need to clean the scrape on your knee."

"Just give it to me. I can do it." I try to take the bottle, but he pulls it out of my reach.

"I'll do it," he says, his eyes glued to the wound.

"Why?" I demand.

His jaw tenses, and he won't look at me. "I'm going to get us a room for the night. We both need to get some sleep before we drive to New York."

The promise of a bed makes the fight go out of me, and I shift in my seat like he asked. He tips the bottle, pouring the water over the bloody scrape. I hiss at the sting.

He winces. "I'm sorry. I know it hurts. I'll be quick."

"Why are you still acting like you care? Your ruse is up. You don't need to pretend anymore."

He puts the water down, rips open an antiseptic wipe, and gently cleans the wound. "I never pretended to care about you," he says quietly.

Lies.

A tear slips down my cheek. All my life, I've been surrounded by liars. By people who have let me down.

I thought he was different.

But he's just like the rest.

CHAPTER 2

NERO

Blake and I cross into Arizona and pull up at a place called the Beaver Trail Motel. When you're running on fumes, even a dump with a name like that starts to look hospitable.

One glance at the map tells me what I already knew—we're in the middle of fucking nowhere, surrounded by nothing but miles of empty desert.

I'd prefer to keep pushing on to get to New York sooner rather than later, but I'm too damn exhausted to trust myself behind the wheel. The last thing I need is to have a car accident.

I've put Blake in enough danger as it is.

Her nostrils flare as I go through the routine of securing her wrist to the door handle. "Is this necessary? We're in the middle of nowhere."

She's right, but I'm not taking any chances after her last escape attempt.

"I'll be right back," I say.

She doesn't answer.

Guilt throbs inside my chest as I walk into the brightly lit reception area. I'm acting like I've got my shit together because I have to get Blake to safety, but I've never felt worse in my entire life.

I was so caught up in finding her and getting her away from Lyle that I didn't mentally prepare myself for what would happen afterward.

Maybe a part of me hoped she wouldn't turn her back on me once she found out who I was. That despite calling me by a new name, she'd still look at me and see the man she'd been dating for the last few weeks.

That was wishful thinking.

Did I really expect her to be okay with all the lies I told her? Did I really think she'd forgive me for starting that fire?

I can't blame her for wanting to get as far away from me as possible right now, but that just isn't an option.

We're tied together now. For life.

However short that might be given what's waiting for me.

I blow out a breath.

There's a selfishly possessive part of me that likes seeing that ring on her finger, but I know I'd like it a hell of a lot more if I hadn't had to force her into this.

Instead of tears of joy on her wedding day, she fought back tears of sorrow. She deserved to stand at the altar in a stunning dress, not in worn-out clothes with a bruise marring her cheek.

I stole that possibility from her. Just like I stole so many other things.

She's probably relieved to know our marriage has a rapidly approaching expiration date.

Maybe after the Ferraros take care of me, she'll find a way to be happy again.

The elderly receptionist at the check-in desk doesn't ask many questions before handing me a key. "Check-out is at eleven."

"Thanks." I grab the key and walk back out.

We can't stay here for long. Eight hours, and then we've got to be back on the road. I need to be back in New York before Gino decides to act on the information that I'm alive.

Worst-case scenario, he puts me on the Menu. That means every made man who wants to earn a quick buck would have an incentive to hunt me down.

I can't allow Blake to get caught up in that.

I've got to get ahead of this fucking thing.

The sooner I make it back to Rafe, the sooner I can get his commitment to protect Blake, no matter what happens to me.

My boots crunch against loose stones as I walk back to the truck. Blake watches me approach through the windshield, her skin pale and her eyes haunted.

A wave of rage sweeps through me. If I could, I'd kill her godfather again for hurting her. And I'd take my fucking time.

I unlock the door, cut the zip tie, and take her hand. As soon as she hops out of the truck, she makes a half-hearted effort to pull it out of my grip, but I keep a firm hold. "No more running. You've hurt yourself enough."

She stares at me with red-rimmed eyes, and seeing her so beaten, hurt, and broken feels like hell on earth.

Fuck. Gino Ferraro will be doing me a favor. I deserve to die for what I did to her.

But that can't happen yet.

I grab the plastic bags with the supplies and lead her to our room.

Inside, it's nothing special. The kind of place that fades from memory as soon as you leave. There's a queen bed, two worn nightstands, and an old armchair slumping in the corner by the south-facing window. I lock the door behind me, deadbolt it, and walk over to the window to test how far it opens—just an inch.

Good.

"I'm not sharing that bed with you," Blake mutters quietly.

"I know." If it was up to her, no doubt we wouldn't even be sharing this room. I can tell she doesn't feel safe around me, and that fucking hurts.

"You want to shower? I bought some extra clothes." I dig inside one of the bags and hand her a T-shirt with "Vegas" printed on the chest. "You can go first."

She takes the shirt out of my hand and disappears inside the bathroom without sparing me a glance.

I sit down on the armchair and listen until I hear the water running.

I'm so fucking tired I can barely see straight. And my emotions are a mess.

I've spent nearly ten years telling Rafaele he should let himself feel things on occasion, but right now, I'd do anything to cut that part of my brain right out.

My throat is tight. My eyes are gritty. It's inching toward three a.m.—the witching hour, the time when bad men are most likely to do bad things.

But I've already committed my share of sins.

I drop my forehead into my palms. I'd been close. So close. If only I'd kept Nero in check like I said I would. If only I hadn't fallen back to old habits.

Blake and I would still be happy. Sandro would still be bossing me around.

My eyes squeeze shut.

I can't believe he's gone. I keep expecting him to call me and ask me where the fuck I've gone. Don't I know we've got meetings to go to?

No, I can't dwell on these thoughts right now. There'll be a time to grieve Sandro, but it'll be after I get Blake to safety and make sure his sacrifice wasn't in vain.

The bathroom door swings open, and a cloud of steam rolls out.

Blake stands in the doorway wearing the oversized T-shirt I gave her, her hair dripping onto the cheap motel carpet.

She looks tired and frail.

I straighten in my seat. "You have to eat something."

"I'm not hungry."

"Starving yourself isn't going to help."

Her eyes flare. "You're right. I'll need my strength if I want to get away from you."

I stare at her. *That's never going to happen.*

She rummages through one of the bags and pulls out a protein bar and a bottle of water. She takes a seat against the headboard on the bed. The sound of the plastic wrapper ripping crackles through the silent room.

"We need to talk," I say.

"I have nothing to say to you."

"Then just eat and listen."

She takes an angry bite and gives me a look so withering it threatens to cave in my chest.

She hates me.

A rising panic clogs my throat. It's not like I deserve any better, but there's a desperate voice inside me that's screaming at me to get on my knees and beg for her forgiveness.

If I thought that would work, I'd do it in a heartbeat.

But we're beyond that. What I've done is unforgivable. Still, I don't want to die without making sure she understands that what we had was real for me.

I swipe my palm over my lips. "I never wanted it to go down like this. When Sandro and I first got to Darkwater Hollow, I was lost. I missed my old life so damn much, I would've done anything to get it back. But then I met you, and everything started to change. I actually wanted to leave Nero behind. I wanted to be Rowan, because that was the only way I could have you."

She swallows.

"I lied to you about a lot of things, Blake. But I never lied about how I felt about you. I—"

"Stop it," she snaps. "I don't want to hear this."

"Nothing made sense until I moved in next door to you. I was barely holding it together in Darkwater—"

"If your life was such a mess, you should've known better than to drag someone else into it. You knew everyone around you could get hurt if your past caught up with you. You knew that, didn't you? You just didn't care."

That cuts deep. It's not that I didn't care. It's that I was too arrogant to acknowledge the possibility that Brett would find a way to nail me.

That fucking arrogance had spelled my downfall.

"I made a lot of mistakes," I admit.

She narrows her eyes. Maybe she expected me to argue with her.

"But do you know what wasn't a mistake? Us. What I feel for you is real. And it's been real this whole time."

"Enough," she snarls. "I don't want to listen to this anymore. Like I said, I have nothing left to say to you, Rowan, Nero, or whoever the hell you are. Just leave me alone."

I watch her turn away from me, the hurt and anger radiating off her in waves. She curls up on the bed, hugging her knees to her chest as if trying to protect herself from more pain.

My body feels cold. There's nothing worse than this—letting down someone you care for to the point where they don't even want you in their life anymore.

I clench my fists against the pain inside my chest. I can't undo the past, but I have to try to make things right, if not for me, then for her.

I get to my feet, grab one of the pillows off the bed, and drag the armchair to the front door. Tonight, I'll sleep with my back pressed against it, because I'm still not convinced she won't try to run. I'll wait until she's out cold and then take a quick shower. I'm in desperate need of one.

After a few minutes, she tugs the blanket up to her chin and turns off the light.

Darkness has never scared me, but tonight is different. Tonight, it presses down on me until my lungs strain to breathe.

"I'm sorry. I'm so sorry," I whisper into the still air.

If Blake hears me, she doesn't say a word.

TWO DAYS LATER, we enter New York State.

Blake's walls are up, and they're impenetrable. I used to be able to read her, but I have no idea what she's thinking anymore. The entire time we've been driving, she's barely said a word.

She breaks her silence when we reach Manhattan. "Where are you taking me?"

Relief pangs through my chest as I glance at her. "You're speaking to me again?"

"Just answer the question." She turns to the window and stares at the skyscrapers towering above us.

My hands shift on the wheel. Does she realize this might be the last hour we have with each other? I get the feeling she didn't believe me when I said the Ferraros are likely to kill me.

Maybe she thinks I'm lying, or maybe she thinks I've got some other plan that doesn't end up with me dead.

I don't.

The only plan I have is to keep her safe.

That's all I've got to do.

Keep her safe.

The line repeats inside my head like a mantra. Whenever I feel myself drifting, losing focus, I pull myself back to it.

"We're going to my old home."

I'm betting on the fact that Rafe hasn't touched the penthouse yet. It's in my name, and he's my beneficiary in case of death.

Still, I doubt figuring out what to do with my penthouse was high on his list of priorities. It's only been six months since I've left.

If I'm wrong, I'll have to take Blake to a hotel, but the penthouse is more secure—impenetrable to anyone whose biometrics have not been programmed into the security system.

The Ferraros won't be able to get in unless they decide to blow up my front door.

The only complication is that the concierge downstairs will call Rafe as soon as we step into the elevator.

But that's fine. I'll only be a minute to drop Blake off before I go to see him.

Reporting for duty.

When Blake and I step into the main entrance, we catch the concierge, Alec, mid-conversation with another resident. "Yes, Mr. Benoit. I'll bring the package to you as soon as it arrives."

The older man nods and shuffles toward the elevators, carefully navigating with a white cane, and Alec turns his attention to us.

His eyes nearly bulge out of his head. "Mr. De Luca! You're..." He wrings his hands, unsure of how to finish that sentence.

"Hey, Alec. I know. I'll explain later."

His eyes flick toward Blake. He hesitates for a moment before asking, "Are you all right, miss?"

I don't need to look at her to know what he sees. Her face is a patchwork of browns and purples. She hasn't complained of the pain, but I know she's hurting. As much as she can't look at me, I can barely look at her. As soon as I talk to Rafe, I'll ask him to send Doc. She's a walking, breathing reminder of how fucking badly I failed.

But I won't fail her again. I'll do whatever it takes to get Rafe to agree to protect her from the Iron Raptors and from the Ferraros, if it comes to that.

Blake shifts on her feet. "I'm fine, thank you."

I glance down at her. I half expected her to tell Alec I'm holding her hostage, but maybe she's finally accepted that trying to run away won't do her any good.

My hand tightens around her arm. "Alec, buzz us upstairs."

He turns paler when he notices the movement. "Of course, sir." He looks uncomfortable, but he knows better than to argue with me. I can guess what conclusions he's jumping to inside his head. I hate that he probably thinks I'm the one who hurt Blake, but I also can't blame him.

At the end of the day, I'm the one responsible for this whole fucking mess.

"And Alec?" His gaze jumps from Blake back up to my face. "Let's keep this between us for now. I'm just going to drop her off before going straight to Don Messero." I reach into my jacket and hand him five crisp hundred-dollar bills.

He takes them uneasily. "I can give you thirty minutes, sir. After that, I'll be in trouble."

"Understood."

In the elevator, Blake huddles in the corner while we ride all the way up to the top floor.

She waits for me to step out first, her footsteps nearly silent as she trails behind me through the foyer that leads to my front door.

23

I press my fingertips against the sensor and wait for the security system to disengage.

When the front door swings open, Blake sucks in a breath.

I walk straight through the circular foyer and lead her into the living area.

Her gaze travels over the Italian-made sofas, the marble coffee table I got from a legendary artisan from Florence, the wall of built-in bookshelves that I never got the chance to fill, and finally to the open-concept kitchen at the back.

Nerves prickle over my nape. Does she like it? I want her to like it. I want her to like just one thing about Nero De Luca, even if it's something as inconsequential as his home.

I clear my throat, anxious for her reaction, but her profile reveals nothing.

Despair wraps around my lungs. It dawns on me then that I'm about to say goodbye to her for the very last time, and there won't be any reconciliation. There won't be any forgiveness. There won't be anything to ease the heavy weight on my shoulders that threatens to buckle my knees.

Men who know they're about to die often pray for peace, but I know there's no prayer that will give me solace. Only this woman might.

She places her delicate hands on the back of the sofa and looks toward the floor-to-ceiling windows. "There were no other doors when we came out of the elevator. Is there no one else on this floor?"

"The penthouse takes up all of it."

A bitter smile graces her lips. "No wonder you thought I'd be safe here. You're putting me inside a gilded cage."

Knowing our time together is down to mere minutes, I don't want to waste a minute arguing. My gaze sweeps over her, drinking in every detail, committing her to memory. "You need to see a doctor. I'll get someone to come."

"Tomorrow."

"Blake—"

"Please. I'm exhausted. I just want to get some rest."

She looks rough, but I know she's not in any immediate danger from her injuries. Rest is probably the best thing for her right now anyway.

"Okay. Tomorrow."

Tearing my gaze away, I leave her to go change, When I return a few minutes later in a pair of black slacks and a white button-up shirt, she's still standing by the sofa.

"When will you be back?" she asks.

"I don't know. I...might not come back at all."

She stares at me, her gaze burning into me for a fleeting moment before the fire goes right out, and all that's left are shards of ice. "And what happens if you don't?"

A crack appears on the surface of my heart. "Someone will stop by and get you all set up. You will never have to worry about money again."

"The moment I get a key to that door, I will leave."

More cracks.

"No, you won't. You know better than that. Remember that even if I'm dead, someone will always be watching you from now on."

Her jaw clenches. "I hate you. I hope I never see you again, Nero."

The cracks spread, break, shatter. Can death feel any worse than this? I doubt it.

I turn away from her and place my hand on the doorknob. "I know."

CHAPTER 3

NERO

An hour later, I pull up to Rafe's mansion in Westchester. The security guard, a man called Hammer, turns pale when I roll down the window.

"Nero! We thought you were..."

"Dead?" I offer.

He swallows.

"I'm not that easy to kill." I wave at the gate. "Want to let me in?"

"I apologize, but I have to check with the don first."

"Do what you need to do."

Hammer smooths a hand down his dress shirt and disappears inside the security booth. He comes back out less than a minute later. "Go ahead. It's good to have you back."

I give him a humorless smile. I'm not convinced Rafe won't kill me on sight.

His instructions to me were simple—stay the fuck away from here. I'm about to throw a wrench into whatever working relationship he and Ferraro have established since I left.

Maybe I should be worried, but instead, I'm just numb. It's like I left my will to live back at the penthouse, inside those mesmerizing blue eyes.

Well, I won't need to keep going through the motions for much longer. All I've got to do is make sure Rafe hears me out and promises to take care of Blake before he pulls the trigger.

I park the car outside the front door and make my way inside the sprawling mansion where I've had many dinners and spent many late nights. Before Rafe married Cleo, we'd have dinner together at least twice a week. His virtuoso cook, Luca, made us the best fucking osso buco on the continent. Veal shanks slowly braised in sauce, served over saffron risotto, and paired with the perfect bottle of wine.

We'd shoot the shit the whole night, starting with work talk and then progressing into more personal territory. When Rafe was still engaged to Gemma, Cleo's sister, I used those nights to needle him about the fact that he had a habit of checking out the wrong sister. He'd kick me out when I annoyed him enough.

I pause inside the foyer as a nostalgic smile tugs on my lips. I didn't think I'd ever be inside these walls again.

For a moment, I stand there and absorb it all. It hasn't changed. Not the round table with the vase of fresh flowers. Not the Renaissance paintings on the walls. Not even the small waiting area where I'd often sit and wait for Rafe to emerge.

The sound of approaching footsteps reaches my ears.

I recognize those too.

By the time my old boss appears, my smile's been put away.

Rafe looks the same as ever. Shiny black hair, clean-shaven face, and a tailored shirt that hides most of his tattoos. I guess he's had no reason to change. It's only been six months, and for most people, that's nothing, but I've traveled through purgatory, heaven, and hell in that short amount of time.

His expression is neutral, but his eyes widen slightly as he takes me in. "Nero."

I spread my arms wide before letting them fall heavily to my sides. "Surprise."

A flicker of what might be a smile appears on his lips.

Rafe rarely smiles. The sight of that small movement makes me clench my fists against the sudden onslaught of emotions. A wrench twists inside my guts.

He fucked up my life, but I've still missed the damn bastard.

Apparently, he shares the sentiment, because he does something completely unexpected. He crosses the room and pulls me into a tight embrace.

A choked laugh escapes me as I slap his back a few times. "My God, Cleo really did a number on you. Look at you, expressing all these emotions."

He ruffles my hair, the way he did when we were teenagers running around New York together, doing everything we could to prove our worth to our fathers. It's so familiar yet so uncharacteristic of adult Rafe that it makes my throat tighten with emotion.

He pulls away, and for a moment, his blue eyes dance with unmistakable fondness. They're lighter than Blake's, but they still remind me of her.

"What are you doing here?" he asks.

I shrug. "Things kind of went to shit."

"Let's go sit down."

He leads me into the living room and walks over to the bar cart. There are a dozen bottles, but he picks out Macallan 15. He splashes some of the amber liquid into two crystal tumblers, hands one to me, and motions at the sofa.

The house is quiet. "Is Cleo around?"

Rafe shakes his head. "Gemma had her baby. Cleo is with her in Italy until next week, and I'm flying there early tomorrow to spend New Year's Eve with everyone."

His words disorient me. I hadn't even realized what day tomorrow is.

Blake will spend New Year's alone.

It seems like something that shouldn't matter, but the thought of her alone in this big city hits me with a fresh wave of regret.

If Cleo were around, I'd ask her to go over there and try to cheer Blake up. Would they get along? They're both strong-willed and stubborn. They have at least one other thing in common—they both got married to guys they despise. Although it didn't take too long for Rafe to win Cleo over.

The thought that I won't get the chance to do the same with Blake tugs at something deep inside of me.

"Well, maybe that's for the best," I mutter.

Rafe's watching me intently as he brings his drink to his lips. "Where's Sandro?"

I glance down at the bottom of my glass. Time to start fessing up to the clusterfuck that happened in Missouri. "Gone."

"What happened?"

"He was killed."

A beat. "Start from the beginning."

So I do. I tell Rafe everything that happened from the moment we left New York. I tell him about Darkwater Hollow and Handy Heroes. I tell him about the Iron Raptors, and how they sniffed me out. I tell him about the pile of bodies I left in Missouri before I drove back to New York.

But I don't tell him about Blake. Not yet.

"The Iron Raptors contacted Ferraro's men and told him they had me cornered. Ferraro would have come hunting for me when those biker rats didn't show up for their scheduled meeting." I lean back and taste the whiskey, savoring the familiar burn as it goes down my throat.

"You made a mistake."

I lift my gaze to Rafe and notice he looks pissed. "I didn't have a choice. This would have blown back on you."

"Giorgio has been helping us plant various false flags since you left. There have been at least five reports of someone seeing you, none of them true. Ferraro no longer pays attention to them. If no one had shown up to the meeting, he would have forgotten about you. You should have done like I said and stayed away from here."

Heat prickles across my nape. "You're kidding."

"I'm not. I knew there was a chance you'd be spotted eventually, so I took precautions. But now it's too late. Now there are photos of you in New York. Camera footage of you entering your condo. Footage the Ferraros are monitoring."

"Can't Giorgio erase it?"

Rafe exhales. "It's not a risk I can take at the moment. Fabi is engaged to Cosimo Ferraro."

Shock travels through me. "You gave your sister to that stuck-up fuck?"

"The wedding will be in spring. Or at least, it's supposed to be. The Bratva have gotten a lot more aggressive, and my alliance with Ferraro needs to be rock solid. It's never quite gotten there after you killed Michael."

So I just seriously fucked him. Ferraro's going to find out Rafe lied to him about my death, and that might put their plans in danger.

I drag my palms over my face. "I didn't come here to beg you to save me. I'm ready to face whatever Ferraro wants to do to me."

He arches a brow. "You came here to die? You should have kept running, Nero."

"I couldn't risk it."

"Why not?"

Time to come clean. "I have a wife."

"A wife?" His surprise is evident.

"I need you to protect her after I'm gone. The bikers I killed were her godfather and his men. Their friends will try to find her and kill her, and I can't let that happen."

Rafe puts his tumbler down, his brow furrowed. "You killed their men. They won't stop until they get revenge."

"Not if they learn she's under the protection of Rafaele Messero." Even those guys aren't reckless enough to attack Blake while she's on Messero turf. Their need for revenge isn't worth their lives. Eventually, they'll let it go, especially once I'm dead.

I wait for my old friend to give me his word, watching as he processes the situation. Rafe doesn't agree to anything until he's considered it from multiple angles. The only person who's ever made him lose his cool is his wife.

Eventually, he nods. "All right."

"Ferraro can't touch her either."

"As of right now, he doesn't even know she exists."

"Let's try to keep it that way."

"Then we have to go see him," Rafaele says, standing up. "Right now. Before he gets a chance to look at footage of you and her or hear about your return from some other source."

I get to my feet. "He'll know you lied to protect me."

"Obviously."

"You wish you'd just killed me?"

Regret flashes inside his pale blue eyes. "No, Nero. But I wish you hadn't come back. Because I can't protect you now."

CHAPTER 4

NERO

I get into the passenger seat of Rafe's Aston Martin and clip in the seatbelt, feeling strangely at peace with the fact that our drive to Ferraro's penthouse in Midtown might be the last car ride I'll ever take.

I suppose it already feels like I'm living on borrowed time. I hadn't expected Rafe to welcome me back like he did, but after meeting Blake, I know what it's like to have a woman change you.

"So what's her name?" he asks.

"Blake."

"Does she know what you're doing right now?"

"She knows."

"She must be devastated."

"Right before I came to you, she told me that she hates me."

Rafe's lips twitch. "If by some miracle you make it back home tonight, I'm sure she'll come around." He stops at a red light and turns to me. "Look at Cleo. She came around even after I forced her to marry me."

I drag my teeth over my bottom lip. "I not only forced Blake to marry me, I also set her house on fire so that she'd move in with me."

Rafe makes a surprised huff. "I didn't realize this was a competition, but all right, you win."

A wry smirk tugs on my lips. "It wouldn't be the first time. Have you found a new boxing partner?"

"Bruno and I go once a week."

"Bruno? Jesus. That's not a real workout. You must wipe the floor with that guy."

"He's not that bad." Rafe glances over. "You look a bit out of shape."

"Liar. I'm in great fucking shape, as always."

"If you say so."

"I'm about to get my head blown off, and you're still giving me shit."

"What else am I supposed to do? Cry?"

"Fuck, no. I have a feeling you're an ugly crier. I don't need to see that in my last hour on earth."

We exchange jabs and talk shit for most of the drive to Ferraro's penthouse. Under normal circumstances, Rafe probably would have told me to shut up a long time ago, but I get the sense he's trying to keep my mind off what's about to happen.

I feel some comfort in the fact that he'll be there with me right up until the end.

Inside, the concierge has to call to see if Ferraro will let us up. Rafe provides him with a fake name for me—the name of his new underboss, Alec Puglisi. A minute later, the concierge gives us the go-ahead.

"How's that working out?" I ask as we walk through the lobby.

Rafe stops in front of the elevator. "Alec? It was an adjustment at first."

"And now?"

He gives me a look. I'm fishing, and he knows it. I'm like a needy divorcée who wants him to tell me that no one could ever replace me.

But by the looks of it, Rafe's doing just fine. He adapted, the way any don worth his salt would.

We step into the elevator.

Did I imagine my departure would be a real hit to his organization? In my worst moments back in Darkwater Hollow, before I moved in next door to Blake, I indulged myself in fantasies of how Rafe would slowly lose his grip on his kingdom without me by his side.

I thought I was important. And maybe I was for a time.

But everyone is replaceable.

I've always known this. I guess it only really sinks in when it happens to you.

The doors slide open, revealing a large fountain in the foyer. A moment later, a member of Ferraro's house staff comes out to greet us.

"Gino is expecting us," Rafaele says.

"I was told it was you, Mr. Messero, and Mr. Puglisi..." The older man trails off, his eyes thinning as he takes me in.

"Change of plans," Rafe says.

"I'll have to ask for your weapons."

Rafe and I hand him our guns.

The man leads us into the living room and offers us a seat, but neither Rafe nor I take one. The air buzzes with anxious energy, and the blood inside my veins feels thick and heavy. This must be what it feels like to walk the plank. To see your death just steps away and know nothing but an act of God can stop it.

Gino Ferraro enters the room.

To his credit, his shock is nearly imperceptible as it passes across his features. Maybe he never fully believed that charred body was mine.

Rafe takes a few steps forward. I wonder if he realizes he's put himself in front of me. "We need to talk."

Gino nods. "I can see that. Let's go into my office."

We nearly make it there when his wife, Vita, comes out of a room.

Her eyes flash as she takes me in. She tilts her head to the side. "You didn't mention we had guests, dear."

Gino drags his palm over his white beard. "A surprise visit."

"Good evening, Vita," Rafe says. "It's true. We didn't give much notice."

Her perceptive gaze flickers between us. "I'll bring us all some tea."

A chuckle nearly escapes me. What a civilized start to an execution.

We follow Gino into his office, which looks like it belongs to a therapist instead of the head of a crime family. Everything is decorated in muted beiges and browns, the windowsill is lined with bonsai trees, and there's the distinct sound of trickling water coming from a small crane-shaped fountain in the corner.

Gino takes a seat behind his desk, and we take the two chairs across from him.

"Your sons aren't around?" I ask.

"If they were, there's a good chance you wouldn't have made it this far."

What he means is they'd shoot me on sight. The Ferraro patriarch is at least willing to exchange a few words first, not that I'm expecting this to be a very long conversation.

Vita comes in carrying a tray with a teapot and four cups. She puts the tray on Gino's desk, and then carefully pours the tea for all of us.

She and Gino have been married for thirty-something years, if I'm remembering correctly. What would that be like? To grow old with someone? To raise a family together?

I'll never get to experience any of that with Blake, and the realization hits me like a knife to the chest.

"Thank you, darling," Gino says. "Should we move to the couches?"

"No need. I'd prefer to stay on my feet. I've been sitting all day," she answers.

Gino nods and brushes his hand over Vita's, but the softness in his eyes disappears the moment they move back to me.

"Nero." He steeples his hands in front of him. "There's a part of me that always suspected we were taken in by Rafaele as far as you were concerned."

Rafaele shifts in his seat. "Gino, he's my oldest friend. And what happened that night was an unfortunate mistake."

Gino ignores him, focusing intently on me. "Why are you here?"

"I was discovered by someone."

"Who?"

"A group of bikers from a Missouri gang called Iron Raptors."

"And where are these bikers now?"

"I left their bodies in a motel parking lot."

Gino arches a brow. "Then why come back?"

"Before I got to them, they contacted your people. I wasn't careful enough, and I didn't want to throw Rafe under the bus. I'm here to face the consequences of my actions."

"How honorable." He takes a sip of his tea and then glances past me.

I follow his line of sight. He's looking at Vita. She's standing by the window, appearing to be focused on the view, but it's clear she's listening to our conversation.

"What happened with Michael was an accident," Rafaele says.

Gino's fingers tap lightly against the desk. "I know that."

"Then you also know now is not the time to fight over past mistakes. There's a reason we've decided to join our families by marrying Fabi to Cosimo. The growing Bratva threat cannot be ignored. We can crush them easily together, or we can fight them separately and lose even more of our men."

"None of that changes the fact that you lied to me. You told me he burned in that fire. How can I partner with someone I can't trust?"

"I lied to you one time. I've never lied to you about anything else."

"You expect me to believe that? The right thing to do would be to call the wedding off and find another wife for Cosimo. You're not the only powerful family in New York, Rafaele."

Vita clears her throat. "My love, can I talk to you in private?"

Gino looks at his wife. Something unspoken passes between them. "Of course. Excuse me."

They walk out, leaving Rafe and me.

"He's as stubborn as a mule," Rafe mutters. "And he likes to hold grudges."

"I was ready for this."

"You should have stayed away."

"What's done is done."

"Fuck, Nero," he says angrily. "It's like you *want* this to happen. What is wrong with you?"

"I don't want it, but I've made peace with it."

Rafe stares at me like he doesn't understand me. I don't expect him to. The mistakes he made with Cleo pale in comparison to how I've hurt Blake.

Gino walks back into the room alone. His footsteps are measured as he moves to reclaim his seat across from us. "My wife seems to be set on this match for our son. Sometimes, she sees things that I don't, but after many decades together, I've learned to trust her intuition. The wedding is still on."

"Good," Rafe says. "I am as committed to our partnership as ever. And Nero—"

"Nero still has a debt to pay."

The hairs on the back of my neck stand straight. In the chair beside me, Rafe stiffens.

Gino stands up and shrugs off his jacket. There's a gun tucked into the front of his waistband. He walks around the desk and leans against the edge of it, stopping just to the right of my chair.

I lift my gaze to his, and whatever lingering hope I had left disappears. There's no mercy in his eyes.

"Get on your knees."

My skin tightens over my bones. Adrenaline rushes through my veins, making cold sweat break out over my back.

This is it.

"Now, Nero."

I won't beg him to spare me. Not when I can tell he's already made up his mind.

And I won't cower. If I die, I'll die like a made man.

I push out of the chair and kneel.

Behind me, Rafe sucks in a harsh breath. "Nero is a capable consigliere. He can help me—"

Gino's laugh is humorless. "You can't expect me to hand him right back to you as if nothing happened."

"Let's talk about this."

"I lost a family member because of you two fucking up, and you want to just go back to business as usual? It doesn't work that way. Nero has to pay." He lifts his gun and points it at my head.

"This is a waste. If he's here, I might as well put him to work. That will help both of us."

"We've managed the past six months without him." The cold barrel presses against my forehead.

I close my eyes and conjure up Blake in my imagination. My death will ensure Blake will be safe from the Iron Raptors and safe from Gino, even if he finds out about her. Rafe will protect her. He'll make sure she's all right.

She's strong, and she'll build a new life here in New York. She can start that bookshop she's always dreamt about right here. But none of these reassuring thoughts manage to expel the regret that I feel.

I failed her.

I was selfish and arrogant. If I'd been more careful like Sandro warned me I needed to be, he'd still be alive, and Blake wouldn't have a target on her back.

"Gino," Rafe says in a low voice, but it holds an undercurrent of desperation. "Can you just put the gun down for a fucking minute? We're in the middle of a conversation."

Gino clicks the safety off. "There's nothing left to talk about."

The chair behind me skids against the floor. "You're acting rashly. This isn't like you."

"That's enough, Rafaele."

"We can use him! He's got the know-how, the network, the credibility. He's a fucking asset."

A ball appears inside my throat. Rafe told me he couldn't save me, but he's trying harder than I thought he would. Even now, he's got my back, the way my own father never did.

I let out a shaky breath and curl my hands into fists at my sides. I don't want to think of that man during my last moments. I only want to think of Blake. Of the way she used to look at me before I broke her heart—like I was someone she could love.

"An asset," Gino mutters, but I barely hear him over the loud drumming inside my ears. *Boom. Boom. Boom.*

A few tense seconds tick by.

What is he waiting for?

I open my eyes. Gino's staring at me with a thoughtful expression on his face.

"You're right," he says, his voice low. "We can use him."

What?

The cold pressure against my forehead eases. Slowly, deliberately, he lowers the gun.

I sag back on my heels. My heart's racing a mile a minute, my dress shirt is sticking to my back, and the room is spinning like a merry-go-round.

Rafe's hand clamps down on my shoulder. "C'mon, Nero."

Gino shakes his head. "He's not going anywhere with you. From now on, I don't want you two to have any contact unless it's absolutely necessary."

There's a beat of silence, and Rafe's grip tightens. "I thought—"

"You thought wrong." Gino tucks the gun back into his belt. "*We* can use him. We will put him to work. He won't be working for you." His gray eyes move back to my kneeling form. "He'll work for me and my sons."

I exhale a harsh breath, my mind scrambling to make sense of what just happened.

He's not going to kill me? Why? I always know when someone's ready to pull the trigger, and Gino was ready.

So what changed?

But the puzzle of Ferraro's motivations fades from my mind, overtaken by something more urgent, more vital.

I'm going home. To Blake. To my *wife*.

And I'm not going to waste this second chance to make all my wrongs right.

CHAPTER 5

BLAKE

Did he mean it?

I close my eyes, rinsing the suds out of my hair and trying to convince myself it's impossible.

"I don't know. I...might not come back at all."

This is another trick, another way Nero's trying to manipulate me. Why would he come back to New York just to die? He wouldn't do that to protect me. My father would have never put my mother's life above his own, and Nero is just like him. A criminal who thinks about himself first and foremost.

There's something he's not telling me. This situation is likely far more complicated than he made it seem. Nero must have a plan to smooth things over with his boss and these Ferraro people. In a few hours, he'll be back.

I step out of the shower and wrap a thick white towel around me. This bathroom is so big it takes me five steps to reach the marble vanity. I drag my fist over the fogged-up mirror and stare at my reflection.

The bruises are beginning to fade. Apparently, they're as impermanent as my conviction, because the question still lingers.

What if he meant it?

If he was truly willing to lay down his life in exchange for saving mine...then I *still* don't know who he really is.

My husband is a mystery to me.

The words I said to him echo inside my head. *"I hate you. I hope I never see you again, Nero."*

My stomach clenches painfully. Why did I say that? If those are the last words I ever say to him, I won't forgive myself. I was so angry that I wasn't thinking straight. It didn't feel good to spit that vitriol at him, and yet I couldn't hold it back.

I'm furious with that man, but I don't want him dead.

What I want is for him to come back here in one piece and tell me that I'm free to leave. There has to be somewhere other than here where I can live safely.

Australia. That's far enough, isn't it? The Iron Raptors won't chase after me if I'm on the other side of the globe. If I can get a fake passport and a bit of money, I'll be set. I'll find a simple job and live a simple life, and I'll convince Del to come visit me once a year.

Since when do you want a simple life? What happened to your thirst for adventure, passion, romance?

It disappeared once I realized living the plot of a romantic thriller is a lot more difficult than simply reading it.

I dry off, pull on some clothes, and venture outside.

My footsteps are quiet as I walk through the palatial penthouse.

The open-concept living space feels like three rooms in one. The kitchen alone is the size of my old house. Arched windows. Dark hardwood floors. Black granite countertops. I grab a rag and wipe off the thin layer of dust that's collected on them since Nero's been gone.

The largest bedroom is a sanctuary of dark tones and extravagantly crafted furniture. I walk up to the heavy wooden desk and sift through the drawers, finding Montblanc pens, lighters, and an old case of Cuban cigars. The walk-in closet is full of crisp dress shirts, tailored suits, and silk ties. There's an entire case of watches that look like they should be locked inside a safe, but I suppose there's no need for that when this entire penthouse is basically a safe.

I find two more bedrooms, an astounding five baths, an office, a sauna, and even a gym filled with equipment.

The level of luxury is hard for me to comprehend. How did a man used to all of this manage to become Rowan, owner of a home renovation company in an inconsequential small town?

I get lost, then find my way back, only to get lost again. Everything in this penthouse screams expensive, but the loudest feature is the view.

I don't have my phone, so I can't check my location, but I'm pretty sure I'm looking at the Brooklyn Bridge down below.

The skyline on the other side of the river is a glittering silhouette against the dark sky.

My fingertips make contact with the glass. It's thick and sturdy, without a latch and no way to open it. There's no way out of here but through the front door.

What if he doesn't come back?

I stare at the city below.

He lied to you. He put you in danger. He destroyed your only hope of getting out of Darkwater Hollow.

He's a criminal. He loves being a criminal.

You fell for him like the world's biggest idiot. You're just like your mother. You have no idea what's good for you.

All of that is true, but other things are true as well.

He took care of you better than anyone else ever did.

Until a few days ago, you've always felt safe around him.

He never told you to stop dreaming. Instead, he tried to help you with your dream.

My chest grows tight. I lift my fingers to my cheeks and discover they're wet. When did I start crying?

I squeeze my eyes shut, and that's a mistake, because immediately, he's there. His image is so clear in my head. He's lying in bed with a lazy grin on his handsome face and his tatted arm tucked under his head. *Come back here, Sunshine. It's not even nine a.m. yet. I want you. I need you.*

The penthouse is empty. There's no one to witness the way I sink to the carpeted floor. There's no one to hear my desperate sobs.

How can one man be so full of inconsistencies and contra-dictions? Which parts of him were real? Which were pretend?

And does it matter that it once felt so right to be with him?

I've seen firsthand what happens to women who let a man like Nero into their lives. In the end, there's nothing but disappointment and pain waiting for them.

The front door opens with a click.

Silently, I wipe the tears off my face and get to my feet. *Nero?*

What if it's someone else? What if he's dead, and the Ferraros have decided they want to kill me anyway, and now someone's here to tie up the loose ends?

Fear sinks its claws into me.

Whoever it is, they're not saying a word.

I tiptoe to the kitchen, swipe a knife out of the wooden block, and tread softly through the living room.

I'm halfway there when Nero steps over the threshold.

The wave of relief that crashes through me nearly brings me to my knees.

Thank God. "You made it back," I choke out, taking a step toward him.

Hope flickers in his eyes as he steps toward me too, but then his gaze drops to the knife in my hand, and he stops.

A beat passes before a sad grimace crosses his face. "You thinking about finishing the job?"

That comment twists my relief into anger. I cried over him. I made myself sick with worry. I regretted every cruel word that had spilled past my lips, and he's acting like it's all a joke?

"What happened?" I demand.

"I work for Gino Ferraro now." He doesn't sound upset, just resigned.

"The man who you said wanted to kill you?"

"That's the one." He rakes his fingers through his hair.

That doesn't make any sense. "How did he go from wanting you dead to wanting you working for him?"

He shrugs, looking exhausted. "Beats me."

I frown. That's not an explanation. "I don't understand. So that's it? Everything is fine now? You're back to business as usual?"

"I wouldn't say that."

I stare at him, tempted to beg him to let me go again. If he's fixed his issues with Ferraro, won't he be able to get me the documents I need to leave the country? Won't he be able to give me some money and put me on a plane?

Yeah. Probably. If he wanted to.

But even if he did, *he'd* know my new name. *He'd* know where I went. And *he'd* always be able to track me down.

That's not good enough. What I need is a real clean slate.

It's going to take me some time to figure out how I can get that.

But I will.

Eventually.

He nods at the knife. "I've got to be up in six hours for my first day of work, and it's been a long day. I need to get some sleep. If you decide to kill me, it's probably better for you to wait until I'm unconscious."

My eyes narrow. "I'm not like you, remember? Not everyone's a murderer, Nero. The knife's for self-defense."

"Self-defense? No one can touch you here. I told you that."

"What about you? Who's going to keep me safe from you?"

His entire face darkens. For a second, I think he's going to say something, but then he turns and walks out of the room, apparently done with this conversation.

I drop the knife onto a credenza and follow him. "So what now? What about me?"

"What about you?"

"What am I supposed to do here while you're at work?"

He moves into one of the bedrooms. "I can get you some entertainment tomorrow."

"You can't expect to keep me inside all day long. I'm not a house cat. I'll go insane."

He takes off his jacket and throws it over the back of a chair before starting to work on the buttons of his shirt.

"It's not forever. But for now, you have to stay put."

"Why?"

"Because I don't know what Gino Ferraro's agenda is. He's planning something, and until I know what it is, it's too risky for you to move around the city. Let me get my bearings. I need a few days to settle in."

"Can I get a phone?"

"Not yet."

"I need to call Del. If she doesn't hear from me soon, she will call the cops. She's relentless. She won't give up until she finds me."

Nero sighs and slips off his shirt. "You can call her tomorrow, but only to let her know you're okay. I'll arrange it."

My gaze slides down his body, over his golden chest and his rippling abs.

I shouldn't find any part of him attractive anymore.

It's infuriating that I still do.

He tosses the shirt into the empty laundry basket and then moves his hands to his belt.

I force my gaze back up.

"Fine. You can have three days to 'get your bearings,' as you say, and then I want a key to this place and a phone."

He unzips his trousers and lets them fall to the floor. "How do I know you won't try to run again?"

I ignore the way my skin prickles with heat at the half-naked view of him. "You've made it abundantly clear there's nowhere else for me to go. But I will not be your prisoner, Nero. If you keep me locked inside this glass box, I'll bring a hammer to your window and hurl myself out of it."

My statement makes his eyes flare with fury. It's the kind of fury that makes even the weakest of men dangerous, and Nero's anything but weak.

He steps out of his trousers and advances on me wearing only his underwear. I back away until I hit a wall.

His tattooed body blocks my view of the bedroom. Palms appear on either side of my head. I'm acutely aware of the few inches between us and how they simmer with heat.

"You can be mad at me," he says in a low voice. "You can hate me. You can wish me dead. But you will never threaten to hurt yourself again. If you do anything to put yourself in harm's way, I swear to God, Blake, I will build a cage and lock you in it."

He's so close that I can make out the gold shards in his irises. My gaze drops to his lips. "I'm already in a cage."

"If you think this is a cage, you've lived a charmed life." He says it so softly that I glance up again. There's something else licking at the edges of his fury now. Something tender and raw that makes my heart pound against my ribcage.

I swallow, unable to keep my face from growing hot. I wish I could erase our history from my memory bank. I wish I didn't remember what he felt like inside me.

"You know I haven't."

"Then take a deep breath and relax." He dips his head, nearly brushing his forehead against mine. "Tomorrow, I'll get you all the creature comforts you could possibly need. You can start to settle in."

He pushes off the wall and takes a step back, but his intense gaze doesn't leave my face. "I need a shower. Unless you want to join me, let's end this conversation here."

Join him? Fury licks up my spine. How dare he?

His masterpiece of a body might taunt me, but I'm not so weak that I'll let myself be tempted by it.

I give my head a hard shake. "Better get used to being on your own, Nero. I'm taking the bedroom next door. Just because we're living together, it doesn't mean we'll see much of each other."

Disappointment flashes across his expression, but before he can argue with me, I leave the room and let the door slam behind me.

CHAPTER 6

NERO

It's still dark outside when I step out onto the street. Ferraro told me to be ready at seven a.m., so here I am. My gun's tucked behind my belt, and I'm wearing a comfortable suit and my favorite pair of leather wingtips.

The only thing missing is my wedding band.

I only wore it for the few days it took us to drive here from Vegas, but I got used to it, and I miss not having it on my finger.

It'll be a while before I can put it back on. I've got no idea what made Gino decide against pulling the trigger, and I could tell Rafe doesn't either. Until I determine what Ferraro's got planned for me, it's better if they don't know Blake exists.

She doesn't want to be stuck inside all day. I get it. But her happiness is secondary to keeping her safe. I'll do everything I can to make her comfortable while I figure out the deal with Ferraro.

And maybe it's naïve, but I still have hope for us. I've got a new lease on life, so to speak, and I'm feeling optimistic. I'll start earning back her trust, bit by bit.

It'll be a steep fucking hill to climb, that's for sure. But I didn't get this second chance for nothing.

I pull out my phone and check to see if I got a response from Rafe to the message I sent when I woke up this morning. Blake needs things, and I've got no way of getting them to her today while I'm busy with my new employer.

> Okay. The last item might be difficult to arrange in the time frame you want. I'll do my best.

A black car pulls up to the curb in front of me, and the door opens, signaling for me to get in.

I hop into the passenger seat and come face-to-face with Cosimo Ferraro.

Just great.

I fucking hate the guy. He takes himself way too fucking seriously.

The eldest Ferraro son scans me over, his lips drawing into a thin line. "It really is you."

"Back to the land of the living." I clip in my seat belt.

"If I were the head of the family, I would have ended you as soon as you reappeared."

"Good thing you're not."

His fingers twitch. He's probably daydreaming about strangling me right here in the passenger seat.

"My father is too forgiving, but me and my brothers are not." He presses on the gas and merges into the traffic, taking us toward the Brooklyn Bridge. "If you think this is going to be easy, you're in for a very unpleasant surprise."

"Shame, I was hoping for a spa day with the boys, maybe a couple's massage. I won't tell if you don't."

"Funny," Cosimo says dryly. "You've always had a sense of humor."

"And you've always had a stick up your ass."

"Watch it. I'm your boss now."

"I think Gino's my boss. And given the current situation, I think you're my driver."

Cosimo's jaw clenches. I know I'm pushing it, but I can't resist getting him riled up. He's an easy target, the same way most firstborn sons are before they finally get the role they're groomed for their entire lives.

To his credit, instead of reacting to my jibes, he simply ignores me for the rest of the half-hour drive.

We pull into the parking lot of a warehouse. It's got a red-brick facade, dusty windows, and looks completely abandoned.

Maybe Cosimo's decided to go against his father and off me after all.

"What is this place?"

"Alessio calls it his palace," Cosimo says.

An uneasy feeling slides down my back. Alessio is Cosimo's brother and the main enforcer for the Ferraros. Everyone knows he isn't quite right in the head.

We get out of the car and walk all the way to the back of the warehouse where there's a heavy steel door. Cosimo bangs on it twice.

"What are we doing here?"

Cosimo turns to look at me, his eyes swimming with satisfaction. He can't kill me, but I can tell he thinks whatever they've got planned for me is almost as good. "You're going to work for Alessio."

Fuck me. No wonder he looks so pleased.

The man himself opens the door and immediately sizes me up.

I do the same. It's interesting to compare the two brothers. Cosimo is all business with his pressed suit, crisp white shirt, and combed back dark hair. Put him in khakis and a polo, and he'd fit right in at Harvard or Princeton.

Alessio, on the other hand, wouldn't fit in... well, anywhere.

The man's covered in tattoos, all the way from his neck to his fingertips, and he's got the kind of energy that makes anyone remotely sane want to skedaddle. There's very little human hiding behind those freakishly light-gray eyes. He's wearing a dark pair of jeans, a leather apron tied around his waist, and no shirt.

There are red streaks on his hands and arms.

Blood.

"Is this my new errand boy?" His voice has a rasp to it. He's not as tall as me, not as wide either, but there's a glint in his eyes that immediately puts me on edge.

It's one thing to be willing to torture and kill for the job. It's another to take pleasure from it. Don't get me wrong, there have been times when cracking someone's bones has brought me pure joy, but it's rare, and only when it's personal. Like it was with those fucking Iron Raptors. I enjoyed every bit of killing those fucks.

Alessio's different. He's extreme. Unhinged. He makes a meal out of every kill. He's famous for it.

Cosimo nods. "In the flesh."

Alessio doesn't offer me his hand. His eyes bore into me as he steps aside and lets us pass through the doorway.

A chemical smell immediately invades my nostrils. Disinfectant mixed with something else. The hallway Cosimo leads me down has a slope to it, like we're moving underground.

I try to piece together what the Ferraros might be doing. Rafe told Gino I'd make a good asset, but Gino's not going to give me any power in his organization. That's obvious. It doesn't matter how smart I am, or how experienced, or how quickly I think on my feet. This business is all about trust, and the Ferraros don't trust me.

So what kind of work is Alessio going to give me?

We take a turn, then another. The wall on the right is lined with steel cage lights that give off an eerie yellow glow. The chemical smell only gets stronger the longer we walk.

We're definitely underground now. There are no sounds coming in from the outside, but I pick up on a strange noise up ahead.

Moans.

I frown. I'm not afraid—I came back to New York ready to die—but this is just fucking creepy.

Alessio's steps are steady behind me. "We're here," he announces just as the hallway opens up to a large room, and we step inside it.

Fuck me.

The scene is straight out of a slasher flick.

There's a big cage with a naked man inside it. He's holding a pair of pliers in his hand, and by the look of it, he's been hard at work pulling out his own teeth.

For whatever reason, the sight of me gives him hope. "Please help!" he calls out in a Russian accent.

I ignore him and glance back at Alessio, waiting for him or his brother to tell me what the fuck I'm doing here.

"Heeelp!"

Jesus, read the room.

Alessio doesn't seem to register the man's cries. He scans me with a detached look. "The Bratva's pakhan has scores of men, and he's not shy about sending them on suicide missions. Most are too junior to know anything, but you never know, so we've got to bring them in."

"Can't cut any corners," Cosimo adds.

"I delegate everything I can to other people in the organization, but I do the interrogations myself."

"Alessio's the best," Cosimo says thoughtfully, his eyes on the man with the missing teeth.

"This is your second chance," Alessio says. "You don't get any more. One fuckup, and you're out for good. You understand?"

I nod. I wasn't expecting anything different. "What do you need me to do?"

"Whatever I tell you to."

Cosimo glances at his watch. "I'll leave you two to it. I've got to go meet Mom for breakfast. You coming tonight, Les? You know she doesn't like it when you skip out on holidays."

Alessio appears to think for a second, and then he nods. "Okay. I'll be there. With Nero's help, I should be done in time."

"Great." Cosimo turns and leaves without another word. Good riddance.

"So what's going on here?" I gesture at his prisoner.

"I told him I'd decrease the process by one minute for every tooth he pulls out."

"The process?"

"I remove some body parts and keep them alive while I do it."

Christ. What happened to a good old-fashioned beating? "Sounds like a lot of work."

"This one killed one of our guys by shooting him in the back. Nothing I hate more than cowards," Alessio explains.

"Sure. Makes sense." It doesn't make any sense.

"Well, have a seat. This might take a while."

IT DOES TAKE A WHILE. Six hours precisely. Six hours during which I get a front row seat to this psycho's interrogation methods, excluding the half hour I take to go pick him up some lunch.

I have to give it to him. He knows what he's doing. The prisoner sings all of his secrets like a little bird.

When Alessio finally puts his tools down, I give him a weary look. "What now?"

He takes off his apron and drops it to the ground. "You're on cleanup duty. I'll be in my office. Come by when you're finished."

I glance around. Blood, guts, and teeth. I haven't had to do this kind of shit since the very early days when I was at the very bottom of the ladder.

It takes me another four hours to clean everything. I have to saw the dude into parts and put them into vats of acid. It's the hardest work I've done in ages.

By the end of it, my body's sweating and sore. Blood's caked under my nails. I seriously regret wearing nice clothes this morning. They're ruined. Everything's going straight into the fucking furnace.

I enter the adjacent office to tell Alessio I'm finished. He's on his laptop, playing Sims from the look of it. I walk closer and study the screen. It's a farm at the foot of a mountain, with sheep and cows and horses milling around. There's a barn and a guy on a red tractor.

Okay then.

"I'm done."

He turns on his gaming chair and steeples his hands in front of him. He's changed into a threadbare black T-shirt that's peppered with holes. "Good. You're ready for your next task then."

I wipe the sweat off my forehead. "What is it?"

"I heard you box."

"I did before I left."

"You any good?"

"Yeah, I'm good."

He stands up, and his desk chair swivels behind him. "Follow me."

He leads me down a hall and into a pitch-black room. When he flicks on the lights, I see it's a gym.

It's huge.

Rows of equipment fill up the side closer to us, and farther up is an elevated boxing ring. Alessio walks around it and takes some hand wraps and gloves out of a plastic bin. "Here."

"This is my next task? Boxing with you?"

Alessio shrugs. "I need a partner. My brothers are busy, and I don't have many friends."

That's the least surprising thing I've heard all day. Did Gino spare me so that his not-all-there son would have a buddy? No fucking way.

I glance down at my ruined dress shirt and pants. "You have something I can change into?"

He nods and rummages through another box before pulling out a pair of shorts. "Here."

Five minutes later, we've both changed, our hands are wrapped, and we're ready to fight.

I flex my toes against the padding on the floor. It's been months since I've done this, but it's no different than slipping on an old pair of shoes. Even if I'm not in the kind of shape I was before I left New York, I'm bigger than Alessio, and in boxing, your arm span is one of the biggest adva—

Pain explodes inside my brow. I stagger back, blinking against the blood dripping into my fucking eye.

"Fuck!"

Alessio cocks a brow. "Did you want me to announce when I'm about to hit you?"

Of course this crazy bastard would skip a warmup.

All right. If he wants to go hard, we'll go hard.

I don't make the same mistake twice. I advance on him, throwing him jab after jab, but he's a quick motherfucker. Whatever advantage I have in size, he's got the same if not greater when it comes to speed.

The first time I land a good one against his mouth, he grins. I think it's the first time I've seen him smile, and it's plain disturbing, especially with the blood coating his teeth.

Doesn't he have a dinner to go to after this? It's New Year's Eve.

And what do you have waiting for you?

Home.

Blake.

This morning, right before I left, I stole a glance inside her room while she was sleeping.

Her bruised face is still a stark reminder of the pain I've caused her. Of the amends I have to make.

My mood darkens. I want to go home, but a part of me feels like I don't deserve to be there. With Rafe helping me arrange all the gifts, she's got everything she needs in the penthouse with her already.

Did seeing all the books I got her make her happy? Will that happiness disappear the moment I show up? Maybe I should let her just enjoy it for a little while.

I beckon Alessio closer. "C'mon."

He dances around me, feigning left and right, and I can see the sweat on his brow glistening under the lights.

I lunge forward with a hook, but he dodges with a flicker of speed and lands a solid punch to my jaw. My head snaps back, and I stumble and grab the ropes to keep myself upright.

Everything falls away except for the pain and the man in front of me.

This is what I need. A way to do penance. A way to pay for my sins.

The next time Alessio moves to hit me, I don't block him. His fist connects with my abdomen, forcing the breath out of my lungs. Then again, and again, and again.

The next punch he throws at my head sends me to the ground. The pain in my jaw is so blinding that for a moment, I wonder if he broke it. My bloody spit collects on the mat. I push myself up using my gloved fist and move my jaw back and forth.

Still attached.

Alessio's feet appear in front of me. "You tapping out?"

I shake my head at the ground. "No."

"You sure?"

"Yes," I snap and roll away from him. My body hums with pain, but I get back on my feet.

We start circling each other, and I dodge a few of his hits before I let him land one on me. Then another.

The next time I end up on the ground, Alessio crouches down beside me.

"There aren't many men in this city who don't know your reputation, Nero."

With a groan, I turn onto my back and meet his cool, assessing gaze.

"That Labor Day, when the city was this close to going up in flames, it was you against six men."

I spit out blood. "Seven."

"That was the night you got your nickname. The Angel of Death."

"If you ask me, there isn't much angelic about death."

"I agree." Alessio cocks his head. "Are you out of practice, or are you going easy on me?"

"Does it matter?" With effort, I get back on my feet. "Let's go."

"You'll be useless to me with a broken arm or leg."

I give him a dark smile. "Then don't break 'em."

CHAPTER 7

BLAKE

The creature comforts Nero promised me begin arriving at noon.

First, the groceries. Alec—the front desk attendant I met last night when Nero and I arrived—opens the door to the penthouse from the outside and explains Nero's given him temporary access for the day. He lets in four men carrying large paper bags. They drop them off in the kitchen and leave without saying a word.

Later, a woman strides in with a rack of clothes. Somehow, every item is my exact size. I ask her how she knew, but she just shakes her head and says she's not supposed to talk to me. Weird.

As I'm finishing up a snack around four p.m., a dozen or so boxes are brought in. These dudes *also* refuse to talk to or even look at me.

I stop Alec right as he's about to follow them out of the condo. "Can I speak with you for a moment?"

He looks reluctant but nods. "Sure."

"Why is everyone treating me like I'm radioactive?"

Alec clears his throat. "Maybe it's better if you ask your husband."

"I'm asking you," I insist. I feel stupid, like I'm missing something.

Alec tugs on his collar. "You are the wife of a very dangerous man, Mrs. De Luca. No one wants to risk doing or saying something that might offend you."

My stomach sinks. Really? So they're scared of me?

"If you'll excuse me." He gives me a quick bow—*a bow*—and leaves.

I blink at the door for a few long moments, trying to wrap my head around my new reality. In Darkwater Hollow, everyone looked down on me, but these people treat me with a fearful respect I've done nothing to earn. I used to be the daughter of a criminal, and now I'm the wife of one. It seems like no matter where I am, a label gets slapped on me.

I push my irritation aside and go to examine the boxes in the living room. Kneeling down, I carefully peel back the tape, lift the lid, and peer inside.

Books. The box is full of books.

A spark of joy ignites as I pull out the first title. *A Discovery of Witches* by Deborah Harkness. I used to own this one.

Hold on. *Darkfever* by Karen Marie Moning? I had this one too.

I pull them out, one by one, reading each familiar title and stacking them into a tall pile.

Then I find it—a signed special edition of Naomi Novik's *Spinning Silver*, the one I know for a fact had a limited print run. My jaw drops.

How did Nero manage to get this?

For over an hour, I sift through the boxes, uncovering every book that was destroyed in the house fire. Every. Single. One.

Something warm yet unwelcome swells inside my chest. I shouldn't be swayed by this gesture, but I'd be lying if I said I wasn't. I'm amazed at how he managed to figure out the entire list of books that burned.

He's trying to make amends.

But this isn't enough. Not even close.

I shut my eyes and let out a breath. I won't allow a gift to sway my opinion of Nero. This doesn't change the fact that I don't trust him or that I'm planning on leaving as soon as I find a way out.

The act of arranging the books on the shelves in the living room feels like a form of meditation. By the time I'm done, I feel calmer. More grounded.

I've just settled down on the couch and cracked open a thick tome when a knock startles me.

This is becoming ridiculous. Another delivery? I already have enough groceries to feed an army, books to last me a lifetime, and clothes for every occasion, which seems silly given that I'm not even allowed to leave this place.

I put the book down on the coffee table, get to my feet, and move into the foyer. "Come in," I call out.

Alec peeks in, a large black box tucked under one arm. He gives me a polite smile. "Last one for the day, miss. And you have a visitor."

He places the box by the door and lets in a wiry, middle-aged man holding a leather satchel.

"Hello, Mrs. De Luca," the man says.

An electric charge zips down my spine at being addressed by that name. *Whoa.* "You're not afraid to talk to me?"

The man's expression turns confused. "If I didn't talk to you, that would make this appointment quite difficult."

"I'm sorry, who are you?"

"I'm the Messero's family's doctor. Call me Doc. I was supposed to arrive much earlier, but we had an emergency at the clinic."

A doctor employed by the mob? Don't doctors have a code of ethics they have to live by?

"Just so you know, I'm being held here against my will."

He doesn't look particularly surprised. "I was warned you might say something like that. Sometimes it takes a bit of time to settle into a new marriage."

I arch a brow. "So this is normal in the circles you run in?"

He shrugs. "Happens more than you'd think. Do you mind if we sit down?"

"Not at all." I walk back into the living room, and he follows behind me. We sit down across from each other on the sofa.

"Before I examine you, Mr. De Luca requested that I let you make a phone call to a friend. Someone named Del?"

My heart leaps inside my chest. I haven't forgotten Nero's promise, but I'd expected him to let me call her only under his supervision. "Yes. Can I call her now?"

He nods. "I have instructions I must read to you first, and then you must promise you will follow them."

I bite on the inside of my mouth. More rules, more conditions. Is everything in my life going to come with fine print now? "Go ahead."

"You will tell her that you've eloped and decided to relocate to New York with Mr. De Luca. You will make no mention of the other circumstances that precipitated this move. You will also make no mention of any distress you may currently feel or allude to any foul play."

"And if I'm honest?"

Doc looks down at the piece of paper in his hand. "530 Hampshire Street, Unit 308. She lives with a roommate and a gray Siamese cat."

A sense of dread settles over me at the implied threat. "Okay. I agree to the terms."

"Good. I'll call her right now." He hands me the phone as it rings.

I try to keep my composure, but the sound of Del's voice over the speaker makes me choke up. "Del," I croak.

"Oh my God, I've been trying to reach you for days! I was getting worried! What happened?"

"A lot," I blubber. Doc hands me a tissue. I crush it in my fist and dab it under my eyes. "I'm sorry. It's been...crazy. I should have called earlier."

"Why are you crying? What's going on?"

Biting down on my lip, I force myself to suck in a deep breath. I need to put a pin in my emotions, or Del's not going to believe a word I say. She knows I'm not a crier.

"I eloped."

"You *what*?"

"Rowan and I are married."

There's a pause so long that I check to see if the call's still connected. "Del?"

"Yeah, I'm here. I just... I can't believe you didn't tell me you were going to do that."

The obvious hurt in her tone makes me wince. "I'm sorry, Del. It happened very quickly. We got a bit swept up, I guess."

"Are you back home now?"

"No. We actually decided to move to New York."

Del makes a strangled gasp. "*New York?*"

"I know it's unexpected. I was just ready for a change, and you know I've been trying to get out of Darkwater for ages. An opportunity came up, and Rowan took it."

"I don't understand. How? Just...*how?* What about his business? What about your house?"

Your guess is as good as mine. I tug on the neck of my T-shirt, feeling my skin turn clammy. Bullshitting her feels awful. "We're still trying to figure all that out."

"Umm...okay. So you just up and left literally everything behind?"

74

I rub the heel of my palm against my forehead. I should have taken a minute to come up with answers to all of these perfectly reasonable questions, but I was so eager to talk to her, I didn't think this through.

I say the only thing that sounds believable. "We kind of did it on a whim. I think we're in that crazy honeymoon period where everything just feels like it'll work out."

Del blows out a breath. "I just hope you won't have any regrets. God, you're Mrs. Miller now! How does it feel?"

"Great," I force out. "Really great."

"When can I come visit you in New York? Blake, I haven't even met your husband. That's completely unacceptable. I'm your best friend, aren't I?"

I don't miss the vulnerable note that slips into her tone. Poor Del thinks I made one of the biggest decisions of my life without even consulting her. She's got no idea I didn't choose to get married.

"Of course you are. Don't be silly. But you'll need to give me some time to settle in."

"Jeez, babe. This is crazy."

"I know. But it just felt right," I add shakily. There's not a single thing in my life that feels right.

"What number are you calling me from?"

"This is Rowan's phone. I lost mine, but as soon as I get a new one, I'll let you know my number."

Doc clears his throat, signaling that I should wrap it up.

"I've got to run some errands. Let's catch up more later?"

"Okay. I love you."

"I love you too. And I'm sorry for not calling earlier."

"It's okay. I'm just glad you're all right."

"If anyone from Darkwater Hollow reaches out, can you tell them what happened? I quit my job at Frostbite the day we left, and I'm not sure how many people know. They might worry."

"Yeah, no worries. I'll call Lottie. The rest of the town will know it by tomorrow morning."

"Thank you. We'll talk soon." I hang up.

Doc watches me with sad eyes. "She sounds like a good friend."

"She is." I put the cell phone into his outstretched hand, and he swiftly slips it back into his pocket.

"What now?" I ask.

Doc nudges his glasses up the bridge of his nose. "I was told you may have been sexually assaulted a few days ago."

My mood sinks even lower. The only good thing about the roller coaster I've been on the past few days is that I all but buried that memory away. "Yes. I was."

"Were you penetrated?"

I nod. "Briefly, with his fingers." It may have only been seconds before Nero arrived, but I'll never forget how violated I felt in that moment.

My stomach roils.

Doc gives me a compassionate look. "Is there any pain right now?"

"No. There was at first, but it's gone."

"I'd still like to perform an examination, just in case. It's best to check to make sure there are no cuts that might lead to infection."

I shake my head. "I'd prefer you didn't."

"Mrs. De—"

"Look, I'm fine. I would tell you if I wasn't." It's the truth. A long night's rest and a few big meals have given me most of my energy back. The bruises are still there, but they don't bother me since I'm stuck inside all day anyway.

"May I at least check your blood pressure? And take a look at the cut on your knee?"

I sigh. "Okay."

Doc's thorough, and it takes him longer than I expected to do a routine check. Nero's orders, I guess. How else would he know about my knee when I'm wearing sweatpants?

Apparently, Nero did an excellent job cleaning the cut in the parking lot of that Walgreens. Doc says it should heal without any scarring.

"All done," Doc announces finally. "Here's my card in case you need anything."

I take it. "I don't have a phone, remember?"

A line appears between the man's brows. "Ah, I see."

"Any chance you can leave yours with me?"

He gives me a sad smile and gets to his feet. "I'm afraid not, Mrs. De Luca. You'll have to talk to your husband about getting you your own phone."

If I keep relying on Nero for everything, I'm never going to be able to get away from here. The fake passport that I need can't come from him, so I need to find someone else who can hook me up. Maybe Doc here can help me get the lay of the land.

"Have you been working for the Messero family for a long time?" I ask as we head toward the door.

"Yes. Over ten years." He presses a button on the landline phone attached to the wall that I've learned today is how the concierge is summoned. Unfortunately, it's not programmed to make any outside calls.

"So you must know everyone well."

Doc smiles. "I've helped a lot of people who work for the don, and I learned a valuable lesson a long time ago. Would you like to hear it?"

"Uh-huh."

"When it comes to men like your husband, Mrs. De Luca, the less I know, the better."

My chest deflates. Well, that's not helpful at all.

A crisp knock sounds against the door.

"That's Alec," Doc says. "I should go. Any plans for tonight?"

"Plans?"

"It's New Year's Eve."

I arch a brow. "Do you think I'm in a mood to celebrate?"

His gaze softens. "Good luck, Mrs. De Luca."

The door closes, and I'm all alone again. My eyes drop to the black box Alec brought in when Doc arrived. It's the only one I still haven't opened. I crouch down and lift the lid. There's red tissue paper hiding the contents.

When I see what's beneath, whatever goodwill Nero managed to earn with his thoughtful gift earlier disappears.

Lingerie.

An angry knot tightens in my stomach.

How dare he?

Did he think his gifts would be enough to earn my forgiveness? Does he think I can be bought?

My anger has reached a ferocious boil when the front door finally opens around nine p.m. I snatch the box off the coffee table and storm into the foyer. The box is so big, I can hardly see around it, but I don't need to.

"You're out of your fucking mind if you think I'm ever going to wear this," I snarl, hurling the open box and its contents at my husband.

Panties, bras, and negligees go flying through the air. The box clatters to the ground.

And that's when I finally see him.

"Oh my God!"

Nero's face is a mess of blood and bruises, and his half-buttoned white dress shirt is stained red. He takes a staggering step, collapses to his knees, and falls onto the pile of lingerie.

"Nero!" I drop beside him, cradling his head in my hands. His stubbled cheek is warm against my palm. "What happened?"

No response. He's unconscious, having used his last ounce of strength to get here.

I glance up. The front door is open. I can walk right out if I want to.

But then I hear Nero's pained moan, and my gaze drops back to him. How can I abandon him in this state?

God damn it. I can't leave him like this.

With a shaking hand, I pull his phone from his pocket, retrieve the card I'd hidden in my sweatpants, and dial Doc's number.

CHAPTER 8

BLAKE

Concussion. Split lip. Bruised ribs.

Someone used Nero as a human punching bag, but according to Doc, things could have been worse.

He cleans Nero up, stitches his wounds, and writes me a detailed list of care instructions. Then he shows me to a kitchen cabinet I hadn't noticed that's better stocked than a local pharmacy.

"This has everything Nero will possibly need," Doc says, and I believe him. Who has this much medicine in their house?

Someone who needs it. Frequently.

Doc pats my shoulder. "He's as strong as a bull, but call me if he gets worse."

"What are the chances he'll get worse?"

"Low. But he'll be hurting when the painkillers wear off."

"Sorry for ruining your evening."

He smiles. "Don't worry, I'm used to being on call at all times. If I'm lucky, I'll make it back in time for my wife to give me a kiss at midnight."

I spend all night by Nero's side, pressing ice to various body parts. Worry buzzes beneath my skin every time he groans in his sleep or makes a low moan. Halfway through the night, I pass out on the bed beside him, and when I wake up in the morning a few hours later, he's still out cold.

At five past seven, Nero's phone starts buzzing on the nightstand.

My head is groggy as I reach over Nero and grab it.

The caller ID says it's Alessio Ferraro.

I don't know who that is, but just the last name of his new employer fills me with rage. Whatever they made Nero do yesterday resulted in him coming home in this state.

I pick up.

"You're late," a voice rasps on the other end of the line. "I told you we're not taking the day off. There's too much work to do."

My hand tightens around the phone. "And you're out of your mind if you think he's coming into work today."

There's a long pause. "Who's this?"

"Blake."

"Blake who?"

"Blake Wo—De Luca."

"And you're his..."

I squeeze the phone in my hand. "I'm his *wife*."

"Oh...shit."

"Yeah, oh shit is right." I get off the bed, too agitated to keep sitting. "Are you the one who did this to him last night?"

"It was a friendly match."

"What?" I ask, confused.

"We were boxing."

"Are you fucked up in the head or something? You call what did this to him a *friendly* match?"

"He was fine when I dropped him off." There's a defensive note in the man's voice.

"He collapsed as soon as he walked through the door, you asshole. What is wrong with you?"

There's a pause. "I'm coming over."

"No, I don't need you—"

"I'll be there in a half hour."

The call ends.

Ugh! I resist the urge to hurl the cell phone across the room and simply drop it on the coffee table.

Fine. If Alessio Ferraro wants to get reamed by me in person, he can be my guest.

A half hour later, Alec calls, asking if I want to let one Mr. Ferraro up the elevator. Moments later, a man who claims to be him is standing in Nero's living room.

Alessio Ferraro is a black ink stain against the cream-painted walls. I thought Nero had a lot of tattoos, but he's got nothing on this guy. With the exception of his face, every inch of him is inked, down to his fingertips.

"Did you know your front door was open?" he asks. "You should keep that locked."

I left it propped open after Doc left last night just in case things took a turn for the worse and he needed to come back before Nero woke up.

I point my index finger at Alessio. "You've got some fucking nerve. If your family wanted to kill Nero, why didn't they just do it the first night he came back? You beat him to a pulp."

He rubs the back of his hand against his cheek and shrugs. "He asked for it. He wouldn't tap out."

"What do you mean?"

"We were boxing against each other. I would have stopped if he'd tapped out."

"Well, why didn't he?"

"I don't know."

A hollow feeling appears in the pit of my stomach.

Did Nero want to get hurt? Why? And also, what the *hell*? Nero must have realized I'd be the one who'd take care of him when he came home looking like that.

Did he think I'd enjoy it? I'm not a sadist. No matter how angry I am about everything Nero did to me, I don't want to see him in pain.

Maybe it's the guilt catching up to him.

No, I'm not holding my breath for that.

I arch a brow at the man in front of me. "You couldn't see how badly you were hurting him?"

Alessio shrugs again. "I do have a tendency to take things too far. Can I see him?"

"He's in the bedroom."

Nero's shifted on the bed since I left him five minutes ago. There's a bloodstain on the pillow from a cut in his brow that's seeping through the bandage.

I go to sit down beside him and start to peel the bandage off, wanting to replace it. Outside, the early morning sun creeps in from between the drawn blinds. I'd kill for some coffee.

"I can call a doctor," Alessio says.

"Someone already looked at him."

"Who?"

"He introduced himself as Doc. He works for the Messeros." The second I say it, I realize I should have kept my mouth shut. What if Nero's not supposed to be in contact with Doc now that he's a Ferraro man?

I glance at Alessio, trying to gauge his reaction, but his face is a blank mask. Only his eyes show small glimmers of emotion.

When they move back to me, they almost seem apologetic. "He'll be alright?"

"Yes." I secure a fresh bandage on the cut, and Nero shifts again. Groans. Cracks open his swollen eyes.

Relief flashes inside them when he focuses on me. "Blake," he whispers.

He sounds terrible.

My emotions surge. It physically hurts to see him broken like this. All night, I tried to convince myself I'd worry this much about anyone who was hurt, but by the morning, I had to admit the truth, if only to myself.

I still feel something for him. In the aftermath of finding out about his lies, I thought every bit of love I had for this man had been expunged out of me, but no, it's still there.

It might be twisted, darkened, and bruised, but it's *there*.

God, I wish it wasn't. It makes me terrified.

I brush the back of my hand over Nero's cheek. "You're an idiot."

He gives me a half smile, wincing when it pulls on his split lip. "Nice to see you too."

That smile vanishes the moment he sees Alessio standing at the foot of the bed.

Nero tries to sit up, emitting a pained groan. "What are you doing here? How the fuck did you get in?"

I place my hand on his shoulder. "Careful."

"I was just telling your wife you should keep your door locked."

Apprehension and unease flood Nero's expression. "Fuck." His gaze pings to me before moving back to Alessio. "Stay away from her."

The tattooed man crosses his arms over his chest. "Didn't know you were married."

Nero blinks once, twice, as if convincing himself that this is real.

Alessio tilts his head. "You didn't come in to work. I thought I'd give you a courtesy call before coming over to kill you, and Blake picked up and explained the situation."

I'm sorry, what? Did he just say what I think he said? "Kill him? You wanted to *kill* him for being late?"

Alessio's gray eyes shift to me. "He knows the deal. No second chances. I thought he didn't show up because he couldn't handle the work."

He must be joking.

"I can handle the work just fine," Nero growls. "Just let me get dressed and—"

I turn around so fast my hair whips against my cheek. "Absolutely not."

"Blake—"

"*No.*" I get to my feet and walk right up to Alessio, who's looking at me curiously. I'm so angry and tired that I don't have the energy to hold my tongue. "I was up all night because of what you did to him. I'm not doing that again. You hear me? You're out of your damn mind if you think he's going anywhere today. He's going to get some rest, and you're going to leave us alone."

Silence descends on the room, so thick you could bite into it.

I glance at Nero. His eyes are wide with shock.

Alessio sniffs and has the decency to look somewhat ashamed. "Fine. He can take today off."

Damn right. I give him a curt nod.

He shoves his hands into his pockets. "By the way, why is there underwear all over your foyer?"

Oh crap. Blood rushes to my cheeks. I haven't bothered cleaning up the lingerie I threw at Nero before I realized he was hurt. "Never you mind," I mutter, refusing to meet Nero's eye. "Are we done here?"

"Yeah, we're done. I'll show myself out." With one final glance at Nero, Alessio disappears from the room.

A few seconds later, I hear the front door open and shut.

"Blake."

"What?" I snap. I'm convinced both these men are clinically insane.

"That was... Wow. Thank you for taking care of me."

I take a deep breath, trying to calm the storm of emotions swirling inside me before I turn to face him. "Did you let him beat you up on purpose?"

Guilt zaps through his gaze.

Suddenly, I'm overcome with the urge to strangle him. "You will never do anything like that again. Not while I'm here. Not while I'm the one who's waiting for you at home."

His skin turns ashen. "You're right. I'm sorry."

I'm sorry too. I'm sorry that I still have feelings for this man, because it only makes it more likely I'm going to get hurt again and again.

It's more urgent than ever that I find a way out of this situation. I won't end up like my mother, in love with someone who only brings her pain.

If anything, last night only confirmed that's what I have waiting for me. Who wants to see their husband come home beaten and bruised? Who wants to worry if he'll make it home at all?

Not me. This life is *not* for me.

And I can't risk forgetting that.

Nero's gaze stays fixed on me. "Maybe when my face looks better, I can make it up to you over dinner. I'll take you to the best place in town."

I give my head a hard shake. "This doesn't change anything, Nero."

His hopeful expression wavers. "Please. Just one dinner."

For a maddening second, I consider saying yes, but instead, I force myself to recall the hurt and anger from last night. "Why did you get me that lingerie, Nero?"

His brows knit in confusion. "What do you mean?"

"Did you think I'd wear it for you after you got me the books? Who do you take me for?"

His eyes widen with horror. "What lingerie?"

"The black box. It was filled with it. Did you think we'd just move on like nothing happened?"

His shoulders slump. "Blake, I just told whoever did the shopping to get you clothes. The lingerie... They assumed. You're my wife, and they assumed."

I search his face for any sign of deceit but find none.

So it wasn't his doing.

"Fine. Good," I grumble.

A few silent seconds pass. "Do you like the books?" he asks.

Of course I do. "How did you know which ones burned?" I clip out.

Sadness flickers over his expression. "Sandro took a photo of your shelves when we came over for Thanksgiving. He sent it to me a while ago."

Sandro.

Some of my anger begins to melt, but I make myself cling to it. I can't let myself weaken. "Thank you for the books, but I want to be clear. There won't be any dinners, any dates. We're roommates, nothing more. Married in name only, Nero."

His gaze darkens with displeasure, but I don't give a damn.

I won't let him get close to me again.

If I do, I'm afraid he'll wash away the line I just drew in the sand like a tidal wave.

CHAPTER 9

NERO

I roll my eyes at the text on my phone.

> Pick up a coffee for me on your way over.
> Extra large, splash of oat milk. From Bar
> Volo. That's the only one I drink.

What is this? The mob version of *The Devil Wears Prada*? Alessio Ferraro is a fucking diva. The coffee shop he sends me to is on the other side of town.

I get into my car and start driving.

My face is a patchwork of bruises. Same with my stomach and ribs. Alessio got me good, but I've had worse, and there's something comforting about the pain. I know how to deal with pain.

What I don't know how to deal with is my wife.

She insisted I take not one, but two days off work, and then she proceeded to ignore me for most of them, only checking in around mealtimes to make sure I ate what she made for me.

As if I wouldn't.

For all her coldness, one thing is keeping my hope alive.

Blake could have escaped when I was unconscious. She could have taken my keys, wallet, and phone, ignored all my warnings, and been on her way to California by now.

But she stayed and took care of me.

And then she scolded Alessio Fucking Ferraro like he's a kid in middle school instead of the biggest psychopath in New York City.

The memory of it still makes me chuckle. I'm going to remember that befuddled look on Alessio's face for the rest of my life.

I pull up to the curb outside the coffee shop, get out of my car, and glance around. This neighborhood isn't in Ferraro's territory. Why the fuck does Alessio have a hard-on for this particular spot?

I walk inside. I'm expecting some gourmet hipster bullshit, but it's nothing special. Behind the counter, the grumpy middle-aged woman with a polka-dot apron tied around her waist pours me two cups out of a stained coffee pot. "Five bucks."

"You got any oat milk?"

She looks at me like I've lost my mind. "No. Try the convenience store next door."

I pay her and snap lids onto the steaming paper cups. As I walk out, two older men playing chess at one of the tables by the door shoot me dirty looks.

The fuck?

I don't understand why Alessio sent me here. But I don't think anyone knows what's going on inside that guy's head.

After I pick up a full fucking carton of oat milk, I get back into my car and drive to the warehouse.

My footsteps echo as I make my way underground.

In the torture room, Alessio's sitting on a metal stool in front of a guy tied to a chair. He's pulling off the guy's nails one by one.

"Brought you your coffee," I shout so that he'll hear me over the man's screams.

He glances over his shoulder and puts the pliers down on the tray beside him before getting to his feet. He walks over and takes one of the cups from me, leaving bloody prints on the white surface. "Thanks."

I tip my head in the direction of his sobbing prisoner. "Who's this?"

"A Bratva runner." He takes a sip. "Junior, but we've heard he's done errands directly for the pakhan. I'm trying to get the location of the safe house where the pakhan is hiding."

"He's in hiding?" He wasn't when I left six months ago.

"Yeah. He's a paranoid fuck. He's giving his vors orders exclusively over the phone. They've got a lot on their plate managing all the men they're shipping here by busload from Boston."

So things have really heated up. "What's their agenda?"

"Business conditions in Boston have become inhospitable. The new mayor has promised to crack down on organized crime, and he's got the Bratva in his crosshairs. The writing's on the wall. They're trying to move into new territory."

"And they chose New York? Don't they know how crowded it's gotten?"

Alessio shrugs. "The Bratva loves New York. They romanticize it. They think if they can rule here, they can rule anywhere. This whole thing is driven as much by emotion as it is by logic."

"I take it you're not negotiating?"

He adjusts his grip on his cup. "We're exterminating. It's taking some time, but I'll find the pakhan eventually. Once he's dead, there will be too much infighting for them to continue this campaign. They'll retreat to where they came from, or they'll pick a new place to try to invade."

A crash sounds from behind a door.

"And that?"

"That's my afternoon appointment."

"Another runner?"

"No. One of pakhan's vors."

My brows rise. A vor is the equivalent of a capo. "How did you manage that?"

"Cosimo set a good trap. We're not going to kill him. Just send a message."

"Uh-huh." I'm doubtful Alessio is capable of such restraint.

"Let me wrap up with this one, and then you can start the cleanup while I talk to the vor."

I nod. "All right."

⁓

THE RUNNER DOESN'T KNOW the pakhan's location. That becomes obvious after Alessio starts sawing off his fingers. The man tells him other things, things that Alessio already knows. He's got nothing that can save him. Nothing valuable to offer.

Around eleven, Alessio appears to get bored of him, and he snaps his neck with no warning.

"I want to talk to the vor," he offers by way of explanation.

"What do you want me to do with the body?"

"Should be some bags in that file cabinet. Chop him up, put him in, and clean the floor. Then you can dump him in the Hudson."

"Easy peasy, huh?"

"Yep," he tosses over his shoulder as he walks into the room with the vor.

I roll my eyes. That guy does not understand sarcasm.

Three hours later, I'm on my knees, wiping blood off the floor, when two Ferraro guys appear.

"What can I help you with, gents?" I call out.

The door to the room with the vor opens, and Alessio drags an older man out. The man's hair looks like a bird's nest, and he's got bruises nastier than mine all over his face. His eyes meet mine, and a second later, there's a flash of recognition.

Does he know who I am? Probably. After all, six months ago, everyone knew who I was.

Alessio rummages in a drawer, pulls out a cloth bag, and tosses it over the vor's head. He shoves him toward the guys. "Take him back."

The two men lead the vor out of the torture room.

"You get anything good out of him?" I ask, my eyes following the men.

Alessio walks over to a fridge in the corner of the room and takes out a shiny green apple. "No."

I get to my feet and wash my hands at the sink. "Why let him go then?"

"I felt like it."

I sigh. I guess he doesn't owe me an explanation.

He bites into his apple with a loud crack. "You're not wearing a ring."

"Huh?"

"Your wedding ring. You didn't wear it the first day or today. Cosimo was surprised to hear you're married."

Nerves prickle over my nape. Now that the Ferraros know about Blake, I've really got to figure out what the endgame is here. How long are they going to have me doing grunt work for Alessio? There are plenty of other guys who could do this shit instead of me, and while it's nasty business, it's far from the worst thing Gino could have put me on if all he wanted was to make me suffer.

"If I die, Blake will be under Rafaele's protection," I say firmly. "Whatever happens between us, you can't touch her."

Alessio takes another loud bite. "I won't hurt her. I like her."

I narrow my eyes at him. "Why?"

"She wasn't scared of me. Most girls are scared of me."

That's because she's got no idea how fucking cuckoo you are.

I lean back against the stainless-steel counter. "What about your brothers? You better not have given them any ideas."

He shrugs. "I don't speak for them, but in general, we don't target women unless they've really earned it. You should talk to my dad about Blake and make sure you've got an understanding."

I nod. "I will." I have no choice at this point.

"You can talk to him tonight. Mom wanted me to invite the two of you for dinner."

Fuck me. I wanted to keep Blake far away from all the mob shit. She's not gonna like it, and she's definitely not gonna be happy that the first time I'm letting her leave the house is to sit down for dinner with my boss and his wife. But I'm not going to delude myself into thinking we have a choice about going.

I run my fingers through my hair. "Let me call Blake."

Alessio pops the apple core into his mouth. What is he, a fucking horse? "Go ahead. You can take breaks, you know? Wouldn't want your wife to yell at me again about the working conditions."

Shaking my head, I walk out of the room and make my way outside.

It's cold as fuck. January in New York is almost as miserable as February. Did Rafe's private shopper get Blake a warm enough coat? I sure hope so, or I'll have to take her shopping. Depending on how tonight goes, Blake's house arrest might be over. If Ferraro promises he won't touch her, my excuse for keeping her locked away will disappear, which makes my anxiety spike. It's better when I know she's safe and sound, but at the end of the day, I know I need to give her a bit of freedom if I want her to ever be happy in this city.

Alec picks up his cell phone immediately. "Mr. De Luca?"

"Can you bring the phone up to the penthouse? I need to talk to my wife." I really need to figure out a better way for us to communicate. Maybe it's time I give her a phone as well.

"Of course, sir."

A minute later, Blake comes on the line. "Hello?"

"Hey, Sunshine. The Ferraros want to have dinner with the two of us."

"Why?" Suspicion bleeds into her voice, but she hasn't snapped at me for using her nickname. I'm going to take that as a good sign.

"I don't know," I admit. "The invitation came from Vita, Gino Ferraro's wife."

"Why can't you go on your own?"

"The invitation is for both of us. I thought you were itching to get out of the penthouse."

"Yeah, but breaking bread with a family of mobsters is not exactly what I had in mind," she grumbles.

A grin tugs at the corner of my lips. She's such a grump sometimes.

She sighs. "All right. Never mind. It's fine."

"Can you be ready by six-thirty?"

"That's two hours from now. Of course, I can be ready. Am I supposed to dress in a certain way?"

"No. Just wear whatever you feel comfortable in. And don't forget your ring," I add after a moment. That reminds me, I need to get her something better than that cheap band from the Vegas chapel. She doesn't need a reminder of our less than stellar wedding on her finger.

She needs something sparkling and heavy, so that whenever she looks at it, she'll think about what we can still become.

CHAPTER 10

BLAKE

"Blake, why don't you tell us how you and Nero met?"

My gaze jumps to our hostess—Vita Ferraro—who's giving me a smile from the other side of the oak dining table. I gulp down my wine. To say I'm feeling disoriented would be an understatement.

If someone asked me what I imagined the wife of a big mob boss to look like, Vita wouldn't be it. She's slim and lively, and she has an air of sophisticated elegance that's both captivating and disarming. I had expected her to be cold and aloof. Instead, she radiates a warmth that makes me feel surprisingly at ease.

It's confusing.

When my dad brought Maxton and me to the trailer park where he and many members of the Iron Raptors lived, there was no mistaking the fact that the people there were criminals. The place reeked of crime. In every corner, there seemed to be whispered secrets of illicit deals and violent confrontations. Conversations grew hushed as Maxton and I walked by—we were outsiders and thus not to be trusted. It was a place where the rule of law had long been forgotten and replaced by a code of survival written in blood.

But it seems the Ferraros operate differently.

Their home—a penthouse even grander than Nero's—is a tranquil setting.

There are no stray dogs with ribs showing, no broken windows patched with duct tape, and definitely no garbage littering the floors.

Instead, subtle notes of pine and lavender waft through the air. The sound of trickling water permeates the space like a gentle lullaby. Everywhere you look, there's something beautiful. Whether it's a piece of art on the wall, an ancient-looking vase on top of a dresser, or the glittering jewelry strung around Vita's neck.

If I didn't know who this family was, I never would have guessed that everything in here was paid for with blood money.

After I got over the initial shock of being invited here, I decided this would be the perfect opportunity to get smart. I'll need help if I want to extricate myself from Nero's iron grasp. I'll need a damned passport, but I have no clue who to ask for that help.

First, I need to understand the rules of the game and the pieces on the chessboard. Tonight is my chance to do that.

Nero squeezes my hand lightly under the table, reminding me Vita's waiting for an answer.

I take another sip of wine before answering. "He moved in next door to me, and then he set my house on fire so that I'd date him."

Nero coughs, nearly choking on his wine, and I can't help but feel a bit of satisfaction at his reaction. Did he want me to make up some story? He should have given me an indication of that if that was the case. Instead, he did his best to avoid answering most of my questions about the Ferraros on the drive over.

It's like he wants to keep me in the dark.

"Well, that's certainly one way to make an impression," Gino Ferraro says with a chuckle, his eyes sparkling with amusement.

Cosimo Ferraro, the only sibling who's joined us for this dinner, regards Nero with a scowl. "So that's what you have to resort to in order to get a woman within five feet of you?"

"At least I didn't need my daddy to arrange my marriage for me," Nero responds without missing a beat.

Cosimo's eyes narrow.

Vita's smile doesn't waver, but there's a slight tightening around her eyes. "Boys, let's not forget we're here to enjoy a pleasant evening."

Nero gives a curt nod and slightly loosens his grip on my hand.

"I have a hard time imagining you in a small town, Nero," Gino says. "You must have been very bored."

"At first, but Darkwater Hollow grew on me. Especially after I met Blake."

A traitorous flutter appears low inside my belly.

God, what's wrong with me? This man forced me to marry him, and here I am *fluttering*.

This is exactly why I have to find my way out of New York, and I have to do it quickly, before I become even more confused about my feelings.

"I wonder how Blake feels about everything," Cosimo says as he cuts into his veal. "Sounds like you brought her nothing but trouble. Blake, I assume you had no idea who Nero was at first."

Beside me, Nero stills. My gaze drops to the tight grip he's got on his steak knife.

"No, I didn't. I only found out recently."

"You must love him a lot to stay by his side." Cosimo's lips curve into a mocking smile.

I can tell Cosimo doesn't like Nero, and for a second, I wonder if *he* might be able to help me.

But the idea makes my stomach churn. Cosimo would never let Nero forget it, and Nero would be so furious he might just try to kill Cosimo.

I bite down on my lip. No. I don't need that on my conscience. There has to be a way for me to slip away without causing anyone to be hurt.

"Oh, there he is," Vita says suddenly, her gaze shifting to the doorway.

I follow her line of sight and see Alessio Ferraro entering the room.

Nero told me that Alessio is the head enforcer of the Ferraro family. He didn't need to give me more details. I know what being an enforcer means.

No wonder Nero seemed so stunned when I yelled at the dark-haired man. I'm guessing most people don't do that sort of thing. But I really wasn't thinking rationally at the time or paying too much attention to anything but my bruised and beaten husband.

Alessio takes a seat beside his brother and gives Nero and me a curt nod. His hair is tied back from his face with an elastic band, but a few strands have escaped, casting shadows over his cheekbones.

Vita smiles. "Blake, Alessio tells me the two of you already met?"

"Briefly."

"It's a shame Rom couldn't be here," she says, referring to the youngest Ferraro brother. "I would have loved for you to meet him too."

My curiosity gets the best of me. "Why?"

This whole evening has just been...entirely too pleasant. It's like they're trying to butter us up for something.

Vita doesn't seem offended by the question. "We think it's important that whenever anyone new joins our family, they feel welcomed."

I glance at Nero. He's cutting his baked potato into neat pieces, wearing a neutral expression on his face, but something's just not adding up.

Nero said Gino Ferraro planned to kill him the day we returned. How the hell does someone go from that to this in the span of less than a week?

"Nero, tell me about this company you ran in Missouri," Gino prompts.

The conversation steers toward Handy Heroes for the rest of the dinner. Cosimo and Alessio stay mostly silent, as do I, but Gino and Vita seem engaged in the discussion, asking questions and nodding along to Nero's stories as if they're old friends.

It's only when the staff come around to take away our empty plates that something in the atmosphere shifts.

Gino folds his napkin into a rectangle and places it on the table. "There's a bit of business I'd like for us to discuss. Would you two join Vita and me in the office?"

"The two of us?" Nero asks, tossing me a look.

"That would be great."

Nero frowns. "Blake doesn't need to be there if we're talking business."

I feel a prickle of agitation at his dismissive tone, but then I remember I genuinely have no reason to be present for a conversation between him and his boss. Why would Gino even want me there?

Gino links his fingers on the table in front of him. "This is something that concerns the two of you."

Nero's profile hardens. He reaches for my hand again and interlaces our fingers, as if trying to reassure me.

Or himself.

"I'll join you too," Cosimo says.

"That won't be necessary, son," Gino says as he gets to his feet. "You and Alessio can get started on dessert. We won't be long."

The dismissal clearly ticks off Cosimo, and he narrows his eyes in displeasure as Vita, Nero, and I rise. Alessio doesn't seem to care, though. He's playing some game on his phone.

Nero tugs me closer to him as we make our way to Gino's office. He leans in and whispers, "Don't be afraid. Whatever this is, I won't let anything happen to you."

I blink at him. I'm not getting a threatening vibe from Gino, but it's clear Nero's worried about something. What is it?

In the office, Nero and I take a seat on one of the cream sofas in the sitting area, while Gino and Vita settle in across from us.

Vita pours us some white wine. When I catch her eye as she sets the bottle down, there's something there that I didn't notice before. Something cunning.

There's far more to this woman than just being the don's hospitable wife.

Nero places a palm on my lower back. "Let's cut to the chase, Gino. What is this about?"

The silver-haired man smiles as his wife takes a seat beside him. "Do you remember the last time you were here, Nero?"

"Of course," Nero says roughly.

"You were right there—" Gino points to a spot in front of the desk "—on your knees before me."

Ice slides down my veins. What?

"Do know why I didn't pull the trigger that day?"

My eyes dart toward Nero. Ferraro came that close to killing him?

It was true. It was all true.

Nero nearly died for me.

The hand on my lower back curls into the fabric of my dress. "No. But I'm guessing you're finally gonna tell me."

"Rafaele's exact words were that you're an asset. And he was right. There's a job that you're uniquely positioned to do for me."

"It sure as fuck isn't what you have me doing now," Nero says.

"No, it's not," Gino agrees.

"What is it then?" A note of impatience slips into Nero's tone.

I force myself to focus on what Gino's saying despite my racing thoughts and the rapid beating of my heart.

Gino smiles, but it doesn't reach his eyes. "We want you to infiltrate the Bratva and help us find the pakhan."

Infiltrate the who and find the what?

Nero seems to know exactly what Gino's talking about. "How do you expect me to do that?"

"Before you left, you were a loyal consigliere. You were the one who killed Michael, but the blame lies with Rafaele. We both know he should have warned you my men would be there. A man in your position would have been rightfully

107

upset about having to give up..." Gino swirls his wine around. "Well, everything."

"What's your point?"

"My point is that it wouldn't be so difficult to believe that you want to get even with your old boss. Especially after he threw you to the wolves when you came back."

"The wolves being you and your sons?"

"Indeed. From the outside, it looks like you got quite the demotion. You went from leading scores of men and holding critical negotiations in gilded meeting rooms to cleaning blood and guts off cement floors after Alessio's interrogations."

Shock crackles through me.

That's...what they're making him do?

Nero's uneasy gaze snaps my way. One look into his eyes tells me he didn't want me to know that.

And that's when something inside me shifts. It's like a lamp's been turned on inside a dark room, casting everything in a new light.

The events of the last few months whirl through my mind.

Nero had to leave New York because of someone else's mistake. He tried to start over. He had a business, a real, honest business that he was running with his partner.

And he was doing fine.

Right up until he moved in next door to me. Right up until getting involved with me put him in the crosshairs of my ex and my godfather. The two men whose actions caused Nero's fake identity to be revealed.

The world tilts.

How did I not see it earlier?

I put all the blame on Nero, but I'm just as guilty we're in this mess.

What would have happened if he'd never met me?

He would have been fine. Sandro would still be alive.

They would still be working in Darkwater Hollow and living their new lives.

Instead, Sandro's gone, and Nero's been forced back here. He's working for a man who nearly killed him. A man who sees him as nothing more than a pawn on a chessboard.

Nero knew exactly what might happen to him upon his return to New York, and he came back here anyway.

For me.

"You wanted that vor to see me today," Nero murmurs. "Alessio didn't kill him because you wanted him to run back to the Russians and tell them what you're having me do."

Gino nods. "Seeing you at that coffee shop also helped paint a picture. It's a laundering front for the Bratva."

Nero's laugh is humorless. "You've really thought this through."

"We wanted the pakhan to realize there's someone in the family who might be willing to turn. Someone who knows a lot of secrets that would be valuable to him and the Bratva."

Even without understanding the terms Gino's using, I'm starting to piece together what he's getting at. He wants Nero to help them take down a rival by pretending to switch sides.

Nero places his wineglass on the coffee table. "The pakhan would be happy to get whatever information he can from me. But what are you hoping to get out of this?"

"His location," Vita answers.

Is this plan her idea?

"No one but those in his inner circle know where he is," she continues. "If we find him and take care of him, the rest of the organization will crumble."

Nero rubs his chin. "How am I supposed to convince anyone to give me his location? Even if he believes I'm willing to betray you, he's not about to invite me over for coffee."

Gino's eyes flash. "That's where your cleverness comes in. Rafe did mention you possess this quality. I have faith you'll find a way in."

"Is this an order?" Nero asks, his voice low.

"It would have been, but unfortunately—" Gino's gaze slides over to me "—we also need Blake's cooperation."

Nero stands up abruptly, his hand lifting from my back. "No."

"We won't involve her if she doesn't want to get involved," Gino says calmly to a man who's definitely not calm.

"She's not getting involved," Nero growls.

Vita catches my gaze. This is why they invited me here—to try and build a relationship. To make me *want* to help them.

"What role would I have to play?" I ask.

"As Nero's wife, you will be subjected to scrutiny," Vita says. "To pull this off, you and Nero will have to work in tandem.

You will have to convince the other side that you're so angry about what happened to Nero that you're willing to risk it all to get your revenge."

My God. It's so crazy, I almost laugh. Me? How am I supposed to manage something like that? I don't belong in this world. I don't know how to exist in it, let alone be an active participant. I'd mess it up on day one.

Nero extends his hand to me. As soon as I take it, he tugs me to my feet. "We're leaving."

Vita's gaze bores into me. "Blake, we'd do everything we can to ensure your success. I would personally prepare you."

"I said no," Nero snaps. "She is under Rafe's protection. You have no domain over her."

"We're aware," Gino drawls. "Which is why we're asking, not ordering."

"This conversation is over." Nero pulls me toward the door.

"Nero, don't you want to hear what's in it for you?" Gino calls out.

"I don't care. The answer is still no. I will not involve Blake in our business, no matter what."

"If you help us end this war, I will make you capo. I will give you a position of power in my organization despite what happened with my nephew. You won't be an errand boy for my son anymore, and you will have the respect you deserve."

Nero's jaw clenches. Silence wraps around the room.

"Blake," Vita says after a few seconds. "What do you think?"

The grip Nero has on my hand tightens. I almost expect him to lead me out without letting me answer, but he stays still, waiting for me to say my piece.

My heartbeat pounds in my ears. I don't know how to do this. I'm just a girl from a town no one's ever heard of. How am I supposed to pull something like this off?

It's impossible.

"I can't help you," I say quietly.

Disappointment flashes inside Vita's eyes, but she quickly collects herself. "I understand."

The evening is over. Gino and Vita walk us to the door, the mood decidedly tense and uneasy.

Vita pulls me into a hug as she says her goodbye. I feel her slip something into my purse. "A burner phone," she whispers into my ear. "Call me if you change your mind."

CHAPTER 11

BLAKE

Nero doesn't speak to me on the way home. He's lost in thought as he drives us back to the penthouse.

Heavy rain pelts against the windshield. It's just above zero tonight, warm for January in New York according to Alec. He complimented us when he saw us leaving earlier. Said we're a beautiful couple.

Just like the Ferraros, you'd never know the truth about us based on how we look.

Their offer circles inside my head like an insistent fly. I have no desire to get more involved with Nero's world than I already am, but there might be something here.

Something that could help both Nero and me.

Now that I finally understand what Nero's given up for me and the part I had to play in our current situation, some of my anger at him has been replaced with a heavy dose of guilt.

He lost everything when he came to Darkwater Hollow, and now he's lost everything again. It doesn't seem like he's even in contact with his old boss or any of his other friends anymore. Did they abandon him now that he's working for the Ferraros?

Does he have anyone in this city besides me?

I've been feeling so alone since he brought me here, yet I never considered he might be feeling lonely too.

He doesn't even have Sandro to confide in anymore. In the midst of all this chaos, has he had a chance to grieve him? Or did he push all of his emotions away?

"We'll program your fingerprints into the security system tonight," he says, surprising me. "Now that the Ferraros know you're here, there's no point in keeping you locked inside."

My house arrest is over. "Thank you," I say softly.

He just nods.

I study him for a few seconds as he navigates the busy streets of this city.

He's still not fully healed from the boxing match with Alessio, but even with the cut on his lip and the fading bruise on his cheekbone, he's painfully handsome.

I push down the sudden urge to lean over and press a kiss to his cheek.

What I learned today doesn't change the fact that I can't ever trust him again, or the fact that it's over between us.

I still want to leave New York.

But I don't want to leave Nero like this.

"What is a capo exactly?" I ask.

"The mob's middle management. A capo has his own crew that he's responsible for. They work for him and pay him a share of their profits. The capo then pays his own share to the boss."

I arch a brow. "Sounds like an MLM. Do you sell Tupperware?"

A chuckle rumbles out of Nero. "Not quite. Unless it's filled with cocaine."

"So is that the core of the business? Drugs?"

He shoots me a sideways glance. "Why so curious all of a sudden?"

"You can't expect me to not be curious after the evening we just had. If it weren't for Cosimo's attitude and Alessio showing up in all his ink, you could have said the family got rich from building an essential oils empire, and I would have believed you. They don't look like gangsters."

"The sooner you learn not to trust appearances, the better off you'll be in the long run," Nero says. "The Ferraros deal in weapons, drugs, and racketeering. They also have a large portfolio of legitimate businesses, some of which act as their fronts. Their empire is vast, and they're well-known in political circles due to their generous donations to promising candidates."

"Promising?"

"The ones whose priorities have nothing to do with going after organized crime."

We stop at a red light.

"Would you want to be a capo?"

Nero turns to me, his hazel eyes assessing. "What does it matter?"

"I'm curious. How would that compare to being a consigliere?"

His lips firm into a thin line. "I was a capo for far longer than I was a consigliere. It would be like slipping into an old pair of shoes, I suppose."

"How did you get involved with all this anyway?"

"The mob? It was never a choice."

My brow furrows. "What do you mean? You were forced into it?"

A hint of amusement appears on his lips as we start driving again. "I'm no victim, Sunshine. I craved this life. From a young age, all I ever wanted was to get made."

"Must have been quite the childhood for that to have been your goal in life." I realize how judgmental I sound only after the words leave my mouth.

Nero just shrugs. "Maybe it was."

"You've never told me about it."

"You've never asked."

"I'm asking now." I think I'm finally ready to learn who Nero is, but I wonder if he's willing to show me.

"My childhood was complicated," he finally says. "It changed a lot when my mom left my dad. My biological father was a weak man who preferred to let my mom and I starve than do what needed to be done to provide for his family."

"You were poor?"

"We lived in a cockroach-infested studio in the Bronx until I was about seven. It's a miracle my mom dealt with it for that long. She was used to a very different lifestyle growing up."

"Her family didn't help her?"

"They tried, but every time my mom accepted any money from her parents, my father would go on an angry rampage. He hated her side of the family, and he had none of his own to rely on."

"Why did he hate them so much?"

"Because they were criminals. He had a rigid moral compass and an unwavering sense of right and wrong."

Heat spreads over my cheeks.

"My mom came from a long line of gangsters. My grandpa was a high-ranking capo for the Messero family. Ma went against her father's wishes by marrying a civilian, and it caused a rift between them. She gave up a lot to be with my father. She loved him. In return, he allowed her to live in abject poverty, refusing help and refusing to take any of the job offers my grandfather extended to him. He was a proud and stubborn man, and he watched his family suffer instead of getting involved with 'those people,' as he liked to call my mother's family."

I exhale a heavy breath. "You make it sound like the only way he could have given you a better life was to work for the mob. I'm sure he had other choices."

"Yeah, well if he did, he didn't pursue them. In the end, my mom left him for my stepdad, and she never looked back. Renzo gave her the life she deserved. He never had any scruples about doing whatever it took to provide for his family."

Something uncomfortable flickers in the pit of my stomach. "Just because your stepdad treated your mom well doesn't make him a good person."

"He didn't care about being perceived as a good person. That's the point. He cared about the people around him, the people he loved, far more than the opinions of others." A muscle jumps in his jaw. "My father was the one obsessed with his image. He wouldn't accept the help his family desperately needed because he was too worried about what the people in his church would say about him if they found out."

The pieces are starting to come together. "Your stepdad was your hero. You think he saved you and your mom."

"I don't think it. I know it. He always treated me like I was his own. He taught me how to be a man."

"He taught you how to be a mobster."

"A very good one." He flexes his hands on the wheel. "I know you look down on this life, Blake, but it saved me and my mom. And my stepdad taught me that the labels society assigns things—the good and the bad, the moral and the immoral—are made up. There are no absolutes in life. Only once you accept that can you find true freedom."

I glance down at my hands, refusing to accept that's true. There are some things in this life that are undeniably bad. And being a criminal, the kind that kills people, is immoral. It's wrong.

But there's no point in arguing with Nero about it. It's clear we won't agree. "Was Gino right about you wanting to get even with Rafaele?" I ask after a few silent minutes pass.

A grim expression unfurls over his face. "No. I would never betray the Messeros."

"Even after what happened? It sounds like he kind of screwed you over."

"It felt like that in the beginning, but I got over it eventually. I forgave Rafe. Sometimes, we're put in impossible situations where there isn't a good way to protect everyone important to us. In those situations we make choices. Choices that define who we are. Rafe made his choice that night. He put his wife above all, even me, his best friend. And you know what? I get it."

My hands curl, my nails digging into my palms. Is he implying that he'd do the same for me? That he'd choose me?

He already has, hasn't he? Only instead of putting me above his best friend, he put me above *himself*.

I swallow, my throat suddenly tight. "Don't you want to at least think about Gino's offer?"

"No." His tone is resolute. "What he's proposing is insane and dangerous."

"The Bratva are the Russian equivalent of the mob?"

"Yes."

"And the pakhan?"

"The pakhan is what they call their leader. The current pakhan of the Boston Bratva branch is a ruthless, paranoid old man who's set on taking over New York, no matter the cost to his people. I doubt he'd even take the bait, but even if he did, the risk isn't worth it. Not even close."

"I'm guessing you've done far riskier things in the past," I prod.

He shrugs as he pulls into the underground parking lot of the building. "Back when I only had myself to worry about, sure. But with you here, everything is different."

Anguish wraps around my lungs. He's sacrificing his only chance at a better life here for me. The Ferraros won't give him another opportunity, that much is clear. The only reason they spared him was for this.

If he holds his ground and keeps refusing to play along... What if they decide they should just kill him after all?

I can't let that happen.

If Nero and I pull this off, he wouldn't have to do Alessio's dirty work anymore. He'd have his own crew, his own people.

And I could ask Vita for something in exchange as well. If the Ferraros are as powerful as Nero says they are, she could get me the fake documents I need.

It would be my way out of here.

Seriously? Don't tell me you're considering working for a family of criminals, the voice of my conscience pipes in.

Unease slithers through me. That's what it would be. No matter how civil the Ferraros seem, they're criminals, and all criminals are cut from the same cloth.

But I won't ever find a way to help Nero and myself if I play by the book.

"You miss it, don't you?" I ask quietly. "Your old life. The way it was before."

"It doesn't matter," his deep voice rumbles as he parks the car. "The only thing I want is to keep you safe. That's the truth, even if you don't believe me."

I do believe him.

But I'll never be safe with him.

Because there's a real chance I might fall for this man again if I stay here longer. And I can't repeat all of my mother's mistakes.

That night, after Nero goes to sleep, I take out the phone Vita gave me and dial the one number saved in it.

CHAPTER 12

BLAKE

The next morning, two men on Ferraro's payroll—a driver and a bodyguard—escort me out of the building. It's lucky timing that Nero gave me the ability to get out of the penthouse on my own just the night before.

As the car winds through the city streets, I track our progress using the navigation app on the phone Vita gave me. Although I can only text or call her, it's a relief to finally orient myself in this maze of a city.

Our destination is a high-end hotel, where I'm meeting Vita for breakfast at its exclusive rooftop restaurant. The bodyguard, Mark, accompanies me all the way to the hostess stand, where a man in a velvet oxblood suit takes over.

"Right this way, Mrs. De Luca."

My cheeks heat. I'm still not used to being called by that name.

Self-consciousness pangs through my chest. Even dressed in the designer clothes Nero bought me, I feel like an outsider. Can everyone tell I don't belong here? Or am I just imagining it? I remind myself I'm not in Darkwater Hollow anymore—no one here knows me. Everyone is just minding their own business, and the stories looping through my head about being inferior aren't doing anything to help me.

Enough.

If I'm going to help execute this plan against the Bratva, I need to summon every ounce of confidence I have.

A moment later, I spot Vita sitting gracefully behind a round table.

Dressed in an elegant floral-print dress, she gives me a friendly wave and rises to embrace me. "Lovely to see you again, Blake. I was pleased to get your call."

We sit down. Vita must sense my unease, because she takes the initiative and orders two glasses of champagne along with our coffee. "It's never too early for some bubbles." Her smile is reassuring.

We exchange stilted small talk until the champagne arrives. I take a few sips of liquid courage, order eggs Benedict from the waiter, and then take a deep breath. "I'm here to negotiate."

Vita's eyes light up with interest. "Smart girl."

"I think I can convince Nero to do this." My voice is surprisingly steady. "But I want something in exchange."

Vita arches a brow. "Your husband's promotion isn't enough of an incentive?"

"Clearly not. You heard his answer. It won't be easy to get him to agree, and I'm not doing that until I know I'll be rewarded."

Her eyes narrow slightly. "What is it that you want?"

I want a ticket out of your world. The words are on the tip of my tongue, but I hold them back.

Last night, as I lay in bed, it dawned on me that I can't simply tell Vita that I married Nero against my will, or that our marriage isn't real. Not if their whole plan for finding the pakhan rides on Nero and me putting on a united front.

If she knew the truth, she might reconsider letting us try at all. Then both Nero and I would be right back at square one.

I have to hide the truth from her, just as I'll have to hide it from the Russians. If anything, this is a good test to see if I can do it.

"I'd like a favor."

"What kind of favor?"

"I can't say."

"I don't understand."

"I want your promise that if Nero and I help you locate the pakhan, you will grant me this favor when the time comes, no questions asked."

Vita's gaze turns calculating. "I'd feel more comfortable knowing what the favor entails. There are things beyond my influence, and I wouldn't want you to expect something I can't give you."

A new passport, a ticket to somewhere far away, and a promise she won't let Nero find me? "I can guarantee that what I want falls within your power."

She assesses me for a long moment and then shifts her attention to the breakfast the waiter just delivered. We both take a few bites of our food. My eggs Benedict look decadently good, but I can barely taste anything. If she says no, I'm not sure what I'll do.

I'm worried about my own fate and I'm also worried about Nero's. Now that I understand how precarious his position is, I don't want to leave him alone here until I can be confident the Ferraros won't retaliate against him.

"All right," Vita says, pressing her napkin to her lips. "I'll grant you your favor, under the condition that it's nothing that will harm my family."

Yes. Relief spreads through me. "Understood."

"Then we have a deal."

"If— Once I get Nero to agree to this, what comes next?"

"You'll make contact with someone in two weeks. One of the pakhan's five brigadiers, a man called Maksim Garin. His wife is a Russian-American socialite and has landed in New York well-equipped with connections. We will arrange an encounter while they're out and about in society."

"Two weeks? I thought you'd want to move more quickly."

"We need to be patient. Let it appear as if Nero is at his breaking point." She takes a measured sip of champagne. "And you'll need to be fully prepared."

"What does that mean?"

"You're new to our world, darling. If you don't want to end up as prey, you need to grow your own teeth."

"I'm not as clueless as you think." I wonder if Vita knows about my connection to the Iron Raptors. Just because I kept my distance from my father's friends after he died doesn't mean I've forgotten what I saw growing up. I know what people are capable of, and I'm not naive enough to think this will be easy.

"It's not about being clueless. It's about being willing to do what it takes. The Bratva men are smart. Their women even more so. Behind their thick accents, plumped lips, and smoky eyes, they conceal sharp minds capable of understanding complex geopolitics and advanced economics. Don't let their appearances fool you. Maksim will task his wife with cracking you open like an egg, and she'll sift through the contents of your mind with her sharp nails."

"How can I prepare for that?"

Vita smiles. "I can help you. But the most crucial aspect will be establishing the right dynamic with Nero. It won't suffice to just share the same story. You must be able to read each other's minds."

My chest tightens. Can Nero and I do that? I won't be able to keep him at arm's length if we want to have a chance of pulling this off. We'll have to work as a team. I'll have to allow myself to get close to him but keep my heart under lock and key.

My nerves spike. I'm already experiencing pangs of longing for him, even though I know he isn't right for me. I could never love a criminal like my mom did. But if this is my only chance to reclaim my life and help Nero, I have to do whatever it takes.

Nero can never know about my deal with Vita. If he gets even a hint of my ultimate goal, he'll never let me escape.

"It's a good thing you're in love," Vita murmurs. "Love makes this kind of deception far easier."

More doubts creep in. Am I still in love with Nero? No, I can't be. Whatever affection I still have for him is nothing but an echo of what used to be there before.

Vita picks up her knife. "The trick is to lean into the truth whenever possible, because that's what will sell your eventual lie. You want to be ninety-five percent authentic and five percent fraudulent."

"What is the truth?"

"You want a better life for your husband." She slices through a piece of smoked salmon. "Right?"

As much as Nero's hurt me, I don't want to watch him suffer at the hands of the Ferraros.

Especially not for my own sake.

I bite down on my lip. "Yes. I do."

"And you don't like my family very much, do you?" she asks casually.

"Not really," I admit.

"Or the Messeros, for that matter. After all, it was Nero's old boss who got him in this situation in the first place." She pops the salmon into her mouth and neatly crosses her cutlery on her plate. "That should be enough. Those are your islands of safety—topics you can always come back to when the conversation veers off course."

I file that tip away in my mental folder—the one where I'll keep all the compromises I'll make, all the sins I'll commit.

Hopefully, one day I can toss that folder out and leave this all behind.

Vita smiles. "Talk to Nero when he gets home tonight. If you manage to convince him, send me a text."

CHAPTER 13

NERO

It's raining again tonight.

The view of Brooklyn outside the window looks like a vast, moody canvas brushed with diffused blue and gray strokes.

I roll the glass of single-malt whiskey between my palms. I'm nursing it alone on the living room sofa.

I don't like to drink alone, but some days demand it.

I needed something strong. Something that would burn as it went down my throat.

There was another Bratva soldier today, and Alessio and I spent eight hours interrogating him. Alessio's convinced the guy knows the location of one of the pakhan's weapon storage facilities.

The fucker's tough. He wouldn't talk no matter what we did to him. We kept him alive. Tomorrow, we'll try again.

The work is wearing on me. The hard part is that it's constant. Every day is the same thing. I'm used to more variety. Unless you've got a few screws loose in the head like my boss, no one enjoys doing this shit day after day.

I'm sure Gino's hoping that it'll break me eventually.

He can keep hoping.

I'm not dragging Blake into this conflict, no matter what it costs me.

"Nero? I didn't hear you come in."

My gaze moves from the window to Blake and... *Fuck me.*

She's standing across the living room dressed in the sexiest little outfit—a fitted gray blouse, a ruffled skirt that shows off her legs, and winter-white boots with a small heel.

I long for the days when I could just walk over and embrace her. She'd probably stab me if I tried to do that now.

Still, just the sight of her eases some of my tension.

I lift my glass to her and drawl, "Honey, I'm home." I can't get over how fucking beautiful she is.

She places her hands on her hips. "You told me you wanted to take me out for dinner."

I want to do a lot more than take her out for dinner, but I swipe my palm over my lips, and say, "I did." *You refused.*

"Let's do it then."

I sit up straight. She wants to go out? What does this mean?

I study her expression. She doesn't seem upset or happy, but there's a bit of nervousness inside her eyes.

Is she extending an olive branch?

Sometimes, it's dangerous to hope, but I don't care. I told myself I wouldn't rush her to process what's happened between us, and now I'm tempted to think maybe I've done exactly the right thing.

She's coming to me.

Good. Great. *Fuck.*

I can't blow this.

My glass makes a sharp clink as I set it on the coffee table. I get to my feet and walk over to her until the distance between us shrinks to mere inches. "Why the change of heart?"

She lifts her gaze to my face and doesn't back away. Another small hint I'm tempted to read a lot into. She's done everything she can to keep her distance from me since we got to New York.

"I'd like a change of scenery."

I pick up on that familiar vanilla scent. The day I had all those things delivered to her, I made sure they bought the shampoo she used in Darkwater. It's become my favorite smell.

"All right," I say softly, already thinking of all the ways I'm going to make tonight count. "C'mon."

There's no better place for an intimate date than Velluto.

Excitement buzzes deep inside my belly as we walk into the familiar art-deco building where Chef Lorenzo makes the best pasta in the city. It's always busy. I wrap my arm around Blake's waist to keep her close to me. She doesn't try to pull away. She seems too distracted studying our surroundings to notice my touch. The walls are covered with eye-catching mosaics from the Amalfi Coast.

Tanner, the manager of the place, spots me over the crowd near the front and comes over to greet us. He shakes my hand. "It's been a while, Nero."

I'm not sure if he knows everyone assumed I was dead for the six months I was been gone, but I'm guessing no. He's a civilian, and he's smart enough not to stick his nose into mob business, even if he regularly hosts our guys. This place is neutral territory.

"Glad to be back. How are the wife and kids?"

"Kids are good when they're not destroying our house. They're at that age now. Clara took them to see our family in Bari this week." His eyes move to Blake.

"This is my wife, Blake. Blake, this is Tanner."

Tanner smiles and nods in greeting, knowing better than to touch her. "Good to meet you. Give me a moment to get your table ready for you."

A group of four walk into the already tight waiting area, and I act out of instinct and pull Blake into my chest. I don't like the thought of her being jostled by anyone.

She feels so right in my arms. Her vanilla scent fills my nostrils once again, and this time, I can't resist leaning down and pressing my nose against her hair.

I hear her suck in a clipped breath.

A second passes. Then two. She's not pulling away.

The hope inside of me grows.

"Nero?"

"What, Sunshine?" A host comes over and leads the group to the table they reserved.

"Are you okay?"

I smile against her hair. "Mm-hmm. There are some people walking behind you. You were in their way."

"Oh." Her breath fans against my chest. "A big group coming in?"

"Yeah. Like ten people. Just give it a bit longer. They'll pass." They're long gone, but my arm tightens around her waist. I'm enjoying every fucking second of having her this close to me.

Too bad Tanner returns all too quickly.

Damn it. For once, I wish he'd made me wait.

We follow him into the dining room, to my usual table in the charming corner nook where Blake and I will have some privacy. I don't need to tell Tanner which wine to serve us. He always has a bottle of my favorite Chianti from a small winery near San Gimignano stashed away just in case.

Blake asks for my opinion on what to order, which strikes me as something she wouldn't do if she was still angry with me.

Fucking hell. I'm going to drive myself crazy trying to read her thoughts, aren't I? But I can't help it. I'm a starving man, desperate for a drop of her affection.

We place our orders. As soon as the waiter leaves, Blake pins those mesmerizing blues on me. "I want to do this."

Elation. Joy. Relief. The emotions rush through me, heady and intoxicating.

She wants to give our marriage a chance. A real chance.

A dazed smile spreads across my lips. "You do?"

"Yes. I want to help Gino Ferraro take down the pakhan."

"You don't know how happy that—" *Hold up.* My thoughts screech to a sharp halt.

I rewind her words.

The surge of disappointment that follows is profound. I'm a little kid again, opening my present at Christmas, and instead of the toy truck Dad promised he'd get me, it's a fucking pair of socks.

It takes me a moment to collect myself, to find my voice again. "That's not going to happen."

"I met with Vita today."

"You did *what*? How did you get in contact with her?"

She reaches inside her purse and takes out a cell phone. "She gave this to me last night."

What. The. Fuck.

Before I can snatch it away, Blake's already slipped it back into her purse. "As your wife, I should have a say in this decision, Nero. Do you think I like knowing the kind of work Alessio is having you do every day? Do you think I like worrying about what you'll look like when you come home each night?"

I push down my anger at Vita for going behind my back—I'm going to have to talk to Gino about the move she pulled—and focus on what Blake is actually saying.

It sounds like she wants to do this for my sake.

"Be careful," I say roughly. "I might start to think you still care about me."

"I care enough to not want to see you hurt."

That stupid hope flickers again. "Does that mean I'm forgiven?"

Her gaze falls to the candle in the middle of the table. "I don't think I can ever completely forgive you. But I also don't want to spend the rest of my life angry with you. What's done is done, and we can't go back in time and change it. I'm ready to move on."

I swallow. "What does moving on mean?"

"I'd like for us to be friends."

My surroundings dim. "Friends?"

"Just friends."

It feels like there's a noose tightening around my neck. "And what if I don't want to be just friends?"

Her eyes narrow. "You don't have a choice. The same way I didn't have a choice when it came to marrying you."

"You want to keep this as some sort of a fake marriage?"

"We started off fake dating. Don't you think it fits?"

"No, it doesn't," I growl. "I made a vow to you, and I take my vows seriously. You are my wife, Blake." My gaze falls to her ring.

Fuck, I still haven't gotten her a new one. My wife shouldn't be walking around with a cheap sterling silver band on that perfect hand.

Her throat bobs. "I know that. But I'm not going to give you my heart again. Not after what's happened between us. The romantic part of our relationship is over for good."

I have to take a deep breath to curtail the storm building inside me. Does she think I'll accept this? I don't believe this is what she really wants.

"What about sex?" I ask.

"What about it?"

"I presume you don't plan on having any with me."

"That's correct."

"Then you'd be fine with me seeing other women?" I demand, trying to provoke her.

Two angry red spots bloom over her cheeks. "Sure." The word is said through gritted teeth. "You can fuck your way through this city, and it wouldn't bother me."

"Right. I can see you're very unbothered."

She turns even redder, but instead of admitting she'd rather castrate me than see me with someone else, she digs in. "That works great for me." Her full lips stretch into a thin smile. "Maybe I'll find a sidepiece as well."

A deep laugh comes out of me. "You have no idea how this works if you think anyone in this city would be stupid enough to touch my wife. They know I'd kill them, Blake. I might not be a consigliere anymore, but my reputation didn't disappear overnight. If another man touched you, I would cut off his dick before I killed him and deliver it to you in a box."

Her mouth parts in shock. *Good.* She already thinks I'm a monster, so she might as well know just how monstrous I can be when someone touches what's mine.

There's a small tremble in her hand as she tucks a strand behind her ear. "That's a double standard, and it doesn't work for me."

I shrug. "Then I guess we're both staying celibate for the duration of our marriage."

"Hmm."

I place my elbows on the table and lean forward. "How long do you think you'll last?"

"Forever if needed," she whispers, her eyes angry even as they drop to my mouth.

She's forgotten what it feels like when our bodies meet. Maybe I should remind her so that she stops talking such nonsense. One kiss would be enough. Would she allow herself to melt for me, or would she stubbornly resist it?

"Why deprive yourself like that?" I murmur. "You know, you don't have to give me your heart to let me make you come again."

Her eyes widen momentarily, but she's quick to school her expression. "I won't be depriving myself at all. I've got two perfectly good hands."

"Is that how you keep yourself busy while I'm at work?" The thought of her getting herself off makes me instantly hard.

She arches a brow. "Not much else to do."

"Doubt you're as good as me, though."

"Maybe not," she admits. "But I'll get better with practice."

Fuck me. "Why don't we practice together?"

"What would be the point?"

"I'll talk you through it. Tell you just how pretty you look with your fingers stuffed inside your dripping pussy."

She gasps.

A waiter appears in my periphery, and only then do I realize our faces are inches away. Blake makes a small sound of alarm and jerks back into her seat.

The waiter refills our wine. "Your appetizers are coming out now."

Blake lifts her hair off her neck and fans herself with her palm, avoiding my gaze, but I've already gotten what I wanted. A confirmation that no matter what she says, she's still attracted to me.

When the waiter leaves, she's once again a picture of composure. "We've gone off topic. Let's get back to where we started the conversation."

"Gino's offer."

"You keep saying you want to protect me. Don't you think that would be easier for you to do if you had a more senior position?"

"Maybe. But you're assuming we can accomplish what Gino wants." I lower my voice. "Deceiving the pakhan and his gaggle of cronies won't be easy."

"You don't think you can do it?"

"I know *I* can."

"But you doubt me."

"You're not exactly a master of deception, Sunshine."

She furrows her brow. "Maybe you should have some faith in me."

"What happened to the utter scorn you have for this entire thing? According to you, the Ferraros are criminals, and thus bad people. Why would you want to help them?"

"I don't want to help them. I want to help you." She takes a sip of wine and stares at me over the rim of her glass. "Despite everything, I don't want you to suffer for the rest of your life. You're not happy doing whatever it is Alessio has you doing."

My chest grows tight. "You want me to be happy even after everything I've done to you?"

A strange emotion flickers over her features. It almost seems like guilt, but that can't be right. What does she have to feel guilty about? I'm the one who's fucked everything up.

"I don't want you to die. Right now, you're disposable. Becoming a capo would make you less so."

"That's true," I mutter. "But I still don't think you understand what you're signing yourself up for."

"Vita gave me a good overview. And she said we'd spend two weeks getting ready. If I feel like I'm in over my head at any point, I can pause things."

The appetizers arrive. I barely taste the antipasti as I think about what she's proposing.

Getting promoted to capo would be a hell of an improvement to my current situation—that much is undeniable. It would get me out of Alessio's "palace" and give me power in the Ferraro family. It would get me a crew. A crew whose loyalty I can develop with time and who could help me safeguard Blake.

But the truth is, she's already safe. The Iron Raptors aren't a threat here, and the Ferraros have made it clear they won't harm her.

Going through with this plot against the Bratva would be far more dangerous than leaving everything as is.

Unless the pakhan wins this war.

Unease slips beneath my skin. Is that a real possibility? Perhaps. The Bratva appear to be gaining ground in this conflict based on the bits and pieces I've picked up from Alessio. Gino and Vita wouldn't have come to us for help if they had other options, would they?

But Blake doesn't want to do this to help the Ferraros win a war.

She wants to do this to help me.

And that makes me think there's still hope for us, no matter what she says.

I miss her.

I want her.

Not as a fucking friend. Just as fucking mine.

She stares at me expectantly, waiting for my answer. There's a determined glint in her eyes. She wants me to say yes.

Maybe this is how we'll fix the rift between us. By working together. By learning to trust each other again.

And it's that thought that makes up my mind. "Fine. We'll do this. But we have to—"

"Be a team. I know. Vita already gave me the pep talk."

"And I will end it immediately if it feels like we're getting too close to the fire," I warn. "I will not risk your life for the Ferraros, Blake. You have to swear you'll listen to me."

She nods. "Okay."

We wrap up the dinner and step outside. The rain's slowed to an annoying drizzle. The valet's busy with a Bugatti that just pulled up to the curb, so Blake and I wait under the awning.

When the valet opens the passenger door, a familiar flash of red catches my eye.

Hold on a sec, that Bugatti looks familiar too...

A woman climbs out of the car and hurries toward us, trying to escape the rain. Her eyes are on the ground, but as she steps under the awning, those green orbs snap right up and land on my face.

Cleo Messero's lips part. "Nero?"

CHAPTER 14

BLAKE

There's a redhead wrapped around my husband.

Moments ago, she launched herself at him with a high-pitched squeal, and Nero caught her midair, wrapping his arms around her waist.

A sharp zing of anger shoots up my spine. Who is she? An old flame?

A dark-haired man walks up to them, a grim expression on his face. He stares at the two of them for a long moment before his gaze slides over to me. His eyes are the clearest blue I've ever seen, and they pierce right through me, unraveling my thoughts before I can even form them.

It's unsettling.

Who is he?

It feels like an eternity passes before the redhead untangles herself from Nero. "How?" she breathes.

Nero raises an eyebrow, gesturing toward the man. "Didn't Rafe..."

The name hits me like a jolt of electricity.

This is Nero's old boss. Rafaele.

The picture I had in my mind doesn't match reality. I expected someone older. Someone who looks like a gangster.

But the man in front of me can't be more than thirty, and he's gorgeous. He could be the CEO of a Fortune 500 company or a high-powered attorney if it wasn't for the dark ink on his hands that spilled out from beneath his sleeves.

"Rafe!" The redhead turns on him, her expression aghast. "Are you kidding me?" She smacks her clutch against his arm. "How could you not tell me Nero's back?"

"You got off the plane three hours ago. I planned to tell you tonight."

"You could have told me over the phone while I was still in Italy!"

Rafaele shoots Nero a look I can't quite read. A cry for help?

Nero clears his throat and gently turns the redhead back to face him with a hand on her shoulder. "Cleo, I didn't give him any notice. It's only been a few days."

Cleo. Rafaele's wife.

The woman Nero saved.

"A few days, huh?" She gives me a dismissive glance. "I see you're having fun already."

A bitter taste floods my mouth. She thinks I'm just a fling.

It's funny how a single sentence can bring all my old insecurities rushing back. I wonder if Nero was as popular in New York as he was in Darkwater Hollow.

In my mind, I picture a long line of gorgeous, flawless women, just like the ones I saw at breakfast today, parading along a conveyor belt.

Monday, Tuesday, Wednesday, Thursday...

Nero takes my hand, intertwining our fingers, and squeezes tightly. "This is my wife."

Cleo's eyes widen, revealing the entire green iris in each one. "You have *a wife*? Are you—" She stops abruptly. When I glance at Nero, he's giving her a frown.

Color creeps up her cheeks. She turns to me and swallows. "I'm sorry. That was rude. Sometimes, I speak before thinking." She offers me her hand. "I'm Cleo Messero."

"Blake," I reply stiffly as we shake hands.

She bites her lip, sending Nero a sheepish look. "Foot-in-mouth syndrome."

"I see nothing's changed," Nero retorts.

A smile tugs on her lips. "I just can't believe this. You're back, and you're *married*. Where did you two meet?"

Nero swipes his thumb over the back of my hand. "A small town in Missouri."

"I want to hear the full story. Can we have you over for dinner? When are you coming back to work?"

Rafaele puts his hand on Cleo's shoulder. "He's not working for me anymore. He's working for Gino now."

"What? Why?" Cleo crosses her arms over her chest, her brows knitting as she glares at her husband.

"It was Gino's condition for moving forward peacefully." Rafaele glances at the valet returning to the stand, ensuring he can't overhear us. The drizzling rain keeps most passersby from lingering on the street.

Cleo's eyes flare, and she shakes off Rafe's hand with a flick of her shoulder. "That's it. We're going home. You've got a lot of explaining to do." She turns to Nero. "What about Sandro? Did he come back with you? Oh my God, I can't wait to see him."

A painful pang hits my chest as Nero and Rafaele exchange a glance. The rain has seeped through the cardigan I'm wearing over my dress, and the cold is biting.

Cleo's expression shifts with a mix of dread and denial. "Nero? Where is Sandro?"

I don't think he realizes that he's doing it, but Nero tugs me closer. My shoulder presses into his chest.

"He's gone."

Cleo's face loses all color in an instant. She looks stricken. Her husband wraps his arm around her shoulders, and this time, she doesn't shrug him off. A tear escapes her eye, runs down her cheek, falls from her chin, and splatters against the surface of her leather boot.

I wonder if she and Sandro were close. Nero told me Sandro was a driver for Rafaele, so perhaps he was Cleo's driver too. That would explain her devastation. My heart aches with pity as she sniffles and wipes her eyes with the back of her hand.

"How?" she asks.

"He was protecting me," I say softly. "He saved my life."

"Come on," Rafaele murmurs, pulling his wife against him. "We'll talk at home."

Nero signals to the valet to bring Rafaele's car around. As we say our goodbyes, Cleo hugs Nero again, whispering something in his ear. I catch her lips forming the words.

I'm sorry.

THE PENTHOUSE IS dark and cold when we step through the front doors half an hour later. I'm desperate to get out of my damp clothes.

I should be happy Nero agreed to go through with Vita and Gino's plan. That was my goal for the evening, and I achieved it.

But I'm not happy. Far from it.

For the first half of the ride home, I was consumed with memories of Sandro. The way he'd looked at me when he'd realized what was about to happen. The moment of his death. The damn unfairness of it all.

But that's not the only thing dragging me into this dark place.

Something unpleasant churns inside my belly, like an agitated snake eager to escape its enclosure.

The more I try to untangle my feelings for Nero, the less I like what I find.

It bothers me that Cleo thought I was some random date Nero picked up within a few days of coming home, as if that's exactly what he would do.

It bothers me to question how many women he's taken to that same restaurant before me.

It even bothers me to remember how Cleo hugged Nero, how comfortable she was touching him—my husband. I know she's married, but that hasn't stopped Nero before, has it? What if they have a history? What if he slept with her?

Damn it all to hell. Why do I care? Why am I *jealous*?

I don't love him anymore. I don't want him anymore.

I *don't*.

"You haven't said a word since we got into the car," Nero says from somewhere behind me.

I kick my shoes off, leave my purse on the credenza in the lobby, and pad toward my room. "I'm tired."

"Is that what this is?" he asks, following me into my bedroom. I should tell him to get out, but I don't.

Instead, I hide inside the walk-in closet, shutting the door behind me to keep him out while I change.

I tie my damp hair into a bun and slip into a T-shirt and a pair of sweats.

There's an angry buzz beneath my skin.

The question bursts out of me before I can swallow it down. "Do you have a history with her?"

"With who?" he asks from the other side of the door.

"Cleo."

There's a long, pregnant pause.

"Does it matter? I thought *we* were just friends." His tone carries a hint of amusement.

Does he think this is *funny*?

I jerk the door open.

His palms are anchored on the doorjamb, and he leans forward, bringing us nearly nose to nose. "Do friends get jealous of each other?"

"I'm not jealous," I grind out, even as the thought of him being with someone else makes my lungs shrivel up.

Now that I've had him, I don't want anyone else to have him, even if I'm determined to never sleep with him again.

You really expect him to be celibate?

Nero's gaze drops to my lips. "You saw another woman embrace me and you practically turned green."

"How could you know what color I turned if you had your eyes glued to her?"

"She's just a friend. She's never been more than a friend. If she had been, I wouldn't be standing here, because Rafe would have murdered me by now. He's like me, Blake. He goes crazy when someone touches what's his."

I push past him and move to the kitchen.

I need a glass of water, an Advil, and a good night's sleep. That should be enough to get these crazy thoughts out of my head so I can calm down.

Nero must sense I want to be alone, because he retreats to his own bedroom instead of following me. There's a stupid ache in my chest, something that can't possibly be disappointment. It's not like I wanted him to follow me. It's not like I need his reassurance.

But when he reappears a minute later, while I'm on my second glass of water, I feel a traitorous flutter—a flutter that shouldn't be there, damn it.

He's changed out of his suit, and now we're in matching gray sweatpants.

Only he's not wearing a shirt.

I can't resist letting my gaze slide down his sculpted torso as he approaches. A pent-up breath escapes past my lips.

Why is he doing this?

He backs me against the kitchen counter, caging me in with his arms.

Heat fans through my body. I'm still attracted to him. I want to leave marks on him. I want to carve my name into his skin. It's ridiculous, because I plan to run away from him, but possessiveness still burns deep inside my belly.

He leans his head down, getting to my eye level. "What do I have to do to make you stop being angry with me?"

"Didn't we talk about it at dinner? I already said I'm done being angry with you. We're good."

He tilts his head. "You call this good? For the love of God, don't bring up that friends bullshit again. I can't stand it."

"I don't know what you want from me."

"I want you to stop denying that there's still something here. Something that's worth fighting for. I was willing to die for you, Sunshine. Do you really think I'm just going to give up on us after I got a second chance to make you mine?"

A shiver rolls down my spine.

No, no. *No*. I can't let him get under my skin.

"I'll never be yours again, Nero. What we had before is gone."

He shakes his head. "You're wrong. I think you still want me, you just don't want to admit it to yourself."

Humiliation tears through me, because it's true.

I don't understand myself anymore. How can I want him after everything he's done?

After all the lies and the hurt?

I twist in his arms, turning so that my back is to his front. So that I don't have to stare into his eyes and feel as if he's seeing straight into my soul.

He presses up against me, and he's as hard as a rock.

"Don't touch me." My voice is weaker than it should be.

His breath grazes my neck, and his lips brush against my ear, sending shivers cascading over my skin. I bite down on my bottom lip to stifle the moan that threatens to spill out of me.

"You have to let me touch you," he murmurs. "We have to be a united front, remember? How will we convince anyone we're happily married if you pull away every time I try to kiss you?"

His hand snakes around my throat, and he turns my head until our lips are a whisper apart. A few seconds of us breathing in the same air pass.

It's pure temptation. Now, I know what a drug addict feels like when she just can't resist her next hit.

My mouth parts.

It's all the invitation he needs.

His lips crash onto mine, his tongue invading, fighting, conquering. The world around us blanks out. There's nothing but him and me, and we're swept up in a tornado of lust and bad decisions.

His grip on my throat loosens as he turns me to face him and presses me against the counter. I can feel his cock twitch through the fabric of his sweats.

I moan into his mouth.

I shouldn't like this. It shouldn't feel like coming home.

And yet it does.

We kiss each other like we're the last two people left on this entire planet. Like if we stop, the world will end.

His palms slide down my sides and wrap around to cup my ass, tugging me into him. There's not a sliver of space left between us, and yet it's not enough. It's like he wants to absorb me into him. I can't say I hate the idea.

He breaks the kiss, dragging his lips to my neck, his hot tongue igniting a trail of sparks down to my core. My eyes drift open, and the first thing I see is his gun lying in its holster on the coffee table. The gun he's used to kill who knows how many people. The haze lifts.

What the hell am I doing? I've lost it.

Panic grips me, and I shove at his chest. "Stop. *Stop.*"

He pulls back with a rough groan. "Baby…"

I slip out from between him and the counter, putting distance between us. My common sense has finally returned. What possessed me just now? He's not good for me, for a million reasons, including how he makes me lose my mind.

I'm supposed to keep my distance from him, not make out with him in the kitchen, for God's sake!

My eyes meet his. "This is a mistake. I don't want this."

Hurt flashes inside his hazel orbs, and I hate that I caused it. But it's better if I hurt him now. It'll be better if I refuse to give him hope.

Because once we get Gino and Vita what they want, I'm getting out of New York.

CHAPTER 15

BLAKE

The next two weeks go by at the speed of light.

Vita comes over at nine each morning, taking care to enter the building through the discreet back entrance where there's little chance anyone will see her. It's doubtful the Bratva is watching the penthouse, but she and Gino don't want to take any risks.

The Bratva can't have any idea what we're planning, and seeing the don's wife coming over here every day of the week would raise questions.

Vita walks me through everything the Ferraros know about the Bratva and how it operates. She shows me pictures of the pakhan, his brigadiers, and his top-ranking vors. She gives me the biography of Maksim Garin and his wife, Ekaterina, also known as Katya. I read this last document over and over until I can practically recite it in my sleep.

Maksim and the pakhan, whose real name I discover is Yaroslav Andreyevich Sokolov, are distant relatives. Their mothers are cousins. According to the information the Ferraros were able to gather from the men they captured, there's been a rift between the two since the pakhan started to have trouble in Boston. Some of the vors think Maksim has been stealing from the pakhan, but there's never been any proof. The familial connection has protected Maksim so far, but one wrong move could be the end of him.

He's looking for a way to win back the pakhan's favor, which is why we need to make contact with him.

"He'll quickly sense the opportunity to get valuable information from Nero, but you will have to convince him that bringing it to the pakhan is worth the risk," Vita advises one morning while we're having coffee in the kitchen. "His wife is well aware of their precarious situation. She will do everything she can to help her husband determine if you are the key to fixing their relationship with the pakhan."

Near the end of the two weeks, Vita takes me out of the penthouse. First, to a three-hour private class on self-defense, and then to a private shopping appointment at a boutique in Manhattan.

Apparently, this mission requires a whole new wardrobe, which feels wasteful given Nero just bought me one.

I start to protest when I see the price tags in the airy, exclusive store that's been closed just for us. "This is too much."

Vita waves me off. "Think of it as a mandatory uniform."

I take a deep breath and try to figure out how the hell I ended up here. Accepting expensive clothes from a woman married to a mafia don. Working for her and her husband.

Even though I know why I'm doing this—to help Nero and to help myself—my stomach still churns with unease.

Your mom helped your dad steal.

I haven't thought about Brett's words much since he spat them in my face back at Frostbite, but now they ring in my ears like a prophecy.

I'm turning into her. I've spent my adult life reflecting on her choices and telling myself I'd never make those same mistakes.

Now look at me.

But this is only temporary. I just have to get through the next few weeks, and then I'll start a new life in Australia, far away from this cruel world and the man I can't let myself fall for again.

I only hope I don't lose too much of my soul in the process.

ON OUR LAST day of preparations, the morning of the big charity gala where Nero and I are supposed to make contact with Maksim, Vita takes me to a small shooting range owned by the Ferraros. The air inside is thick with the smell of gunpowder. There's no one here but us.

My heart pounds as I take the gun Vita passes me, the cold metal feeling foreign and heavy in my grip. My hands tremble slightly as I point the gun at the outline of a man on the target.

"Steady," Vita murmurs. "Take a deep breath. You can do this," she says before she places the earmuffs over my ears, muting the world into a dull throb around me.

A drop of sweat trickles down my spine.

This seems pointless. If that were a real person in front of me, I'd never shoot them. That's where I'd draw the line.

But in this world of shadows and secrets, I have to be prepared for anything.

I take a deep breath, trying to quiet the chaos inside me and focus on the target.

My finger pulls on the trigger, and the gun recoils. A small hole appears in the outline's chest.

I lower the gun, my heart racing, and look at Vita. She nods approvingly, her eyes holding a mixture of pride and something else—something like understanding.

"You're doing great," she assures me, placing her hand on my arm. "The gun will go home with you."

"I don't want it," I protest.

But she's undeterred. "This is just a precaution. The goal is diplomacy, not violence."

That afternoon, I spend a long time getting ready. Two hours before Nero and I are meant to leave, I'm already standing in my walk-in closet, trying to pick what to wear.

On the left side are the clothes Nero bought for me. They're beautiful, high quality, and fit my style. They're far nicer than anything I've ever owned before, but at the same time, they fit my character. It's like he purposefully instructed whoever did the shopping to not go over the top so that I wouldn't feel uncomfortable.

But Vita obviously had a different agenda when she shopped for me.

Rubbing the heel of my palm against my forehead, I walk over to the right side and carefully take out one of the designer dresses she selected.

It's an extravagant midnight-blue evening gown embroidered with silver and gold beads that shimmer against the light. It takes me a moment to realize they're meant to resemble the night sky, with the moon outlined on the right side of the bodice.

The process of putting it on is nerve-wracking. I'm worried I'll tear something as I slide it carefully over my hips. When it's finally on, I move to stand in front of the mirror.

There's an impostor staring back at me.

I'm a girl who grew up in a trailer park, but I'm wearing a dress worthy of a princess.

My leg peeks out from the slit that goes all the way to the top of my right thigh. The low V-cut does nothing to hide the flush creeping up my chest, or the way my throat bobs on a nervous swallow.

I drag my fingertips over the beads, skimming over the stars until I reach the crescent moon.

The dress is gorgeous. A work of art.

And I look like I want to bolt out of it.

Vita's instructions come back to me. *Straighten your back. Tip your chin up. Keep your thoughts in your head and off your face.*

The red lipstick helps. As does the heavy makeup. It feels like armor. A mask I can hide behind.

I reach for the diamond stud earrings Vita gave me and pop them into my ears.

Just as I clasp the sapphire pendant necklace behind my neck, the front door opens with a distant clang.

Nero's voice filters through the walls. "Blake?"

"I need a few minutes!"

"I'm going to go change," he calls back. "Meet you in the living room."

Meeting Maksim isn't the only thing I'm nervous about tonight. Nero and I haven't had much privacy since our preparations started. Vita's been here nearly every evening when he's gotten home. She's helped us rehearse our story and prepare, and by the time we're done, both Nero and I have been too exhausted to say more than a few words to one another.

The kiss in the kitchen feels like something out of a hazy dream.

The fact that it hasn't happened again makes me feel like we've made it back onto steadier ground with each other.

As friends.

But tonight, I'm not supposed to act like his friend. I'm supposed to act like his wife.

I drag a brush over my straightened hair a few more times and slip my feet into a pair of high-heeled shoes with a pointed toe.

It's time.

When I walk into the kitchen, Nero's already there, one hand wrapped around a glass of water, the other holding his phone.

I stop dead in my tracks.

He's dressed in a black tuxedo that clings to him as if it's been tailored to every muscle and contour of his body. His hair is swept back from his face, and his beard is perfectly trimmed, highlighting his strong jaw. There's a watch glinting on his left wrist and hints of black ink swirl from under his crisp white cuffs.

The effect is devastating.

I manage to force two word past my dry throat. "I'm ready."

He looks up from his phone, and when his eyes land on me, they widen.

The glass slips out of his hand.

CRASH.

I suck in a harsh breath, but he doesn't even flinch. There's a dark, hungry storm inside his eyes as he takes a step forward, the broken glass crunching beneath his leather shoes.

My pulse picks up speed. He prowls toward me—slowly, purposefully—like he wants to give me time to prepare myself for what comes next.

Kiss me.

What? No. That's *not* what I want.

But the closer he gets, the less I can avoid looking at his lips.

He stops a half step away, close enough for his scent to hit me with full force. Pine, leather, smoke. "You look like a dream."

My heart's ignoring my head, and it's now doing strange pirouettes inside my chest.

He lifts his hand and curls it around my neck, threading his fingers through my hair.

"What are you doing?" I whisper, feeling drunk even though I haven't had a single sip of alcohol all day.

I should tell him to stop touching me, but the words die on my tongue when his thumb gently strokes the side of my neck.

A flutter appears in the pit of my belly before it moves lower.

"I got you something," he murmurs, his breath coasting over my face.

His hand remains on my nape as he retrieves a small black velvet box from his pocket. With a flick of his thumb, he opens it and holds it up for me to see.

A wedding ring.

And *what* a ring.

Baguette diamonds set seamlessly side by side in a gleaming gold setting. They form a continuous sparkling band that dances with light.

"What do you think?"

It might be the most exquisite ring I've ever seen. It's extravagant. Impossible to ignore.

And I fucking love it.

I love it so much.

"You don't like it."

My gaze lifts to Nero's face. I must have been staring in mute shock at the ring for long enough to make him worried.

Uncertainty and a tinge of vulnerability dance inside his eyes, and for a moment, I almost give in to the urge to kiss him before I remember that I can't.

I *can't.*

So instead, I force myself to speak. "How could I not like it? It's beautiful."

His lips quirk up. He removes his hand from my nape, drags it down my arm, and picks up my left hand. The ring he put on me inside that Vegas chapel comes right off, and then he slowly slides on the stunning new band.

It's a perfect fit.

"What if someone steals it?" I whisper.

Nero huffs a low laugh. "That's not going to happen. No one's that suicidal." He lifts my hand and presses his lips against my knuckles, making me lose my ability to breathe.

God.

How can he still have this much power over me? And why does it feel like it only grows with each passing day?

I have to pull it together. I can't be weak.

He glances at me from under his brows, his eyes piercing through me. "Shall we, my darling?"

CHAPTER 16

NERO

The plan is simple.

Blake will approach Maksim when he goes to look at an early edition of Pushkin that's up for bidding in the silent auction. According to Vita, he's got a fucking hard-on for that book. Vita's got a friend on the gala's organizing committee who told her Maksim tried to get them to sell the tome to him outright, but it didn't work out, so he'll be salivating over it tonight.

Just like I'm afraid he'll be salivating over my wife.

One glance at Blake in that fucking dress is enough to turn my brain to mush, and the same is obviously true for every other bastard that's dared to look at her. I've lost count of how many jaws dropped when she walked into the room. I can't blame them, but at the same time, I still want to kill them all.

All I want to do is find an empty hallway and have my way with her against a wall. I'd feel better if she had my cum dripping down her thighs while these fuckers stared at her.

We're at the cocktail reception right before dinner, standing by a high-top table where we have a good view of the whole room.

Blake shifts her weight from one foot to the other, a glass of champagne in her hand. Her gaze darts around the room, looking at anyone but me. She's avoided eye contact ever since I slipped that sparkling new wedding band onto her finger.

I can tell that she likes it, because she keeps glancing at it.

But I want her to be glancing at *me*, damn it.

"Have I already told you that you're stunning?"

The object of my obsession blushes a pretty pink. "Yes. At the penthouse and on the ride over."

"Ah. Well, a lot could have changed since."

"Did it?"

"Indeed. Somehow, you look even more stunning now than you did ten minutes ago."

I swear, there's a smile tugging on those perfect lips.

Fuck, I've missed her. These last two weeks have been hell. Vita Ferraro all but moved into my penthouse, leaving me barely any time alone with Blake. In the mornings, I'd leave before Blake woke up, and when I got back, Vita was there. We sat through hours of planning and strategy meetings, dialing Gino in for some of them.

Given the sensitive nature of our mission, practically no one in the Ferraro clan knows what we're doing. Not even Cosimo, which is a fucking delight. He's going to be so fucking pissed when he discovers he's been kept in the dark. I can't wait to rub it in his face for the next few years.

Out of the three brothers, only Alessio has been brought into the loop. He knows his parents are keeping me busy, and yet he still puts me through the wringer at work. It's all part of building my story, but I think the sadistic bastard enjoys it a bit too much.

Put all that together, and I can count on one hand the number of times Blake and I have been awake and alone in the house. And she's done everything she can to cut even those brief interactions short.

I can guess what's going on inside her pretty head. She doesn't like what that one hot kiss in the kitchen revealed— that the attraction between us is alive and well.

I lift my hand and allow my knuckles to graze the underside of her jaw. Her skin is soft and warm. "I can't stop looking at you."

"Is there something on my face?"

"Definitely. Eyes I could spend the rest of my life gazing into. Lips I'd really like to kiss. And a mouth I'd love to taste and fu—"

She spins away from me and snatches another champagne glass from a passing tray.

I wipe my hand over my smile.

She's remembering how fucking good it was between us. She just needs to realize it can be like that again.

If only I can convince her to give our marriage a real chance.

I snake my arm around her waist. "You're the most beautiful woman here."

"Do you see him?" She swivels her head, pretending to not hear me. "What if he doesn't show up?"

"That dress fits you like a second skin. Will you let me peel it off you when we get back home?"

"I'm not a piece of fruit," she grumbles.

"Your pussy sure tastes like one."

She sucks in a harsh breath and starts chugging her champagne.

I stop her. "Careful. You don't want to get drunk."

"Then stop making me need it, Nero," she hisses. "Whatever you're doing, that's enough."

"Just admit—" I begin, but a familiar face by the entrance catches my eye.

Maksim. And his wife.

I lower my lips to Blake's ear. "They just walked in. The wife is wearing a green dress."

Blake gives her half-empty glass to a waiter and throws a discreet glance toward the other side of the room. "Yeah, I see. I recognize him from the photos. He looks older though."

"Maybe it's the stress from the last few weeks. The Ferraros have been picking off their vors like flies. The pakhan can't be happy."

"Then why does Gino need us if he's capturing so many of their men?"

"Because the pakhan has a near endless supply of soldiers he can throw at the problem. He imports them from Siberia, where his brother has built a private army."

Blake arches her brows and shakes her head, her gaze sliding back to Maxim. "I'll never understand why someone would want to throw their life away by working for someone like that."

"You're judging them too harshly. For most, it's their only chance at a better life. Not much upward mobility in the remote regions of Russia. People do what they have to in order to survive."

She looks like she wants to debate, but this isn't the time or place. I press a kiss to her cheek. "C'mon, let's go to our table. Dinner is about to start. We don't want them to notice us just yet."

Blake loops her arm through mine, and we merge with the crowd moving into the room next door.

It's fun watching her astonishment as she takes in the grand ballroom. The gala is being held in a glitzy hotel called The Admiral. The place is full of crystal chandeliers, marble columns, and Baroque art on the walls. I think I got very drunk in the lobby bar once.

"So beautiful." Her hand tightens on my wrist, her brand-new wedding ring sparkling in the light. Seeing it on her hand makes my chest swell with pride.

Mine, the caveman inside of me growls.

The tables seat twelve people, so we spend a good five minutes on introductions. By the time we take our seats, Blake looks uneasy.

"I already forgot most of their names," she whispers to me. "I'm terrible with that. Who's the woman with the gold brooch in her hair?"

I shrug. "No clue."

"Very helpful," Blake mutters as she hangs her purse on the back of her chair.

"These people don't matter. There are only two we need to pay attention to. They're three tables to our right."

Her brows furrow as she searches for Maksim. She confirms she found him with a small nod. "I see them."

An elderly man in a tux comes up to the podium to deliver introductory remarks about the organization benefiting from the gala—the Wallace Arts and Literature Foundation.

He drones on about the foundation's beginnings and its accomplishments to date. I genuinely couldn't care less.

I scoot my chair closer to Blake's. "Have to give it to Lottie for keeping her introduction short and sweet at the mayor's Christmas auction."

"I was just remembering that, too," she admits quietly. "I'm as nervous now as I was that night."

"Why were you nervous then?"

She gives me a funny look. "Are you serious? I was convinced no one would bid on my class. That Lottie would have to crack an awkward joke and move on to the next item, and everyone would laugh at me." She takes a swig of her champagne. "Seems silly in retrospect."

"Yeah, it is silly. Especially since that class was the highest bid of the night."

"That was all you."

"Damn right, it was. And let me tell you something, Sunshine. Anytime you ever donate anything to an auction, you can bet I'm going to win it." I lean in closer. "After all, that class was exceptional. Worth every dollar."

A deep blush spreads across her chest before creeping up her neck. Is she remembering that night at Frostbite Tavern and the way she came so beautifully for me?

I shift in my seat. I'm as hard as a rock from the imagery flashing through my mind.

The old geezer on stage finally wraps it up, and a waiter appears to take our drink order.

"I'd like an old-fashioned." It's the same drink I licked off her tits that night.

Blake swallows hard. "Water, please."

The dinner service begins, and I make sure Blake eats her bread and pass her mine too. She needs something to soak up all the champagne she's had, and the leek soup that's brought for the first course ain't going to do it.

She mumbles a quiet thanks.

When she finishes eating, I place my hand just above her bare knee, my pinky lightly brushing her inner thigh.

She glares at me. "Nero."

"What?"

"Why are you touching me?"

"Because I'm obsessed with you, baby. Haven't you realized that by now?"

A waiter comes around to take our empty soup plates away. Blake sits there stiffly until he leaves, then she reaches under the tablecloth and flicks my hand away.

"You're taking advantage of the situation," she mutters. "If we were here under normal circumstances, I'd throw my wine in your face."

I grin. "Thank God for abnormal circumstances, then."

Her expression flickers between bemusement and exasperation, but at least I've made her forget about her nerves. As long as she stays calm when she talks to Maksim, tonight should go off without a hitch.

I'm still uneasy about this whole thing, but every time I thought about calling it off, I couldn't bring myself to do it. Yes, there are risks, but I've managed far riskier situations as Rafe's consigliere.

And the potential reward has never been as great. It's not money on the line or the fucking promotion Gino's dangling in front of me.

What's on the line is my and Blake's future. Working together is how I'll earn her trust back. It's how I'll show her that we're meant to be.

She leans in. "That kiss in the kitchen shouldn't have happened. We should have talked about it before we came here to clear up any confusion."

"Don't worry. There's no confusion at all."

"I think there is. You can only touch me when it's mission critical, got it?"

"Understood."

She gives me a wary look. "Really?"

"Yes. We just might disagree what mission critical means."

She huffs in frustration. "Groping me under the table at dinner, where no one can see, can't possibly be mission critical. I said I want us to be *friends*, and I meant— Shit, he just got up."

My eyes snap to Maksim and Ekaterina's table. Maksim is out of his seat, heading toward the room where the Pushkin book is on display.

A prickle of unease coasts over my nape.

Blake swipes her handbag from where it's hanging on her chair. "This is it. It's just a conversation, right?"

We lock eyes. I force a smile. "Just a conversation. I'll be there before you know it. You got this."

She nods, squeezes my hand, and stands up.

As I watch her walk all the way through the room, I have to hold myself back from getting up, going after her, throwing her over my shoulder, and taking her out to the car.

She disappears into the hallway, and for a moment, I can't breathe. Seconds tick by, each one heavier than the last. I try to focus on the room around me, on the clinking of glasses and the murmur of conversation, but all I can think about is Blake.

I really fucking hope I'm not making a mistake getting her involved in this.

CHAPTER 17

BLAKE

It's official. Nero is driving me insane. He knows exactly how to get under my skin with his words and his touch.

If it wasn't for this thing with Maksim giving me a way out, I'm not sure what I would allow my husband to do to me. Because with every passing minute in his presence, a little voice in my head wonders if it really would be so bad to give in.

I promised myself I wouldn't. My mind knows that I *shouldn't*.

But my body doesn't seem to care about any of that.

How I wish that I still hated Nero with the same intensity as when he drove me to New York!

But I don't.

And Nero can sense it, can't he?

What if you give in just once?

No, it's never just once. That's how it starts, and then it happens "just once" again and again.

It's not like Nero is some stranger from a bar, and after we sleep together, he'll just go on his merry way, and I'll never see him again.

We live together. He's my fricking husband. A husband who wants to repair our relationship. A husband who's shown me he's willing to die for me.

A heavy weight lodges inside my belly. I keep comparing Nero to my father, comparing my story to my mother's, but my dad would never have laid down his life for my mom. For his kids. For his family.

Nero is…different.

I clutch my purse close to my chest as I walk out of the ballroom.

He might be different in some ways, but he's still a criminal. I can't forget that. And I can't risk doing anything that will shake the walls I have erected around my heart. The walls that already feel like they're crumbling, which only makes it more urgent that I get the hell out of this place before I lose myself even more.

I roll my shoulders back, force myself to breathe, and amble around the showroom for a few minutes, stopping by the glass displays to look at the items enclosed. The starting bids aren't shown, but they're listed in the app I scrolled through on the drive over, and they're not for the faint of heart. Our tickets alone were ten grand apiece.

With the dinner still in progress, there are only a few people here. I wait until the couple standing close to Maksim drift away.

He's older—in his forties—and well groomed. The tailoring on his pinstripe suit is precise and flattering. This is a man who takes pride in his appearance.

The sound of my heels clicking on the marble floor alerts him to my approach. As I stop across from him, his gaze lifts to meet mine over the top of the display.

He considers me for a moment before asking, "Are you a collector?"

"No," I reply with a smile. "Just a book lover."

"That's how it starts," he says, a knowing glint in his eyes. "I must compliment your intuition. You're looking at a second-edition *Eugene Onegin* by Pushkin, the greatest Russian poet who ever lived. Have you read any of his work?"

"I haven't."

He tsks. "You must. The translations are never as good as the original, but there's some literature that simply cannot be ignored." He drags his thumb over his mustache. "*I was prepared to love the world, but no one understood me, so I learned to hate.*"

Goosebumps scatter over the backs of my arms. "A quote?"

"Indeed. Onegin was a cynic, disillusioned with society." He steps around the display, his eyes gliding over me with a subtle, unnerving interest. I feel a sticky unease creeping over my skin.

"That's a beautiful dress," he murmurs.

"Thank you."

Without asking, he reaches into my personal space and flicks his finger over the beaded moon embroidered on my hip. "I'm a man who appreciates good craftsmanship."

I force myself to stay still, resisting the urge to step back.

"You must give me the name of the designer so I can get something for my wife. I promised her a gift tonight, but nothing at the auction has caught her eye."

I swallow, hoping he can't sense the deception beneath my uncertain smile. "My husband wants to get me something too. I haven't picked yet." My gaze drifts back to the old book.

"I'm afraid it won't be the Pushkin. I've been waiting to add him to my collection for a very long time, and tonight is the night."

"What if someone outbids you?"

"They won't." He clasps his hands, contemplating the book with quiet confidence. "When I see something I want, I always find a way to get it." His gaze slides back to me, and my instincts flare, warning me of the predator behind his polished exterior.

This man is dangerous. It's not that I didn't already know that, but now I *feel* it.

A drop of cold sweat rolls down the valley of my spine.

"So where is your husband?" Maksim asks.

"Finishing his meal. I was too excited to wait."

"It's better to look at everything when there aren't so many people around. I dislike crowds, but even they weren't enough to keep me away tonight. Did you know there are only ten known copies of this edition left on the planet?"

That would explain why the bidding on the book starts at three hundred thousand dollars.

"I had no ide—"

"Maks! There you are."

A dark-haired woman teeters over to us.

Ekaterina.

She's got a glass in one hand, and judging by her unsteady balance, it's far from the first one she's had tonight.

Maksim's lips thin for a moment, but when Ekaterina reaches us, he masks his irritation with an obliging smile.

He clasps her by the elbow to steady her. "This is my wife, Ekaterina. Kotik, meet my new friend..." he trails off, obviously expecting me to fill in the blank. We haven't exchanged names.

"Blake."

Ekaterina eyes me with suspicion. "Nice to meet you." Her accent is heavier than Maksim's. "Dorogoy, chto ty tut delayesh'? Ya uzhe nachala volnovat'sya."

Maksim sighs. "Pochemu? Ya zhe tebe uzhe govoril pro knigu. Posmotri syuda." He points at the book and then lifts his gaze to me. "Ty vidish', kakaya ona krasivaya?"

Ekaterina scoffs at the display case. "Gospodi. Kniga kak kniga. Zachem tebe eto nuzhno?"

I have no idea what they're saying, but their body language and the way Maksim rolls his eyes at his wife suggest she's managed to annoy him. I wonder if the stress of not knowing where they stand with the pakhan has put a strain on their relationship or if they've always been like this. Vita made it sound like they married for political reasons.

Maksim drags his tongue over his upper teeth. "My wife doesn't appreciate literature the way we do."

Ekaterina reddens and narrows her eyes at me as if I'm guilty of something.

My nerves spike. This isn't good. The goal was to make friendly contact with the two of them, not piss Ekaterina off.

I give her a smile. "That's all right. I love meeting people with different passions from mine. The world would be boring if we were all interested in the same things, wouldn't it?"

Ekaterina's brows pinch together. "How nice." She unlaces her arm from Maksim's and takes a step back to look past him. "Did you already look at that Swiss pocket watch we talked about? My dolzhny ikh dostat' dlya Slavy. Yemu ponravitsya."

My ears perk up at "Slava." That's the short form for Yaroslav—the pakhan.

Just then, I spot Nero under the arched vestibule that connects the two rooms, and I give him a wave.

Maksim glances over his shoulder. "Is that your husband?"

"He's very tall," Ekaterina notes as Nero moves toward us. There's a hint of appreciation in her tone that I don't like.

Maksim doesn't appear to notice it though. His eyes stay glued on Nero, and a notch appears between his brows.

He recognizes him.

My nape begins to prickle. His reaction once Nero intro-
duces himself is important. If he turns hostile, the whole
plan might fall apart.

Nero arrives at my side, slipping his arm around my waist.
"Hey, baby. Having a good time?"

Ekaterina's eyes flare with interest, and without thinking, I
get on my tiptoes and press a kiss to Nero's cheek. "I am."

Nero's grip tightens slightly as he shifts his attention to
Maksim. "Thank you for keeping my wife company."

Maksim sizes him up. "It's been my pleasure."

For a moment, tension coils in the air, and I half expect
Ekaterina to bristle at Maksim's words, but her gaze is fixed
on Nero with an almost predatory curiosity. I can practically
see the hearts dancing in her eyes.

That green monster wakes again.

What is it about this man that brings out my jealous side? I
never felt this way with Brett, even though plenty of women
liked to ogle him too.

Nero extends a hand toward Maksim. "Nero De Luca."

Maksim accepts the handshake with deliberate slowness. "I
know who you are."

"Have we met before?"

"I don't believe so, but you're a famous man among some
circles."

Understanding flashes in Nero's eyes. "And you are?"

Maksim cocks his head to one side. "Maksim Garin."

"Ah." The single syllable hangs in the air, dropping the temperature a few degrees. "And here I thought we might make some new friends tonight."

"You used to be a man with many friends," Maksim counters, his tone lightly mocking.

Nero shrugs. "Things change."

"I suppose they do. You've only recently returned, right? For a while, word on the street was that you were dead."

"I know. I helped start those rumors."

Maksim chuckles. "But you discovered life's charms once more?"

"Something like that." Nero takes a sip out of the tumbler in his hand. "Although this isn't quite the life I imagined I'd return to," he says under his breath.

My heart picks up speed. He's just thrown the bait.

Maksim's smile remains frozen, but his eyes narrow. "Things change quickly in New York. We heard you've got a new boss now."

"It's no secret," Nero says easily. "I was...reassigned."

"Ferraro's known for holding grudges."

Nero's response is a tight smile. He's playing this perfectly. He can't seem too eager to complain, or it will be obvious.

Maksim lets the silence linger for a few moments. He wants to see if Nero will volunteer something else. Vita's advice rings inside my ears. *Don't let them coax things out of you. Say your part, and then shut up.*

"Well, life can't be too unpleasant with such a magnificent wife by your side," Maksim says finally, breaking the tension with a nod in my direction.

Ekaterina sighs dramatically, rummaging through her tiny purse for her phone.

Nero draws me closer. "She does make even the most difficult situations bearable."

"I'll bet—"

"Maks, Angelica and her husband are here," Ekaterina interrupts, her tone laced with impatience. "We have to go say hello."

"Of course, Kotik." Maksim clears his throat. "Well, enjoy the rest of your night."

"You too," Nero says, watching them retreat into the crowd.

I wait until they're far enough away that they won't overhear, and I turn to Nero. "Do you think that worked?"

His gaze is glued to the back of Maksim's head. "We'll find out soon enough."

CHAPTER 18

NERO

I'm in bed and drifting in and out of a fantastically explicit dream featuring my wife, when I get a call from Gino the next morning.

"Well done last night."

The sound of his voice makes my dick deflate instantaneously. I swear I can hear his fountains fucking gurgling in the background. I don't know how he lives like that. I'd have to piss all the time.

I sit up against the headboard and rake my fingers through my hair. "What happened?"

"They put eyes on you this morning."

Huh. He's moving fast. Blake will be pleased to hear our efforts have paid off. "You got some more details?"

"The penthouse is being watched. There's a black Mercedes parked half a block east, and there are guys on each of the exits. They're dressed in athletic gear and caps."

Great. Who doesn't love having a few trigger-happy Russians on their doorstep? "Do you think Maksim is acting on his own or with the pakhan's blessing?"

"It's doubtful he went straight to the top. Given his position, he won't tell the pakhan about you until he's absolutely certain he's got you leashed."

Irritation spikes through me. Me, on a fucking leash? I thought my pride went out the window the moment Gino told me to get on my knees in his office, but it looks like it's still here, because that image makes me want to shove Gino's face into a fucking wall.

"And how is he going to do that?" I growl.

"We have to wait and see. Another accidental run-in would be too suspicious. But if he's put his guys on you, you've clearly caught his attention."

Did I?

Or did Blake?

I didn't miss the way Maksim looked at her last night. He practically frothed at the mouth over my wife.

My. Fucking. Wife.

"If I had to guess, he wants to monitor who's coming in and out to see you. Vita won't be stopping by anymore. Every discussion from now on will take place over this secure line. I'll make sure Rafaele also gets the memo. I don't want him around you at all. We need to sell the idea that there's a rift between you two."

I sniff. "All right."

That won't be hard. Rafaele has kept his distance, and I don't know if it's because he feels weird about what almost happened in Gino's office, or if it's something else.

An ache spreads through my chest. There was a time when we were inseparable.

But Maksim was right about one thing last night. Things change.

"You need to get him to trust you, Nero. He'll do whatever he needs to do in order to get a feel for where you stand."

"Yeah, I got it. You don't need to hold my hand." Frankly, if all I've got to do is convince Maksim I'm hungry for revenge, it won't be hard. I'd never betray Rafe, but Blake's right. My current situation isn't good. She deserves better than a husband who's got less power and influence than a low-level soldier.

"Is that disrespect I hear in your tone, De Luca?"

Fucking Ferraro. He's giving me plenty of frustration I can channel into the lies I'll feed Maksim.

"Just getting in character, Your Majesty. We'll be in touch." I toss my phone on the nightstand and let out a sigh. I hate being bossed around by this asshole. Rafe was never a condescending piece of shit like him.

Irritation buzzes beneath my skin as I throw off the blanket and sit on the edge of the bed. Outside the window, the city I once ruled goes about its business as usual.

Seriously, though, why the fuck did Maksim look at Blake like that? There was a certain glint in his eye—a glint that a married man shouldn't have, especially not with his wife standing right beside him. A glint that a man speaking to the wife of the Angel of Death shouldn't dare possess. Unless, of course, that nickname doesn't carry the weight it used to.

Working with Rafe always felt like a partnership. Yes, he had final veto power, but it rarely came to that. He listened to me, respected me, and valued me.

Gino doesn't.

If my boss treats me like a nobody, soon enough, everyone else in the city will catch on.

I swallow hard. My problems seem to be multiplying, but they will be solved if Blake and I pull this thing off.

Even though the main reason I agreed to the plan was because I think it'll bring Blake and me closer together, it will be nice to be a capo again.

Gino's capo. And eventually, Cosimo's.

But that's better than being Alessio's lackey.

I roll my shoulders back and let out a long breath. I can handle Maksim. I've handled men far more clever and dangerous.

But something about this doesn't sit well with me. Was it right to allow Blake to get involved in this?

Forget the fact that she's the one who wanted to do it. She doesn't understand how quickly things like this can go off the rails. It's my job to make sure they don't, but it's a hell of a lot easier to control a situation when you've got an arsenal at your disposal, and right now, all I've got is me.

I might be putting her in danger. Again.

I let out a sigh.

She won't agree to call this off so quickly, not after fighting so hard to do it in the first place. And wasn't last night great for us? Didn't it feel like I was getting through to her? I made her smile. I made her blush. I offered her the support she needed without her even asking.

There's a selfish part of me that doesn't want to give that up, despite my anxiety.

The next few days only serve to agitate my nerves even more. The black Mercedes is out there day and night. Blake doesn't leave the penthouse while I'm working, but I worry about the men staking out the building. They wouldn't dare try to come inside. Then again, the Bratva are daring and not always logical. I ask Gino to station a car with three guys a few blocks away, just in case the Russians make a move. He agrees.

On Wednesday, my phone rings with an unknown number just as I pull into the parking lot of the penthouse. I turn off the ignition and pick up the call.

"Mr. De Luca." The accented voice on the other end of the line is instantly recognizable.

"Garin. I don't recall giving you my number."

"Where there's a will, there's a way."

I roll my eyes. "To what do I owe the pleasure? In case it wasn't obvious at the gala, I'm happily married, so if you're calling to ask me out on a date, the answer is no."

He chuckles. "I've heard you have a sense of humor."

"From whom?"

"Some mutual friends."

I flick through my mental Rolodex. Everyone in the underground knows about the turf war between the Italians and the Bratva, and most have picked sides, except for—

"There's a poker game at Red Vines on Friday. I wanted to extend an invitation."

Ah. Red Vines is neutral territory. Been that way for a few decades. It's a club run by a Greek called Yannis. I wouldn't call him a friend, but I've been to some of his game nights. Maksim must have spoken to him about me.

I toss my car keys in my palms. "Those seats usually get taken quickly."

"There's room for one more. I thought you might enjoy a friendly game."

As in, he wants an opportunity to put me under the microscope.

Gino will be happy. I hate making him happy.

I rub my jaw with my palm. "It's been a while since I've played."

"It'll be a good time."

"I'm sure it will be, but you know, I've got a packed social calendar."

"Oh?" Annoyance creeps into Maksim's voice. He knows it's a lie given I haven't gone out or had anyone visit me since he put his guys on watch.

But I can't seem too eager.

"Let me check my agenda." I swipe through the promotions tab in my email for a full minute before I finally say, "Looks like I'm free that night."

"Great." There's a bite to his tone. "My wife is hosting a dinner that same night with a few of her girlfriends at a restaurant not too far from the game. She took a real liking to your lovely wife at the gala. Would Blake like to join them?"

No.

I pinch the bridge of my nose. I'm supposed to say yes. Vita spent two weeks preparing Blake so that she could hold her own with those women. "I'll have to ask."

"She must be lonely, not knowing many people in the city."

"How do you know she doesn't?"

"She's not from New York, is she?"

So he's looked into her. It doesn't surprise me, but it still pisses me off.

"I'll talk to her and see what she thinks. What's the address?"

Maksim rattles it off. "I hope she can make it. It'll be good for her to get out of the house."

I bite on the inside of my cheek. "Thanks for the invite. Looking forward to it."

Upstairs, Blake is munching on some pasta when I walk into the kitchen.

She glances at the clock. I'm home earlier than usual. When she sees the expression I'm wearing, she frowns and puts down her fork. "What happened?"

I walk over to where she's sitting at the kitchen island and steal a bite from off her plate. "We've received two invitations. Me to a poker game with Maksim, and you to a dinner with his wife."

"That's good, right?"

The moment I take the stool beside her, she pushes her half-finished plate toward me and gets to her feet.

Frustration pulses inside my chest. She's been trying to avoid me since the gala, going to sleep before I get back home from work, and now she's running away from again.

My hand shoots out to grab her forearm, and I tug her back into her seat. "Sit with me."

Her gaze drops to where I'm touching her, to where her soft skin is pebbling with goosebumps.

Lightly, I swipe my thumb over her inner wrist. "Blake, we spent all evening together at the gala, and now it's like you can't stand five minutes in my presence. What happened?"

Slowly, her gaze rises to meet mine.

How is it that I used to be able to read her? To understand her? Now, she's a black box to me.

"We were working," she says softly.

A stab goes through my heart. "So you'll only spend time with me while we're working?"

"Nero, you spent all evening taking advantage of the fact that I couldn't tell you to back off. I thought I made myself clear. We can be friends, but nothing more."

My nostrils flare. That word used in relation to me and her makes me want to punch a fucking wall.

"If you can't accept that and keep pushing for more, I have no choice but to keep my distance."

I lean in, inhaling her vanilla scent. "Do you remember when you tried to be my friend back in Darkwater Hollow?"

Pink spreads over her cheeks. She tugs on her bottom lip with her teeth. "That's old history."

"Sunshine, history tends to repeat itself."

She exhales a low breath, her eyelashes fluttering. I'm so close, I could count them all one by one if I wanted to.

Her body betrays her true feelings by tilting closer to me. When will she stop fighting this? What will it take to get her to drop her defenses and trust me again?

Maybe it'll happen when you stop putting her in danger.

My jaw clenches. This time, it's me who lets go of her and leans away.

She sounds a bit breathless as she says, "Tell me about this poker game."

I give her the rundown of my conversation with Maksim.

Blake's brows are furrowed. "Isn't Maksim worried about being seen with you in public? If he's already thinking about trying to turn you, he'd want to keep your meetings private, no?"

"He picked well. The two of us being seen on neutral territory like Red Vines shouldn't arouse suspicion. In his mind, even if it gets back to Gino that he and I were there together, our attendance could be easily explained as coincidental." I take another few bites of her abandoned pasta. "What do you think about this dinner with Ekaterina?"

Blake shrugs. "I have to go. It's the kind of thing Vita told me to expect."

"You'll be there on your own. I don't like it."

"It's not like she's going to do anything to me in public. What are you afraid of?"

"I don't know." Something uncomfortable gets lodged inside my throat. Should I tell her how I'm really feeling?

Fuck it. I've got nothing to lose.

"I'm worried I'm putting you in danger. I promised you I'd keep you safe, and this doesn't fucking feel like me fulfilling that promise. This feels like me doing the wrong thing for selfish reasons again."

Her eyes widen, like that was the last thing she was expecting me to say.

"What are you talking about? I'm the one who convinced you to do this. I *want* to do this. You becoming capo..." She swallows. "It will make everything better, won't it?"

No more twelve-hour days when I barely see her. No more blood caked under my nails when I get home. No more men doubting that I could disembowel them for giving her lingering looks.

And to top that all off...I just have this gut feeling that once we make it to the other side of this, she'll be mine again.

"Yeah, it would. But at what cost?"

"I can handle this. I don't want to see you hurt, Nero."

"It's not your job to fix my problems, Sunshine."

Unease flickers across her expression. "It is when I'm the one who contributed to them."

I frown. "What are you talking about?"

"Brett was my ex. Uncle Lyle was my godfather."

Is she seriously blaming herself for what happened? "You're kidding, right? Don't tell me you're doing this out of some misplaced sense of guilt."

"You know, in the beginning, I was so worried about the people in my life causing problems for you. And then when I found out about how you'd lied to me, I was so full of rage that I became blind to my own part in what happened to us. But if it wasn't for Brett and Uncle Lyle, you would have stayed Rowan Miller. You'd still be running Handy Heroes with Sam, and you wouldn't have had to risk your life by coming back here. So yeah, I do feel guilty, and I don't think my guilt is at all misplaced."

My heart breaks all over again.

This woman. How can someone be this fucking pure and good?

She's wrong, of course. She's blameless. If I'd handled Brett differently, he wouldn't have gone to the Iron Raptors and demanded they look into me.

But I can see now that this has been weighing on her.

I swipe my hand over my lips, trying to contain the flood of conflicting emotions suddenly rushing through me. "You don't have to do this."

"I know. But I want to. You've taken many choices from me, Nero. Don't you dare try to take this one from me as well."

She's right. She's fucking right. If I want to ever win her back after forcing her to marry me against her will, I have to start letting her make her own decisions. She will never allow herself to love me again if I insist on ruling with an iron fist.

I take her hand in mine, interlacing our fingers and marveling at how soft her skin is. "Fine. I won't."

A second passes, and then she squeezes my hand back. "It'll be all right."

I want to believe she's right, but doubts still swirl inside. And maybe I'm imagining it, but I swear there's a hint of something false inside her piercing blue eyes.

CHAPTER 19

NERO

The air in the back room of Red Vines is thick with the heat of bodies and cigar smoke. A lone overhead lamp illuminates the table and the men sitting around it with dim light.

The room goes quiet as I step over the threshold.

Maksim's gaze meets mine. He puffs on his cigar and gives me a small wave. "Welcome," he says out of the corner of his mouth. "Have a seat."

Yannis walks over to shake my hand. "Welcome back to New York, Mr. De Luca. We missed you around these parts."

I pat Yannis on the back. He's not a bad guy, although I wonder if his neutrality will continue to stand if this war keeps heating up. It's nice to mix and mingle in times of peace, but when the dead keep piling up, few men will be willing to leave their grudges at the door of Red Vines.

Taking a seat, I do a quick inventory of who's here. There are two men I don't recognize, three Greeks that I've seen hanging around Yannis, Sergio Delvagio—a free agent previously associated with the Santoro family—and Mick Smith. Fuck that guy. I'm certain that's not his real name. He's a trafficker and someone I don't like to associate with.

Given the malicious look in his eyes, he knows it too.

"Do we need to make any introductions?" Maksim asks.

I nod at the two men I haven't seen before. "We haven't met."

Turns out they're Albanian smugglers here on vacation. Friends of Yannis.

What a merry fucking crew.

Yannis makes sure we all have drinks and then the game begins.

The dealer, a younger Greek I recognize but whose name I can't recall, shuffles the deck with practiced hands.

To determine the button position, each player is dealt one card face up. I get a seven. One of the Albanians gets a king, earning the button, making me the big blind. The agreed-upon big blind is four hundred dollars. I slide my chips into the pot, waiting for the dealer to deal the starting hands.

Mick's eyeing me with a smirk that's starting to piss me off.

I swipe my palm over my chin. "Got something on my face?"

He flashes me his yellow teeth. "Must be nice to take a six-month sabbatical from all this. Want to share some tips? I'd love a vacation."

Two cards appear in front of me. I glance at them quickly before stacking them together. "Plenty of people around these parts who'd like to send you on a permanent vacation, Mick."

He cackles. "Still got your sense of humor, I see."

We start the first betting round. Mick folds. The rest check. I raise. The dealer deals three cards on the table. I mentally run through the possible combinations.

I've got nothing.

Maksim brings his drink to his lips. "Nero came back to New York with a beautiful wife."

This fucking prick.

"Oh yeah?" Mick drawls. "How is she liking it here?"

I crack my knuckles. "She's warming up to it."

Maksim's eyes glint from across the table. "She seemed quite at ease at the event where we ran into the two of you. You should bring her out more often, Nero. No need to hide her away at home."

My gaze drills into the cards on the table while a fantasy of putting a bullet right between Maksim's eyes plays on repeat inside my head.

I better channel the anger pulsing through me into the act I'm supposed to be putting on.

We start another betting round. I fold.

"And you? How you've been since your return?" Mick asks.

He's up my ass, and I have a feeling Maksim's the one who put him up to it.

"Just fine."

"Is that right? A lot of things have changed since you left. Can't be easy adjusting to it all."

The dealer reveals another card.

"Not as hard as you think," I grind out.

After we go around the table once more, only Sergio, Mick, and one of the Greeks remain in the game.

The dealer flips the final card. A jack of hearts.

Across from me, Sergio throws his cards onto the table—he's got a full house.

The guys who were still in the game curse.

"Sergio takes the pot," the dealer says before he starts collecting our cards off the table.

Mick's grin is all shark teeth and malice. "Hey, Nero, remember when you used to be someone important? You know, before you became Alessio's errand boy?" Laughter echoes around the table, sharp and biting.

I force a tight-lipped smile. "Times change, Mick. We play the hands we're dealt." My voice is calm, betraying none of the bitterness that swirls in my gut like a bad meal.

I'd expected this. These games are always full of jibes and underhanded insults, but they usually slide right off me like I'm made of Teflon.

Now, they burrow under my skin.

I am a fucking errand boy.

But not for long if we manage to nail the pakhan.

We start again. Cards are dealt, bets placed.

"I'm just kidding with you," Mick says. "You're not the kind of guy who stays at the bottom for long. You'll work your way back up in no time."

"If they let him, that is," Maksim adds. "Forgive me if I'm wrong, but I don't think Gino Ferraro is interested in giving any power to a man who killed one of his nephews. No matter how capable he might be."

I bite on the inside of my cheek. "Time will tell."

"I just wonder if your wife will be patient enough to wait," Sergio chimes in, tossing his chips into the center with a clatter. "If not, and if she's as beautiful as Maksim says, tell her I'll be happy to take her off your hands."

Chuckles erupt, but they're tense. Probably because they can tell I'm contemplating murder.

"You say one more thing about my wife, and I'll break your neck."

Mick scratches a spot on his cheek with his thumb. "Don't you need Gino Ferraro's permission to do that?"

Sergio laughs, but he stops quickly when he registers the look on my face. He tugs on his collar and sniffs. "Take a joke, will ya?"

"All right, let's not bring the ladies into this," Maksim says smoothly, like he's the magnanimous referee.

Our eyes meet. Every instinct inside me demands I hide how the snide comments from him grate against me, but I make a point to let the frustration bleed into my expression.

This is what he's looking for. This is exactly what he wants to see. A man who's been reduced to nothing. A man who'll do anything to get back what he lost.

His lips twitch before he looks away.

The final hand comes around, and the air tenses, thick with anticipation.

When the dealer reveals the fourth card, excitement flares inside my chest. I've got a flush, all cloaked in hearts. A winning hand, finally.

I raise. So do Maksim, Mick, and Sergio. The pot grows to thirty grand before the dealer reveals the last of the five cards.

I reveal the two cards I've got, and the table falls silent as the realization dawns. Mick's face turns an interesting shade of red.

"Well, fuck me," he spits, his hand empty except for a useless pair.

"What he said," Sergio grumbles.

Maksim just sniffs.

I rake in my chips, the clink of them sounding sweet to my ears. "Just playing the hand I was dealt, gents." My smile is all teeth now, no pretense of friendliness.

"Let's take a break," Yannis says.

"I've got to take a leak," Mick mutters, shouldering past me on his way out.

Maksim and I walk over to the bar set up in the corner. "Well played. You've lost a lot, Nero, but you haven't lost your edge."

Despite my win, I'm tense. "Yeah. Thanks. Whiskey, neat."

Maksim nods at Yannis. "One for me too."

Yannis pours it for us. "Here you go."

"I can tell you've got a fire in you," Maksim adds as we pick up our drinks. "Gino hasn't managed to extinguish it."

He's fishing. Looking for me to slip and say something I shouldn't while I'm still pissed. I'm fucking sure he told Mick to be on his worst behavior just to rile me up.

I let my anger slip into my tone. "Not for the lack of trying."

"Has it been difficult?" he says, lowering his voice.

"What do you think? I've spent my whole life doing right by the Messeros. And this is how they repay me."

Maksim lets the silence linger.

I huff and give my head a shake, letting my agitation roll off me in waves. "Never mind. It is what it is."

"It's not fair what they did to you."

"Loyalty only extends in one direction in that family."

Satisfaction flickers inside Maksim's gaze. I think I have him.

"One day, it might come back to bite them," he says smoothly.

"Yeah. One day."

We stare at each other, an understanding solidifying between us, and a conspiratorial smirk lifts up the corner of his lips.

"I'm glad we met." Maksim raises his whiskey. "To new friends."

I clink my glass against his. "To new friends."

The alcohol burns as it slides down my throat. Around us, the other players have broken into small groups, their chatter filling the room.

But one person is missing.

Placing the empty glass on the bar, I give Maksim a nod. "I'll be right back."

Mick's washing his hands when I walk into the bathroom. His eyes meet mine in the mirror, locking onto my reflection like a hawk tracking its target.

I walk toward him with slow, measured steps, enjoying the way all color seeps out of his face.

He turns off the tap. "Hey, Nero. All good? I didn't mean to offe—"

"I'm not here to chat," I growl.

I drag him to the toilet, shove his head into the bowl, and flush until he nearly drowns.

The satisfaction I get is even sweeter than winning that hand.

CHAPTER 20

BLAKE

"Andrey Arkadiev's wife had no idea how to use the fish knife, so she went in and took the bones out with *her fingers*. She saw how shocked I was and asked me what was wrong. I couldn't believe it. I had to say something though, so I went, 'I'm sorry, but I've never seen someone eat it like that before.' You should have seen how red she turned!"

The women around the table cackle, and I eye the formal setting in front of me with unease. Four knives, five forks, two spoons. Vita went over table manners in one of our lessons, but the topic didn't seem all that important at the time.

Now, I wish I'd done a better job committing every word she said to memory.

I squint at the smallest fork. Nope. No idea what that's for.

If Ekaterina is hunting for more stories of social faux pas to add to her repertoire, I'm sure I'll give her plenty of material to laugh about before this dinner is over.

Maksim's wife sits across from me, enveloped in a cloud of pink chiffon that matches the champagne-hued wallpaper of this gilded, extravagant private dining room tucked away in the back of a one-star Michelin restaurant.

I feel woefully underdressed in the silk wrap dress I chose for the occasion.

There are four other women around our table. They all said hello to me when I first arrived and have been largely ignoring me since. Based on their accents, all of them are Russian, and I'd bet all of them have husbands in the Bratva.

I wasn't sure what to expect from this dinner, but so far, it's been uneventful. Kind of boring, to be honest. They've been gossiping about people in their circles for the past fifteen minutes and laughing at jokes with punch lines I don't understand.

Why did Ekaterina invite me to this?

She appears to be the leader of this group, but as she delves into lengthy monologues, I notice a few women exchanging mocking glances. I can't help but wonder if they all know her husband has lost the boss's favor.

As Ekaterina begins yet another story about someone's wife, I check my phone for an update from Nero.

Nothing.

He's at the poker game with Maksim, while I'm here with the wives.

We never said we'd keep each other in the loop tonight, and I'm seriously regretting that oversight.

I'm on pins and needles. Ever since we talked last night and opened up with each other about how we've been feeling about this mission, something inside me has shifted.

Last night, I lay in bed wondering where the anger that used to burn so brightly was.

I couldn't find it.

I've...forgiven him.

And I'm starting to trust him. I can tell that he's trying to do right by me, even at a great personal cost.

Yesterday in the kitchen he confessed he wants to call off our plan because he's worried for me.

And yet, he didn't. Because he listened to what I want and need.

My heart clenches.

It's getting harder and harder to keep my walls up when Nero shows me with each passing day that he's not the man I thought he was after he revealed his true identity to me.

He's not my father. And he doesn't treat me like my father treated my mother.

But this still isn't the life I want. I don't want to live in the shadows, where everything could be torn away from me by cruel hands in the blink of an eye. I don't want to be in a marriage that I was *forced* into. How can anything beautiful grow on such a rotten foundation?

It can't. Which is why I have to leave, no matter what I'm starting to feel for my husband.

"Blake, I heard you were born in a small town somewhere in Missouri?"

My head snaps up.

Ekaterina is looking at me with a mean glint in her eyes. Nero warned me they'd done their research on me, but her comment still catches me off guard.

It's a bit concerning how quickly they were able to figure out who I am.

"That's right. Born and raised."

"Missoooouri," one of the women, Frida, exclaims with a weird drawl that's a poor attempt at the accent. "I don't know anything about it."

I smile. "It's the birthplace of Mark Twain."

Ekaterina purses her lips. "Did I forget to mention that Blake is a big fan of literature? She's one of those bookish types," she says with a dismissive wave.

She's trying to make me feel uncomfortable, but I don't think my love of reading is anything to be ashamed of, so I just smile. "It's true, I love to get lost in a good story."

Ekaterina narrows her eyes. "Moving from Missouri to New York is quite the fairytale. Has it been everything you expected it to be?"

A fairytale. Yeah, maybe one of those dark ones where the children get lured into the witch's hut with sweets. The kind where dreams twist into nightmares, and the prince is as likely to be the villain as he is the hero.

"It's been an adjustment. For both me and Nero."

She perks up at the mention of Nero's name. "Your husband used to be a well-known man in certain circles."

"It seems he still is."

"It must be devastating for you to watch him lose it all." She taps her fingertips against her chin. "Then again, you didn't know him when he held his old position, so maybe you haven't noticed the difference. I'm sure he feels it though. Fate can be such a cruel thing."

My teeth clench even though this is what we wanted. We wanted Ekaterina to dig her claws into me so that she can judge if I'm the kind of person who'd support Nero going rogue.

"I don't believe in fate, but I believe in my husband. Whatever challenges he's facing now, he'll find a way to overcome them."

"Will he?" Ekaterina takes a sip of her drink. "His situation seems to be quite tricky."

"You must be very angry," the woman beside her says. "If my husband lost his position..." The woman makes a dismissive movement with her hand. "Let's just say he wouldn't stay my husband for long."

How sad. Is this what marriage in the mob comes down to? Using each other for personal gain? It didn't seem like Maksim had much affection for his wife at the gala, but he's clearly putting her to work with me.

If I'd married Nero consensually, I don't see why I'd give a damn about his position or rank. It's not his power I care about. I just don't like seeing him be treated like crap by Gino Ferraro.

But I know that would be the wrong thing to say. I'm supposed to drop hints that I'm unhappy. That he's unhappy.

So unhappy he's ready to betray the Italians.

I smooth the napkin spread over my lap and mutter, "It's their loss."

Ekaterina tips her head slightly to the side. "What's that?"

"I said that it's their loss if they can't appreciate my husband's value. He's got a lot of experience, and he knows more about the way things are run in this city than most of the men above him do."

"Does he? Even after being gone for six months?" Her tone is casual, but I can tell she's trying to draw information out of me.

"He may have been gone for six months, but before he left, he worked here for ten years. It's not like all the things he knows became irrelevant in that short amount of time. With the exception of the don himself, there's no one in the Messero family who knows as much about its dealings as Nero does."

Ekaterina's gaze goes from mocking to assessing. "For someone who's new to this world, you sure seem to have caught on quick, Blake."

"I don't like feeling left in the dark. And I learn quickly."

"Some men prefer keeping their personal life separate from their business."

"Is that what your husband prefers?" I ask.

Her eyes narrow again. "Maks tells me everything."

I can't resist giving her a condescending smile. "You two seem like a great couple."

"We are." There's a defensive note to her voice that suggests otherwise.

Our server comes around with another bottle of champagne. I've lost count of how many we've gone through by now. These women drink it like it's water.

The server—a woman in a perfectly pressed uniform with the restaurant logo embroidered on her chest—pauses by Frida and refills her glass before moving to Ekaterina, who has already turned her attention away from me to launch into another story. Ekaterina talks with fervor, her hands constantly in motion, and when the waitress pours champagne into her glass, Ekaterina's arm swings out at the same time.

A collective gasp echoes around the table as the champagne glass tips over, drenching the front of Ekaterina's dress.

"You idiot," she hisses at the waitress, even though it was hardly her fault. "What have you done?"

"I'm so sorry."

"This is *couture*." Ekaterina's face darkens with rage. "Is your job really so fucking hard that you can't even refill a glass properly? Or is this your first day here, you dumb bitch?"

My eyes widen at her outburst. *Holy anger issues.*

"Madam, it was an accident." There's a hint of panic in the server's tone.

Ekaterina snatches a napkin off the table and dabs it against her dress. "It's ruined. I hope they pay you well here, because you're going to buy me a new dress."

The server's shoulders slump, and her eyes brim with tears. The women around the table watch the scene unfold in silence, making no move to intervene. That's when it dawns on me. If I don't stop this, no one else will.

I open my mouth, but I'm too late. Ekaterina has already grabbed the bottle from the server and—

"Stop," I shout, just as Ekaterina flips the bottle and empties the rest of its contents over the server's clothes.

"Katya!" someone gasps.

The server inhales sharply, standing frozen in shock. "Y-you can't do that."

A cruel laugh escapes Ekaterina. "I can do whatever I want. Do you know who I am?"

The server looks down at the ground. "Yes."

"Then clean up this mess." She drops the bottle to the floor. "*Now.*" She smiles, but it's a chilling expression that doesn't reach her eyes. "If you keep wasting my time, I'll insist you lick the floor clean, so you better hurry instead of standing there like a statue."

The server scurries away, tears streaking her cheeks.

A beat passes, and I hope those around the table feel even a fraction of the shame I'm experiencing from being associated with this madness.

But that's too much to hope for.

Beside me, Frida forces a laugh. "What an idiot."

The rest of the women mutter their agreement.

Ekaterina's gaze lands back on me, a challenge glinting in her eyes. *This is who I am*, her eyes say. *Do you dare question me?*

My palms are sweaty. Acid creeps up my throat.

There's nothing I can do. Even though I want to fling my plate at her head, I have to sit here and pretend like what just happened is totally normal.

These people are twisted and cruel. And am I any better? After all, the reason I can't say anything is because I can't let Ekaterina think I'm the kind of woman who'd talk her husband out of betraying his side.

I have to pretend I don't have any morals.

The longer I stay in this world, the less I recognize myself.

And that's why I need to get out.

CHAPTER 21

BLAKE

Back at Frostbite Tavern, there's a sign on the wall that says, "Lord, give me coffee to change the things I can, and wine to accept the things I can't."

Wise words.

When I hear Nero come through the front door about an hour after me, I'm on the living room sofa nursing a glass of red wine and trying to find just a little bit of that acceptance.

The soft satin robe I wrapped around myself feels rough against my raw skin.

I spent a good thirty minutes scrubbing myself in the shower, and yet I still feel dirty.

The image of that server keeps flashing in front of my eyes. That could've been me in my old life. That could have been me they were humiliating.

Those women are sick, plain and simple. And for the duration of that dinner, I had to pretend to be no different from them.

My stomach churns, and I feel disgusting.

Nero steps into the room. There's an uneasy air about him and a storm brewing inside those hazel eyes.

"How did it go?"

"Fine." He loosens his necktie with a sharp tug and undoes the top button of his shirt.

"You don't look fine."

He walks over to the small bar in the corner and starts pouring himself a whiskey. "Neither do you."

I put the wine down on the coffee table. "These people are psychopaths."

"What happened?" he asks, keeping his back to me.

"A waitress spilled a drink on Ekaterina, and you should have seen how she reacted. She humiliated her. Poured champagne on her and threatened to force her to clean the spilled drink off the ground with her tongue. Who the hell talks to people like that? She has serious issues. I don't want to imagine how she'd behave if her side ruled this city."

Nero walks over to sit on the couch beside me. He looks down into his glass, his jaw clenched.

"You don't have anything to say to that?" I prod.

"What do you want me to say? Did you really think they'd be nice people when you signed us up for this? You're not supposed to like them, Blake. You're supposed to want to take them down."

Goosebumps scatter over my arms. Take them down?

Sounds pretty good, doesn't it? Ekaterina deserves it.

What? No. I don't want to take anyone down. Where did that thought even come from?

I swallow, unsettled. That's not why I'm doing this. I just want to help Nero and then put as much distance as I can between myself and these people.

"Is that it? How was the rest of the evening?"

I look over at Nero. "Uncomfortable. She prodded me about you."

He sniffs. "What did she ask?"

"She kept bringing up the fact that your position has changed. I guess she tried to see how I felt about your demotion."

Nero's expression grows even more tense. "So did Maksim. They must have decided that's the weak spot they need to exploit."

Worry runs through me. I can't imagine Nero responded well to that.

His knuckles turn white around his glass. "How *do* you feel about it?"

"About what?"

"My position."

"I acted as if I'm angry on your behalf. I think she bought it. She kept trying to imply that you're weak. I think she wanted to see if that bothers me."

"Does it?" His voice is clipped.

"Of course not. I don't care about what position you hold."

"Don't you? You seem determined to make me capo."

"Yeah, because if you keep doing what you're doing now, you're far more likely to end up dead."

His jaw moves as he stares into his glass for a few moments, and then he tosses the whiskey back.

"How did it go for you?" I ask.

"You came up."

"Did I?"

"Maksim said I have a very beautiful wife. He wanted to know how you liked New York. I lied and told him you're warming up to it."

"Maybe you shouldn't have. Maybe you should have told him I'm miserable, and that you're desperate to make me happy. If you make him think your life is in ruins, he'll believe you're willing to do whatever it takes to—"

"This was never supposed to have you at the center of it, Blake," he snaps. "And I don't fucking like it. Every time he mentioned you, I wanted to shove my gun between his lips and pull the trigger."

The raw fury in his voice makes the hairs on my arms stand up straight. "He's just trying to push your buttons."

"Maybe you're right. If so, he's doing a hell of a job of it." He slams his empty glass on the coffee table, rises to his feet, and walks over to the window. "I keep thinking about how he looked at you at the gala. Like you're something he wants to own."

There's something in his tone that sends a shiver through me. "He liked my dress, that's all."

He anchors his palms against the window frame. "A year ago, no man would've dared look at you that way. Not if they knew you're mine. But now, they're not afraid of me anymore."

My gaze slides down his body. He's tense, and his back muscles flex under the fabric of his shirt. I wonder if we both feel caged, albeit in different ways.

He's not used to being bossed around. To not being at the top. He doesn't have to pretend to be upset about how much he's lost.

Some force pulls me to my feet. I walk up to him. I want to comfort him, to embrace him, to tell him it will be okay.

But as I reach for him, my hand freezes halfway.

The more closeness I allow between us now, the more he'll be hurt when I leave.

I don't want to hurt him, but I can't stay in this world with him. I'm afraid of what will happen to me if do. My mother betrayed herself over and over again for the sake of a man who lived in the shadows, and I had a front row seat to her heartbreak and pain. And it didn't even end after my father died, because then Uncle Lyle started knocking on our door and dragging us back into the darkness.

I refuse to let history repeat itself.

There is no happiness for those who love criminals, and it would be naïve to think that I could be the exception to that rule.

Nero will miss me when I'm gone—for a bit at least—but being made capo will soften the blow.

It won't take him long to find someone else to keep by his side. After all, he's never had trouble with that.

I drop my hand back down. "This is temporary," I say softly. "You can't let Maksim get to you."

Nero whips around to face me. "He wants you," he growls, his eyes flashing with anger and frustration. And then he wraps his fist around the knot holding my robe together. His knuckles press just below my breasts, and he tugs me toward him.

I make a surprised gasp.

"Can't you see it?" he demands.

"He's married," I whisper.

"You think that matters to him?" His eyes drop to my lips, and I feel an unwelcome rush of heat in the pit of my belly.

It drives me crazy how he can still make me feel this way. How one look can send me reeling. How one touch can set me alight.

I fight to keep my voice steady. "How could I forget that men in your line of work are never hindered by things like marriage vows?"

He tugs me even closer, until the hard points of my nipples make contact with his chest. Our close proximity makes my pussy clench.

"You're putting me in the same category as Maksim?"

I'm not. By now, I know Nero would never cheat on me. He was willing to die for me.

But I need to wedge something between us, something that will push him away. "Do you have to ask why? Have you forgotten the conversation we had at the restaurant? You asked me if I'm okay with you sleeping with other women. If I'd said yes, you would have gone out and done just that."

His laugh is darkened at the edges. "I know you're not being serious right now."

"I am."

Frustration rages through his features. "*God*, Blake. I want to bend you over my knee and spank some sense into you."

The imagery makes me squeeze my thighs together. That statement should piss me off, not turn me on. There's a building panic inside my chest as my resolve begins to slip.

He bends his neck, bringing our faces close together. "When are you going to understand that other women don't exist for me anymore? There's only you. There will only ever be *you*."

A wave of heat crashes through me. As his heady scent envelops me, I can feel my control unraveling bit by agonizing bit. I shouldn't have drunk more when I got home. The alcohol's taken the edge off my restraint, and that's a dangerous thing when Nero is around.

His long fingers unwind from around the knot of my belt, and he takes a half step back. At first, I think he's about to walk away, but then he pinches one of the tails of the belt and stretches it taut.

He waits.

Waits to see if I'll stop him. If I'll rip it out of his hand like I should.

But I'm frozen. Ensnared by his gaze. There's an energy swirling inside my body, desperate to be released after being bottled up for so damn long.

His eyes stay glued to my face. "It's killing me that I can't have you. That you won't trust me."

I do.

"That you won't forgive me."

I already did.

But if I tell him the only thing still keeping me from accepting this new life is my belief that I can never be truly happy with someone like him, someone who lives in the shadows, someone who *forced* me to marry him, I'm afraid he will make it his mission to prove me wrong. I'm afraid he'll convince me to believe in a fairytale, a story that's not real.

So I lie. "There's nothing you can do," I breathe. "What you did is unforgivable."

Pain flashes inside his gaze. "I had to lie to you. I had to lie to everyone." He shakes his head. "It wasn't easy. On more than one occasion, I thought about telling you the truth, so that you'd know all of me. See all of me."

"But you didn't."

"Because if you saw me, you would leave. Just the way I think you still want to leave now."

My heart stutters on a beat. Does he know about my agreement with Vita?

No. He's guessing. He's trying to see how I'll react. I stay silent as I hold his gaze and pull on my bottom lip with my teeth.

He starts to tug the silk belt open. "Don't you feel the pull between us?" His voice is raw and filled with hunger I recognize all too well. "It's still there. It never left."

An embarrassing wetness trickles down my inner thighs. "No," I whisper, without any conviction.

The knot comes undone with a twist. A breeze would be enough to part the robe now, but in the still air, it hangs frozen, giving Nero only a narrow glimpse.

He lets out a heavy breath. "I dream of you every night, Sunshine. Of having you writhe beneath me again. I dream of your moans and the way you used to gasp my name when I buried myself deep inside of you. I dream of nipping on your perfect lips with my teeth and then kissing them better. And I dream of that moment when we'd both reach our peak and it felt like we were the only people left in this entire wretched world."

My heart is a frantic drum inside my chest. I know I should put an end to this, but the truth is...I can't bring myself to do it. I miss him too. I miss the way things were between us before I learned the truth.

He drags the tip of his finger in a line between my breasts. "I've hurt you, so let me make it better. Let me give you pleasure to make up for the pain."

My eyelashes flutter. It feels like my entire lower body has started to liquefy, and it's getting hard to maintain a grasp on any rational thought.

If I let him open the robe, he'll know. He'll see the red flush over my chest. He'll see my nipples sharp as points. And when he dips his hand between my legs, he'll find me drenched.

And he'll *know* I want him too.

My body throbs with need. My control makes a last gasp at the edges of my conscience and then dies a quick death.

I take a step closer.

Nero's eyes flash. He grabs the robe by the lapels, opens it, and lets it fall off my shoulders. Ravenous dark eyes slide down my body. It's as if he's looking at the best damn meal he's ever seen.

He lifts his hand to my chest and rubs his thumb over my nipple, shooting sparks straight to my swollen clit. "You belong in my bed, beautiful wife," he murmurs. "But since you won't come to me there, I will make you come for me right here."

A hand slides over my belly, going lower and lower, until it's *there*.

"Oh God," I gasp when his warm hand cups my sopping pussy. My head tips backward as two thick fingers slide inside of me and curl.

"That's my fucking girl," Nero growls, eating up the remaining distance between us and pressing his fully clothed body against my naked front. He grabs a handful of my ass and presses his lips to my neck while finding my clit with his thumb.

I moan at the sensation. I moan at having him wrapped around me once again. There's safety and comfort in his embrace, but it's an illusion.

An illusion I can allow myself to believe just for a little bit.

He carries me to the sofa with ease and makes me straddle his lap, his face a mask of dark lust. His hands trace over my chest, his touch gentle but sure, as if he wants to remind me how well he knows exactly what makes me tick.

A swipe of his tongue along the underside of my breasts. A pinch to my nipples. Hot, wet kisses over my sensitive flesh.

I pant and writhe against him, rubbing myself over the hard ridge of his cock. The added friction from his trousers being in the way is enough to drive me insane.

That's exactly what I feel like. Like I'm losing my mind.

"Fuck, baby," he swears. "You're gonna make me come in my pants if you keep grinding yourself on me like that. This isn't supposed to be about me at all."

I don't have time to formulate a response before my back hits the sofa and he buries his face between my legs. His hands curl in a possessive hold over my thighs. The world tilts a little more with each thorough lick, each hungry suck.

Shivers race down my spine as he plunges his tongue inside of me before moving back to circle my clit. I wrap my palms over his strong shoulders and hold on for dear life.

There's a buzzing sound inside my head. My inner muscles spasm. I move my hands to tangle in his hair, and I tug him closer. He makes a rough sound somewhere between a moan and a growl. Stars appear. Then fireworks. And then a supernova rushes through me in a wave of liquid heat.

"Nero," I choke out as he pins me with his dark eyes.

My hips rise off the sofa while he holds me tightly and helps me ride the waves of my orgasm.

It's so, so good.

I let myself drift in and out of this orgasmic bliss, but when the waves finally stop cresting, reality comes crashing down.

I blink at the ceiling and slowly let go of Nero's hair.

What have I done?

His shadow falls over my body as he rises to his feet, but I don't meet his gaze.

I can't.

Guilt and shame and longing slowly press down onto my chest. It feels like a cruel curse to love a man who isn't right for me.

I pick up my robe off the floor with trembling hands, wrap it tightly around me, and slink away, leaving my husband standing against the backdrop of the city below.

It's only after I lock the bedroom door that I allow my tears to fall.

CHAPTER 22

BLAKE

Mrs. Blake De Luca and Mr. Nero De Luca,

You are cordially invited to the Full Moon Soiree at the Seven Lives Social Club.

Join us for an unforgettable evening under the glow of the full moon, where fantasy will meet reality. We welcome you to indulge and fulfill your deepest desires without restraint.

Your utmost discretion is requested. The details of the night remain our little secret. Please present this invitation to guarantee your admittance.

Awaiting the pleasure of your company,

Maksim Garin

I slide my fingertip over the embossed logo in the top right corner—a black cat with a curved tail—and let out a slow breath.

The invitation arrived yesterday morning. Nero spent all day trying to figure out what this place is, but all he and Gino Ferraro's security team were able to discover was that the property was quietly purchased by Maksim a few years back.

There's no business license, no references online, not even a sign above the black steel door Nero photographed when he discreetly checked it out last night.

We have no idea what we're about to walk into.

Nero's hand tightens on the leather wheel as he pulls up to the curb. "That valet stand wasn't here yesterday."

"I'm guessing neither were those security guards." Two men dressed in black suits wait outside the door. A couple approaches them—a man and a dark-haired woman dressed in a long fur coat—and one of the security guards says something to them. The man produces a piece of paper that looks just like our invitation.

"I don't fucking like this," Nero mutters.

"Neither do I." But what can we do? Gino thinks this might be the night Maksim makes Nero an offer to work together. Maksim's clearly taking care to get us somewhere far from prying eyes. According to Nero, this place isn't anywhere near established Bratva territory.

"If anything feels off, we're leaving." Nero turns off the car and slides his gaze over me. "I've got a bad feeling about this."

I reach over and grab his hand. "We'll be all right."

He flips his hand over so that our palms touch and laces our fingers together.

My heart aches.

It's been two days since he made me come on the sofa in the living room.

Two days since I realized how weak my conviction to leave him has become.

I keep telling myself that Nero and this life are wrong for me, but I'm not sure I even believe that anymore. All I know is that when he held me in his arms that night, it was the first time I'd felt like everything would be all right.

I've been trying to stay rational and realistic about my situation, but now, it's as if my emotions are tired of being repressed, and they're demanding I listen to them instead of logic.

Is that what I should do? I don't know.

I'm grateful that at least for tonight, I can leave that question on the back burner and just focus on our mission.

Whatever it might entail.

Nero brushes his thumb over the back of my palm. "C'mon."

The valet takes the car, and the guard at the door follows the same procedure with us as he did with that other couple, taking our invitation and then checking my purse before letting us inside.

The dark and narrow hallway beyond the front door doesn't give us any hints as to what this place is. Our steps are punctuated by the heavy beat of a slow, seductive song streaming through speakers hidden in the ceiling.

We stop by a coat-check stand, where a young woman in a low-cut sequined dress takes our jackets. A few feet away, thick velvet curtains hide whatever lies at the end of this hall.

The coat-check girl slides Nero a tag with a number. "First time?"

"Yeah." Nero swipes his thumb over his lip, eyeing the curtains with suspicion. "We got an invite, but it didn't have a lot of details on it. What is this place?"

She just smiles. "It's better to go in blind. You're in for a memorable night."

Nero and I exchange a look, but strangely enough, I'm not nervous. It takes me a second to realize that it's because...I'm with him.

Whatever we're about to walk into, I trust Nero will keep me safe.

The thought sets off a flock of butterflies inside my belly.

Nero snakes a protective arm around my waist and tugs me against his side. "All right. Let's do this," he mutters in a low voice.

Mischief flashes in the girl's eyes as she pulls the curtain aside. "Welcome to Seven Lives."

We step through the opening and...

I stop in my tracks.

Holy. Shit.

The room beyond the curtain is a lavish space. It reminds me of the photos I've seen of old European palaces. There are high ceilings, crystal chandeliers, and intricately painted walls. But it's not the grand bar that stretches along one wall or the gilded cages that hang from the ceiling, each with a dancer swaying to the heavy beat of the music, that capture my attention.

About ten paces ahead, on a small circular stage, a woman is tied to a cross. A man's kneeling between her spread legs, devouring her pussy with intense fervor.

Her moans, loud and unabashed, can be heard even over the music.

"Umm." My wide eyes jump to Nero. I've never been to a sex club before—it doesn't take a genius to conclude that's what this is—but has he?

What if this is part of the whole mafia schtick?

The tendons in his thick neck are taut as he stares at the scene in front of him. "Toto, we're not in Kansas anymore."

I choke out a mildly hysterical laugh. "We sure are not."

His eyes lock onto mine. "You okay?"

Am I? My cheeks feel as if they're melting off. "I don't know. This is—"

"Ohhh!" the woman exclaims, her moans getting louder as she starts to come.

Nero laces our hands together and tugs me forward. "Come on. Let's grab a drink at the bar, and we can try to decipher why the fuck Maksim invited us here."

We move through the throng of people gathered around the stage. Some of them glance at us as we walk by them, but for the most part, everyone's attention is on the woman on the cross.

Nero and I are definitely wearing more clothes than anyone else in here. The women are in lingerie, and the men are in their underwear. There's one man who's wearing nothing at all, and his erection bobs as he shifts on his feet.

I avert my eyes and focus on the edges of the room. Velvet booths wrap around the perimeter, many of them occupied by couples in various stages of undress.

My blood pulses in my cheeks. I don't consider myself a prude, but I need a few minutes to process all of this and acclimate. It's a lot to take in.

At the bar, there's a wooden sign that says, "Two drink limit."

"I guess I can see why they wouldn't want the patrons getting drunk," I say quietly to Nero.

He orders me a gin and tonic and a whiskey for himself. "I've heard places like this often limit alcohol."

"You've never been to one?"

He gives me a smirk. "No, Sunshine. Believe it or not, exhibitionism isn't really my thing."

The bartender, dressed in only a slinky negligee, comes back with our drinks and slides them over the counter.

I pick up the G&T. "We're so overdressed."

Nero grabs the whiskey and leans against the bar. "It's better this way. If you were wearing any less, I'd have to kill any man that looked at you, and it would turn into a whole mess." He takes a sip of his drink.

I give him a weary look. "It never fails to amaze me how casually you talk about murder."

"It's just a part of life, like paying taxes or being stuck in traffic."

I roll my eyes. "Please, there's no way you pay taxes."

"What do you mean? I pay some."

"Oh yeah? What do you put down as your job?"

He smirks. "Waste management."

"There's something seriously wrong with you," I say, but disturbingly enough, I'm smiling. Since when do I find dark humor funny?

"Handsome couple."

I glance over Nero's shoulder at an older woman who's standing at the bar a few feet away. Her lips tip into a flirtatious smile as she catches my eye. "Mind if I watch?"

I blink at her, stunned. She wants to watch Nero and I do what exactly? Anything? *Everything?*

"Not this time," Nero says smoothly, turning to face her. "My wife's a bit shy."

"Oh, how sweet," she croons. "First time at Seven Lives?"

Nero smiles. "Indeed. Are you a regular?"

"I've been coming here once a week since they opened six months ago."

"Do you know the owner?"

"Maks? Yes, he's a darling. It's always a fun time when he's playing." The woman takes a glass of sparkling water with a lemon slice from the bartender and raises it to us. "Enjoy your evening."

I wrap my hand around Nero's wrist once she walks away and tug him toward me. "You're quick on your feet. I had no idea how to answer that question."

He grins. "A simple no would have done the job. C'mon, we both know you don't have a hard time enforcing boundaries."

"That's true, but I'm feeling a bit out of my depth right now."

I sip on my G&T and survey the room again. The woman is still writhing wildly up on the cross, and there are more than a few couples doing their own thing in the booths. In one of them, a girl with bright-pink hair is riding a tanned, tatted man who has his inked hand wrapped around her throat.

Goosebumps erupt over my skin. I'm shocked to discover I'm getting turned on. I used to love it when Nero held me by the throat like that...

I clench my thighs to try and calm the steady pulse between my legs, but that only makes it worse.

Nero points at an unoccupied alcove with a small sofa. "Let's go sit over there."

Moans echo around us as we walk. The alcohol sends a pleasant buzz through my veins, and it makes me bolder. I don't look away so quickly when my gaze lands on something I like.

Jesus. I'm kind of enjoying this. I'm acutely aware of the wetness gathering inside my panties, especially when Nero and I sit down close enough for his thigh to press against my own.

He throws his arm over the backrest behind me and props his ankle on his knee, his eyes on the crowd.

I scan him over, a bit annoyed at how unruffled he seems for someone who's never gone to a place like this. I almost want him to be just a little worked up so that I don't feel like such a deviant.

This isn't me. I'm not into things like this. I like...normal people things.

You sure as hell liked it when he fucked you on top of the bar at a restaurant owned by your ex. Yeah, that was so normal.

I bite down on my lip. Have I been lying to myself about who I am, or is Nero just corrupting me? Maybe spending all this time in his world has gotten to my head.

I've always prided myself on knowing right from wrong, but this place doesn't feel *wrong*. It's just different.

A drop of sweat rolls down the valley between my breasts. "I swear they turned up the temperature. I'm boiling in this blouse."

Nero's dark gaze slides over to me. "Should I take it off you?"

A shiver scatters down my spine. He's so close that I can feel the caress of his breath against my cheek. My gaze drops to his lips. "You're no longer worried about others seeing me in a state of undress?"

His big hand appears on my thigh. "You're right. We can grab a private room to help you cool off."

I swallow. "I think that would be quite counterproductive. I can't believe you've never been to a place like this."

He starts tracing circles on the inside of my thigh with his thumb. "I've been inside a few, but only when I had business to sort out with the owners. I never stuck around to participate."

"Why do you think he invited us here?"

Nero presses his nose to my neck and inhales. "Who?"

My gaze dips down to Nero's lap. There's a pronounced bulge there.

"Maksim."

He pulls back to look at me. "I have no clue, but have I told you that you look really fucking pretty when you turn all pink like this?"

My pussy flutters. "We should stay focused," I whisper, trying to regain control of the situation as Nero's hand begins to move higher beneath my skirt.

"We should." The words rumble inside Nero's chest. "Shit, baby. You're already wet."

Panicked, I scramble to my feet and press myself against the wall, needing to put some distance between us because I'm enjoying his attention a bit too much.

I'm enjoying *all* of this a bit too much.

Nero steps closer, trapping me against the wall with one arm while his gaze drops to my chest. Damn it, why did I wear such a flimsy bra? It's not enough to hide the hard nipples poking through my blouse.

"You sure you don't want to find a private room? Who the fuck knows how long Maksim will take before he decides to show up."

"I'm sure," I choke out.

"I could take care of you so well," he murmurs. "It pains me to see you suffer in those soaking panties."

I glance down at the outline of his erection. "You seem uncomfortable too."

His eyes darken, and he moves closer, pressing his body against mine. "Why do you think that is?" His words rumble inside his chest at the same time that his hard length twitches against my thigh.

A moan catches inside my throat. "Is being here turning you on?"

"Watching you get all flustered is. You're so worked up that you're grinding against me."

My eyes snap wide open. Oh God, I am. When did that happen?

"You know, maybe we should split up for a bit," I squeak out.

A woman lets out an excited moan from somewhere outside the alcove, and I instinctively lick my lips.

His eyes drop to my mouth. The tension between us is palpable, charged with electricity. "You're not going anywhere without me."

"Oh, there you are," a familiar voice calls out.

CHAPTER 23

BLAKE

The hunger in Nero's eyes fades as annoyance takes over. He steps back, pulling me in front of him and wrapping his arms around my waist, holding me close against his body. "Maksim."

Maksim studies us, his lips stretched into an enigmatic smirk. "Having fun?"

Nero's grip on me tightens. "A warning might have been nice. We'd have come better prepared if we'd known we were walking into this."

"I apologize." That smirk keeps playing on his lips. "I thought you might appreciate the surprise. What do you think?" His gaze moves to me.

"It's...like nothing I've ever seen before," I answer.

"I wanted you to step out of your comfort zone. Do you know the club's philosophy?"

"Enlighten us."

"Here at Seven Lives, we embrace a singular truth: unlike our feline friends, we are granted but one life. It's our belief that we should savor it."

"How inspiring," Nero says in a bored tone before releasing his grip on me and pulling out his phone from an inner pocket of his jacket. His brow furrows. "Fuck. I've got to take this call."

Maksim smiles. "Would you like to take it in my office? It's quieter in there."

"Yeah. Thanks."

Nero grabs my hand, and we follow Maksim to his office. "It's that bastard Cosimo," Nero says, his voice hushed. "I have no idea what he wants, but I can't ignore him."

"Doesn't he know we're busy?"

"No. He's not involved with this."

That's right. I forgot Cosimo Ferraro doesn't know about what we're doing with Maksim.

The music is muted as we step into Maksim's office.

The room is more like a suite, divided into two sections—a sitting area at the front and a room with a large wooden desk behind a set of French doors.

Maksim gestures toward the sitting area. "Will you be comfortable here, Nero? While you take your call, I can show Blake my small library."

Nero frowns, his hazel eyes narrowing on Maksim before moving to me.

A silent conversation passes between us.

I don't trust him alone with you, his expression seems to say.

I tilt my head. *You'll be able to see us through the French doors. He's not taking me far away.*

Nero clenches his jaw and nods in agreement. "I won't be long." His phone rings again, and he answers it with annoyance. "What is it?"

Maksim fixes his tie. "Shall we?"

I follow him into the second room, while Nero switches to speaking in Italian on the phone.

"Where's Ekaterina?" I ask.

"At home. She doesn't like coming to the club." We enter the second room, and Maksim closes the French doors with a quiet click. His shoulder brushes against mine as he moves past me. "Can I offer you a drink?"

"Just water, thanks."

A large bookshelf takes up one of the walls. It's filled with ancient-looking leather tomes. I take a few steps closer, examining the titles. The bottom two shelves hold encyclopedias, while the rest are classic literature. There are titles in English, French, and Russian.

Maksim comes up to me and hands me a glass of water. "I decided to split up my collection after I heard you lost yours in a terrible fire."

My head snaps up to look at him. "How do you know about the fire?"

His thin smile twists my stomach into knots. "I like to thoroughly research things that fascinate me."

My pulse quickens. What game is he playing now?

"Have a seat," he says, gesturing at one of the armchairs next to the desk.

Surprisingly, instead of taking the seat across from me like I expected, he settles into the armchair beside me. His fingers hang off the armrest, just inches away from my own. I quickly withdraw my hand and place it in my lap.

"I find you incredibly fascinating, Mrs. De Luca," Maksim murmurs.

I stay silent, waiting for him to say more. Nero's voice filters through the French doors—he's arguing in rapid-fire Italian.

"Your husband doesn't sound too happy with his circumstances," Maksim remarks. "Are his masters tugging on his leash too tightly?"

I pause for a moment, choosing my words carefully before responding. "I'm sure Nero wishes things could go back to the way they were before."

Maksim nods. "Perhaps. But we all know that's not possible. The past cannot be undone. However, we can shape the future. Your husband desires power, correct? A power he will never attain if he remains under Gino Ferraro's control."

I raise an eyebrow, giving space for him to continue.

"I can give him a way out. Not only that, I can help him take down the people that destroyed his life." He gives me a thin smile. There's something in his gaze that makes me want to recoil in disgust.

"How?" I force myself to ask.

"I can persuade the pakhan to take Nero under his wing. After all, the enemy of our enemy is our friend. Especially when Nero could be a very useful friend. But I would be taking a personal risk by vouching for Nero. To make it worth my while, I'd want something in exchange."

"What?"

Maksim lifts his hand and trails a knuckle over my cheek. "What I want is one night with you."

A crater opens up inside my gut. "Wh-what?"

Maksim's eyes bore into me. "One night, Blake. Don't you love your husband enough to do this for him?"

My thoughts race in confusion. He wants me to sleep with him in exchange for helping Nero. He believes I would do anything to aid my husband escape a situation he despises.

It becomes clear to me then just how depraved Maksim truly is. He is pretending to be doing Nero a favor, but it's all for his personal gain.

This is his way of testing the waters, of seeing how desperate Nero and I are to change our circumstances.

I swallow hard. I could never do what he's asking for. The thought of being with Maksim twists my stomach.

But refusing would be the end of our mission. It would be giving up Nero's chance at becoming capo. It would be giving up my only possibility of getting that passport—my ticket to freedom.

A ticket I'm not so sure I even want anymore.

"So..." Maksim leans back in his armchair, steepling his fingers in front of him. "What is your answer?"

I don't know. I feel dizzy and a little sick.

Suddenly, the French doors swing open, and Nero strides in. "I'm finished, and I'm getting a bit bored of this scene, so let's cut to the chase, Maksim. Why did you invite us here?"

"I was just talking to Blake about that."

Panic swirls inside my chest. What will Nero do when he finds out what Maksim wants?

He'll probably lose it.

But what if he doesn't? What if he thinks it's a fair price in exchange for getting what we want?

"Blake?"

I stare at my lap, my vision turning blurry. There's a loud whooshing sound inside my ears. And then Nero's right there, kneeling beside me.

He cups my cheek with his warm hand and forces me to meet his worried gaze. "Blake."

A tear slides down my cheek, and his concerned expression turns to pure stone.

"What happened?" he asks in a rough voice.

When I can't get an answer past my tight throat, he directs his attention to the man beside me.

"What *the fuck* did you say to my wife?"

CHAPTER 24

NERO

Maksim rises out of his chair and walks around the desk, as if realizing it's better if there's something standing between him and me right now.

How the hell did this scumbag make Blake cry in only five minutes during my pointless phone call with Cosimo Ferraro?

That jerk-off didn't even have anything important to say to me besides demanding my presence at some fucking meeting he's organizing for his made guys tomorrow night. I told him where he could shove his meeting. He didn't like it, but I don't give a damn. If he's upset, he can go cry to his daddy, who'll tell him I have more important things to do than stroke his ego.

And now I'm even more pissed about that useless exchange, because clearly, I never should have left Blake alone with Maksim.

The Russian places his hands flat on the desk. "I simply made Blake an offer."

"What kind of an offer?"

"A fair one. One night with her in exchange for my help in getting you out of the mess you're in."

It takes me a few moments to register what he means. When I do, my eyes immediately snap to Blake.

The look in her eyes rattles me. Why does she seem so unsure?

Is she actually considering his offer?

No way. There's no fucking way she could even imagine going through with it.

Why didn't she slap him as soon as he said the words? Why didn't she storm the hell out of this office?

I shove all those questions away until after I've dealt with Maksim. "Do you have a death wish?"

Maksim smirks, crossing his arms over his chest. "You want to get revenge against the Ferraros and the Messeros. You want to reclaim your power. I can help you do that."

"How's that exactly?"

"If you tell me where they store their weapons, I'll pass the information to the pakhan, and he'll do the rest. You won't have to do a thing for Gino Ferraro anymore, because he'll be dead. Wouldn't it feel great to know your information causes their downfall?"

This motherfucker. He's playing on my ego. He thinks the satisfaction of being the one responsible for the Italians' demise will be worth more than anything to me, but he couldn't be more wrong.

"You make it sound like you'd be doing me a favor. But let's be real, your boss stands to gain a lot from my intel."

Maksim waves a dismissive hand. "Your information would certainly be valuable, but we can still win this war without it. The pakhan is not worried."

And now he's bluffing.

"All I want is one night. Surely you can spare Blake for that long."

I see red and tightly clench my fists, feeling my nails dig into my palms.

I can't kill him right now. Not while Blake is here, and I am outnumbered by the guards he has scattered throughout this place. It would put her in danger, and I'm not willing to risk that.

But when the time finally arrives... Oh, I will relish it. I will rip him apart, piece by piece, until there's nothing left but scraps for feral dogs to feast on. I'll make sure he won't even get a proper burial.

I walk up to him, stopping only when we're practically nose to nose. "No amount of revenge or power is worth you putting your grubby hands on her. There is *nothing* you could give me, nothing you could promise, to justify a price that high."

I watch with satisfaction as his smirk melts away and his expression darkens.

Before he can utter another damn word, I grab him by the collar and slam him against his bookshelf. "If you ever make a proposition like that to my wife again, it will be your last sentence. Do you understand?"

Behind us, Blake sucks in a harsh breath.

My grip tightens. "Do. You. Understand?"

"Yes," Maksim wheezes out, his face turning red.

I give it another few seconds, and then I let go of him. He slumps and rubs his neck, his eyes flashing hatefully in my direction. "You're making a mistake. This is—"

I have no interest in hearing what he has to say, and I don't plan on sticking around to listen. My hand reaches for Blake's, and I pull her out of the office, stopping only to grab our coats before we step outside.

This is over.

Our mission is done.

∾

THE DRIVE HOME feels like sitting inside a pressure cooker. I don't think I've ever felt so many damn things at once.

Anger, resentment, confusion, fear.

It's not Maksim or Ferraro that I fear. What I fear is the fact that I no longer understand my wife.

Something is seriously wrong. I knew it the moment I got on my haunches beside her and saw the uncertainty in her eyes.

She was uncertain about something that should have been crystal clear.

My hands twitch around the wheel. I want to press hard on the gas and scream. Instead, I force myself to drive calmly all the way back to Manhattan.

As soon as we enter the penthouse, Blake grabs me by the arm. "Nero, we have to call Vita and Gino and tell them it's over. We failed."

Is it just me, or does she sound defeated?

I can't shake the feeling that there was a part of her that actually thought about taking Maksim's offer.

It's driving me insane.

"I'll call them after I understand one thing," I growl. Taking her hand, I walk her into the living room and sit her down on the sofa. She wraps her arms around herself and blinks at me with tired, resigned eyes.

"Why didn't you just say no to him, Blake? I was right there, on the other side of the door. You knew I'd come to you if he so much as raised his voice, so it couldn't have been fear that kept you silent."

The way her gaze slides to the rug makes rage pulse inside my chest.

"Our mission—"

I crouch down in front of her and lift her chin with my knuckle. "You're telling me you considered his offer for the sake of our damn mission?"

Her lips waver. "I just froze. I-I didn't know what you'd want to do."

I can't believe what I'm hearing. "You didn't know what *I'd* want to do?"

"No."

"What did you think I'd say? 'Sure, Blake. Go ahead and fuck that slimy scumbag. I'll wait for you at home.' Where are we? On Mars? On what fucking planet do you think that would have happened?"

Her chin quivers. "You hate working for Alessio. You hate being powerless. I saw how upset you were after that poker night, and you weren't faking it for Maksim's sake, Nero." She sniffs. "I knew you wouldn't like what Maksim was proposing, but maybe you'd think it was worth—"

My fingers dig into her knees. "For fuck's sake, of course I don't. I would rather spend ten lifetimes working for Alessio than have Maksim lay his hands on you for even a second."

She sucks in a shaky breath. "In your world, wives are pawns, aren't they?"

I frown. Where is this coming from? "Why would you think that?"

"Why wouldn't I? Just look at Ekaterina. It's clear Maksim doesn't love her, and he has no problem using her to help him achieve his own goals. Her help doesn't even earn her his loyalty. I was so angry at her after that awful lunch, but now I feel sorry for her. What a miserable life she must live."

"Their relationship has nothing to do with us," I say firmly. It's slowly starting to make sense. She's trying to understand the rules of our world, how relationships can work in it, but she's got no good reference for it. All she had were her parents—hardly a good example of a partnership—and now Maksim and Ekaterina.

"Blake, you can't assume everyone is like Maksim and Ekaterina. Their dysfunction would likely be there whether Maksim was part of the Bratva or not."

"You're really telling me what they have isn't the norm amongst the people you know?"

"Do relationships like that exist? Yes. Is it the norm? No. If only you knew how fucking crazy Rafe is about Cleo, or the kind of relationships her sisters have with their men, you would realize that there are plenty of us who find Maksim disgusting for how he treats his wife. Look at Vita and Gino—"

"Vita is a player in her own right," she snaps. "Maybe that's what she's had to do in order to survive. But I will never be like her. I don't *want* to be like her. So where does that leave me, Nero?"

"Exactly as you are." Doesn't she understand that she doesn't need to change a thing?

She gives her head a hard shake. "Sometimes, I wake up in the morning and feel like I'm drowning. I have no agency, no autonomy. You forced me to marry you. You forced me into this world, and even after weeks of trying to make it here, I still don't know how to. I froze completely in Maksim's office, and I'll freeze again. Maybe in a situation where it might cost me my life. Or yours."

"Baby—"

"I'm scared!" An angry tear slips down her cheek. "I'm scared that I will never have the strength to make it here unless I do things I don't want to do and become someone I don't want to be."

My chest grows tight. I wrap my arms around her and pull her against me. It kills me that this is how she feels, because I know that for her whole life, she's never felt like she was enough.

Not in Darkwater Hollow, and not here either.

But there's one place where she will always be enough. Where she will always belong. Right here with me.

I just need to make her see it.

When her quiet sniffles recede, I lean back and look at her face. "You're not a pawn, and I will never treat you like one. We tried to do something very difficult, something most mob wives would never even attempt to do. You're so fucking brave, baby. And so damn *good* for trying to help a bastard like me."

A strange drama plays out across her face. There are so many conflicting emotions rushing through her eyes that I struggle to understand them.

I brush the hair from her face. "But you don't need to be brave for my sake, Sunshine. I know you're feeling guilty for what happened in Darkwater Hollow, but you have nothing to feel guilty for, and it's about time you accept that."

I thought my words would comfort her, but instead, her gaze turns haunted. She pushes my hands off her and rises to her feet.

"It doesn't matter anymore. We've failed."

I stand too. "Do you know why I agreed to do this even though it made me sick with worry to bring you into it all?"

"Because becoming capo would help you keep me safe."

"Yes. Of course. But that alone would never have been enough. I agreed because I thought this experience might help bring us back together. *That's* why I did it."

Her eyes grow very wide. "What?"

"It was always only about you. What I want is *you*. If I had you... Fuck, I'd be happy doing anything Ferraro wanted me to."

That fucking guilt flickers again on the edges of her expression. She stands by the bookshelf just staring at me. "You're really not upset we blew it?" she asks eventually.

"Not at all."

She places her hand on one of the shelves, but her eyes don't stray from me. "I just...find that hard to believe."

I rake my fingers through my hair. "My God, you still don't get it, do you? Isn't it fucking obvious by now?"

"What are you talking about?"

I walk up to her and cage her in with my arms. "I told you I wouldn't lie to you anymore after we got to New York. I stuck to that promise. But there's something I've been holding back. And isn't that just as bad? I don't want to play these games anymore."

She tips her head back against the shelves. "What are you talking about?"

"I fucking love you."

Her lips part on a harsh breath. She stares at me with her glistening blue eyes for a long moment, as if she's trying to see into the very depths of my soul, and then she ducks under my arm and flees down the hallway to her room.

No. I'm not going to let her run away from me.

She tries to close the bedroom door, but I fling it open. She moves inside, but I catch her, grabbing her by the waist and pulling her against my chest. She struggles for a moment before she grows still.

I press my lips to her ear and whisper, "I'm in love with you. And I know you're not sure if you feel the same way about me because I'm not the kind of man you ever imagined yourself with."

Her chest rises and falls with heavy breaths.

"But, Sunshine, the more I see you fight the feelings that are trying to burst out of you, the more determined I become. I will wait for you for however long it takes. I'd rather face your scornful looks and your righteous anger than exist in a world where you're not *mine*."

I turn her around and hold her by the arms. "It's torture to have you so close to me yet so far. It's torture to remember how we were. When I think back to our days in Darkwater Hollow, the pain I feel is visceral. It's worse than the pain of being in that ring with Alessio. I'd let him wreck me again and again if it meant I'd have a hope of getting us back."

A whimper comes out of Blake. The sound is devastating. "It's never going to be like it was. Not here."

"Believe me, I know. But I also know that as long as my heart beats, I'm going to keep trying to find a path back to you. Back to *us*."

Her shining eyes pierce through me as she sobs.

I press my forehead to hers. "You're it for me. You are my first love. And you are my last."

She makes a choked gasp and shoves at my chest. "Damn you, Nero."

And then she crushes her lips to mine.

CHAPTER 25

BLAKE

The kiss is an explosion. A supernova. The energy released pours into my veins and takes up residence, setting my body aflame.

Our plan is ruined. There's no way out for me anymore. No hope of leaving. The idea that I'm stuck in this world forever should devastate me.

Instead, I feel a deep sense of relief I hadn't felt since we arrived in New York.

It's almost better that the choice has been taken from me. It saves me from the agony of trying to decide between what I want and what's "right."

For the first time in my life, those two things don't align.

What I want is Nero—a criminal who'd die for me, who'd kill for me, who'd give up everything for me.

And now there's no use in resisting my true feelings anymore. I can simply give in to Nero and this new life.

We move apart only long enough to rip each other's clothes off. His hands are greedy as they slide down my bare hips and grab handfuls of my ass. We stumble backward to the bed, my feet tripping over his in my eagerness to get us horizontal. The sheets billow out around us in a white cloud when we finally collapse onto the bed.

Nero's solid, muscled body presses down on me. He's everywhere—his scent, his flesh, his warmth. The air in my lungs becomes so filled with him that it's hard to breathe, but I don't mind.

I've missed this. God, how I've missed this.

"Open your eyes," he commands. "No more hiding from me. I won't let you go somewhere else inside your head."

Our gazes snap together. The gold shards in his eyes are brighter than usual, as if they're lit from the inside out. His body radiates heat, and when his lips travel down my neck, nipping and licking, he leaves a trail of fire in their wake.

"Fuck, you feel good," he groans as he fills his hand with my breast, flicking his thumb over my nipple in a way that makes sparks travel all the way down to my clit.

I writhe beneath him, needing more. "Nero..."

He sits up on his knees and trails his hand over my chest down to my pubic bone before gently sliding his thumb inside my pussy. He gathers some wetness and then moves his thumb back toward my clit and presses down.

My breath catches in my lungs. "Oh God."

"Do you know how many times I've been in bed on the other side of the wall and imagined you touching yourself just like this?" He drags his thumb in a slow, wet circle, his eyes glued to mine. "It drove me fucking crazy. I kept picturing this perfect pink cunt, and your delicate fingers going in and out, in and out."

"I thought of you when I did it," I choke out. "Every single time. Even when I hated myself for it."

His eyes spark. He changes the angle of his movements, and he gets it so damn right that my hips jump off the bed.

A groan tears out of me. He pushes two fingers inside me while his thumb keeps playing with my clit. I throw my head back and bite down on my lips to contain the screams that threaten to pour out of me. Does he know how good that feels?

A hand appears around my throat. "Show me how you make yourself come, Sunshine. I want to see you do it."

I reach down and cover his hand with mine. He stops rubbing my clit, but he keeps his fingers deep inside me even as I slide one of my own in as well, covering it in my wetness before bringing it up to my sensitive nub.

His lips part as he watches me make small, tight circles. The grip he's got on my neck tightens. "Fuck, baby, you have no idea how gorgeous you are."

I speed up, and the tingles spread. My heart is beating so hard against my ribcage. It feels like there's a drum in my chest. Nero curls his fingers inside me, hitting just the right spot, again and again.

"Pinch those pretty nipples for me. I want to see you play with your tits," he says in a rough voice.

I do as he says. I roll my nipple between my index finger and my thumb, and *God*, it feels amazing. My back arches, chasing the high that's so, so close.

He squeezes the sides of my neck. "That's it. You're almost there. I told you it would be even better if I talked you through it. You look so fucking pretty with that cunt dripping all over my hand. You're doing such a good job. Let me see it."

My toes curl. My breaths are no more than tiny, harsh puffs. There's a live wire running through my entire body, and just when I think I can't possibly take any more—

"There it is," Nero groans. "I can feel your cunt starting to flutter. I can't fucking wait to destroy it with my cock."

I explode.

Wave after harsh wave.

Spasm after hard spasm.

There are no words to describe the mind-melting pleasure that overtakes my body. No damn words besides my unintelligible moans.

Nero buries his face between my legs, lapping up the wetness gushing out of me, and then he rolls us over so that I'm somehow sitting on his face. My hands grip the headboard for support while he sucks and licks my aching slit, his fingers pulling me apart to give him better access.

By the time he gets his fill and drags me down to straddle his thighs, I've managed to come back to my senses.

Kind of.

The smirk on his lips suggests I'm staring at him like he's God, but screw it. He was right. It's *so* much better when he talks me through it.

I lower my gaze to his impossibly hard length. It's wedged between our naked bodies, leaking precum from the tip.

"Are you ready for this, Sunshine?" He tucks my hair behind my ear. "If you need me to wait, I'll wait. I'll wait until you're so eager to fuck me again, you're begging for my cock."

My pussy clenches, making it very hard to hold a coherent thought.

But something vulnerable slips into Nero's gaze, something that makes me look inward to see if I really am ready.

It's true what I said to him earlier. I am scared of who I'll have to become to survive by his side. But maybe I don't have to become Ekaterina or Vita or my mom. Maybe I can just take it one day at a time. Nero doesn't expect me to be anyone but myself.

And who is that? You're far from the selfless good girl he thinks you are. How would he react if he knew about the deal you made with Vita? How would he feel if he knew you've been lying to him?

I'll have to come clean. One day. But I don't want to think about that tonight.

Tonight, I just want to be with him.

Reaching between us, I wrap my palm around his erection. I lift myself off his thighs and press the tip to my pussy. "I want it. I'm ready. I want you inside me."

He groans and wraps his hand around the back of my neck, pulling me down to crush our lips together. His tongue invades my mouth at the same time that his cock nudges inside.

My eyes go wide. It's been so long that I forgot how big he is. I'm drenched, but he still stretches me with every inch he squeezes in.

I estimate he gets in about halfway before my gasps turn into whimpers. I press my palms to his chest and sit up. "Nero, slow down."

His eyes are so darkened with lust they look nearly black. I can feel his chest rise and fall with harsh breaths. "Breathe through it, baby. You're doing so well."

The praise alone makes me sink down another inch.

His abs flex. "Oh, fuck."

I roll my hips, taking him just a bit deeper. Other than his ragged breaths, he stays as still as a statue, letting me control the pace.

"I don't know if I can do it," I whine when it feels like I'm about to burst at the seams.

"You've done it before, and you can do it again. Your body remembers me, Sunshine. You just have to let go. Can you let go for me?"

I release a harsh breath and then slide all the way down until he's buried in me to the hilt.

He cups my cheeks. "You okay?"

I nod. He's right. My body remembers. When we're like this, everything is perfect. We fit so damn well.

He grabs my thighs and flips me over while staying buried deep inside of me. "If it gets too much, stop me, because I won't be holding back." He kisses my forehead.

"Okay."

And then he pulls out and rams into me so hard I see stars.

"Ohmigod," I gasp.

He's ravenous. Relentless. He pounds into me with his hard thrusts until my eyes roll to the back of my head. It feels better than anything ever has before. Sex with him is so removed from the sex I had before him that it feels like an entirely different act.

Our bodies meld perfectly together, two puzzle pieces waiting to click. His cock fills me completely, reaches parts of me only he has ever reached. He's lightning to my thunder. Gasoline to my flame.

"I'm going to..." My body feels boneless, spent from that first orgasm, but incomprehensibly, another one is building deep inside my core.

"You're going to come for me like the good girl that you are," he growls against my ear. "Your pussy's going to milk me dry, baby. Let me see it."

In the moment of my orgasm, my neural circuits go haywire. I scream as it tears through me, violent and all-consuming.

Nero presses his face to the crook of my neck and groans as he spills inside me, his thrusts slowing to something more languid as his cum mixes with my own.

We hold each other for a while, and I revel in our closeness. I've denied us this for so long, and I'm lost in the blissful haze of the moment.

I let myself believe that this is it—this is when everything changes for us for the better.

I just hope I'm not wrong.

CHAPTER 26

BLAKE

When I wake up the next morning, the sun is high in the sky, and Nero is no longer in my bed.

I sit up against the headboard and wince at the dull ache between my legs.

Maybe I should have taken a bath at four a.m. after Nero woke me up again, but at that point, I'd come so many times, I was no more than a puddle of tingling nerves. I would have likely drowned.

I let out a low groan and roll my head back and forth to stretch my neck. There's a constellation of hickeys marring the swells of my breasts. I'm sure if I look in the mirror, I'll find more.

Gingerly, I get out of bed. As I walk to the en suite bathroom, Nero's words come back to me, constricting my chest. *"I'm in love with you. And I know you're not sure if you feel the same way about me because I'm not the kind of man you ever imagined yourself with."*

I anchor my palms against the vanity and heave out a breath.

It's true, I never imagined myself with a guy like Nero. On paper, he sounds exactly like the kind of man I swore to stay away from after seeing how my mom suffered with my dad.

But it's time to face reality and admit that I've fallen for him. Thoroughly and completely. Regardless of who he is.

Rowan Miller. Nero De Luca.

Turns out they're not so different after all, at least not as far as my heart is concerned.

I splash some cold water against my skin and meet my own gaze in the mirror. My hair is in a terrible state. I grab a brush and start combing out the knots, taking my time with each one so that I can gather my thoughts before I get out there and face the man.

Nero was honest with me last night. He's been honest with me since he put that cheap ring on my finger. But I haven't been honest with him. He has no idea about the deal I made with Vita behind his back.

While he was telling me last night how good and selfless I am for trying to help him, all I could feel was a crushing sense of guilt.

When did I become a liar? And a hypocrite as well?

I was so angry with Nero for weeks after I found out how he lied to me in Darkwater Hollow. I declared I'd never forgive him for those lies.

While he's been trying to bring us back to each other these past few weeks, I've been scheming about how I can run away from him.

That seemed justified at the beginning when I was brimming with anger and hurt, but it doesn't feel justified anymore. And would I have kept up the lie if Maksim's disgusting offer hadn't forced us to call off our plan last night?

Probably. I would have continued to let Nero believe I was doing all of this only to help him. I would have gotten that passport from Vita, and then I would have had a big decision to make.

To stay or to go.

It's so clear to me now that if I'd left, it would have crushed Nero. It would've been the worst possible thing I could ever do to him. It would've been a cruel betrayal. But I don't have to worry about that anymore. My hand has been forced. It feels like fate's telling me to trust my heart instead of my head, and I'm going to listen.

I can forget about the favor Vita promised me. I can pretend it never happened. I place the brush down on the vanity, grab my robe from the hook, and wrap it around me. What if Vita mentions it to Nero herself? I never told her what the favor would entail, but Nero could likely guess the gist of it. It's so damn obvious what I would have wanted all those weeks ago when I met with her.

Should I tell him the truth? Confess?

I don't want to. It'll be agony to see the hurt inside his eyes when he realizes how cruel I'd planned on being.

I just want to move on from all this and start fresh with him. But can I do that without coming clean?

My feet carry me to the kitchen, where I find Nero staring down at the ingredients spread out in front of him on the marble counter.

My heart stills. He's wearing nothing but his boxers and an apron tied around his waist, and he looks so damn sexy that I have to take a moment to just appreciate him.

Heat stirs between my thighs. I'm sore as hell, but I still want him.

His eyes lift to mine, his lips curving into a tantalizing smile. "Morning."

My feet carry me right to his side. He puts the knife in his hand down on the wooden board and turns to face me.

Something vulnerable passes through his eyes.

I didn't tell him that I love him last night, and even now that I know I do, the words get stuck inside my throat. Why can't I say it?

I take a step forward and press my cheek against his chest.

His ribs expand on a deep breath. I can hear the steady beating of his heart as he brushes his hand back and forth over the small of my back.

I tip my head back. "What are you making?"

He bends down and places a quick peck against my lips. "Breakfast. French toast and scrambled eggs. I didn't think you'd be up so early. I was going to bring it to you in bed to help you recover from last night."

"How thoughtful," I say with a soft laugh. "Is that your peace offering for what you did to my insides?"

Concern flashes over his expression. "How bad is it? Should I call Doc just in case? If you're in pain, maybe he can prescribe something."

I swat at his arm. "You are not going to call Doc and tell him about how you destroyed my vagina last night. I'll be fine."

"Wait right here." Nero walks around me, pulls open the thoroughly stocked medicine drawer, and plucks out a small bottle of pills. "Take this."

I'm about to protest that he's being ridiculous before I realize it's ibuprofen.

Eh. That can't hurt.

He hands me a glass of water to chase down the pill and starts cracking eggs into a bowl.

I sit on a stool across from him. "Have you talked to Gino?"

"Not yet."

I search his tone for a hint of regret—maybe now in the morning light he's realized what he's losing by giving up his one chance at a promotion—but I don't find it.

He splashes some milk into the bowl and picks up a whisk. "Listen, I want us to get away from here for a few days."

"Yeah?"

"I was thinking about what you said last night before I, as you said, 'destroyed your vagina.'"

I groan, feeling my cheeks heat.

He throws me a mischievous look. "Your words, not mine."

"I shouldn't have said that," I grumble. "Your ego is big enough as it is."

He laughs, and the low, throaty sound makes my stomach flutter with butterflies.

"What I was trying to say is, you've been cooped up in here the last few weeks—alone or with Vita for company. And then we jumped straight into this Maksim and Ekaterina bullshit, which is no fun. We haven't gotten a real chance to do anything that makes life here enjoyable. I want to show you that being here with me wouldn't just be all this mob bullshit."

Oh. "It wouldn't be?"

"No, baby. You've been thrown right in the deep end, but that's not how it'll be from now on. I promise you that."

Nero's phone starts buzzing on the counter. He leaves the whisk in the bowl and glances at the screen.

"Gino?" I ask.

"It's Maksim." His eyes flash with barely restrained fury as he glances at me from beneath his brows.

The blood in my veins chills. For a moment, I think Nero won't pick up, but then he grabs the phone and presses it against his ear. "Hello?"

I wrap my palms around the edges of the counter and just watch him. What does Maksim want now? Anxiety churns in the pit of my belly. What if he decides to come after Nero or something insane like that?

Seconds tick by and then turn into minutes. Nero's responses are curt and indecipherable. He hangs up, puts the phone down, and picks up the knife again.

"He apologized," Nero says, sounding irritated as he chops the veggies. "Said he was out of line. Wants to meet to discuss how we can help each other."

My stomach drops.

So it's not over. Not yet.

If Maksim is willing to come back to the negotiating table, it means there's still a chance we can pull this off.

"Why the change of heart?" I force past my dry throat.

"He said he was bluffing last night. He thought he could convince you he'd be doing me a favor by putting me in contact with the pakhan. He needs something to convince the pakhan he's still a useful asset."

Nero's phone pings with a notification. He opens it and scrolls for a little while. "Might have something to do with this." He slides the phone to me.

It's a newspaper article with the headline, "FBI pursuing investigation into alleged turf war between the Italian Cosa Nostra and the Russian Bratva outposts in New York."

"The Bratva don't have as much sway with the authorities as we do. They want to finish this quickly. This is the perfect time for Maksim to appear as their savior."

"What are you going to do?"

"What do you think I should do, Sunshine?" He places his hand on top of mine.

My lungs feel stiff. It's difficult to breathe.

I should tell him about my deal with Vita. If there was ever a time to come clean, it's now.

But there's a little voice inside my head that disagrees. *You might still have a way out of here. Won't it be nice to at least have that choice?*

I want to stay with Nero. My fantasy of escaping overseas doesn't appeal to me anymore, not even a little bit.

But what if that changes? What if you go down this path only to realize it's not for you? Sometimes, love isn't enough. You know that. It's good to have an exit plan, even if you never use it.

I swallow. "If you meet with Maksim...maybe there's a way we can still pull this off. You could still be capo."

A muscle in Nero's jaw twitches.

"We're so close. You said a lot of things last night, Nero, and—"

He walks around the island and comes up to me. "And I meant every word. We don't need to do this. I will be fine just the way things are right now, Blake."

"I know. But I would feel better knowing the debt Gino Ferraro thinks you owe him is paid. Having you infiltrate the Bratva was the reason he spared you. If we walk away when we don't have to, and he finds out, who knows what he'll do to you?"

It's not a lie, but it's not the full truth either, and I wonder if Nero can see hints of my deception as he cups my cheek and peers into my eyes.

Nero's gaze is intense, searching, but he doesn't find what I'm afraid he will.

"Fine. But you're not getting involved in this anymore. I will deal with Maksim alone."

"But—"

"No buts. At this point, your job is done. If he's willing to negotiate, it means we have him."

A lump forms in my throat. Now I understand how Nero felt when he thought he might be putting me in danger for selfish reasons.

Aren't I doing the same?

No. You're doing what's smart. For him and for yourself.

CHAPTER 27

NERO

After Blake and I finish our breakfast, I go to get ready for my meeting with Maksim. I'm not looking forward to seeing that slimy fuck.

In the bathroom, I give myself a silent pep talk in the mirror. As much as I'm itching to toss him in the trunk, take him to Alessio's palace, and make him die a slow, painful death, I can't do that today.

Fucking bummer.

Though it might feel even better to watch the life drain out of his eyes after he realizes how we've played him for a fool.

We meet at an upscale bar in Midtown. Maksim's already there, sipping on a glass of wine at a table in the back, his eyes scanning the room as I approach. He's on edge, fidgeting with the stem of his glass, but he's trying to appear nonchalant.

He doesn't fool me for a second.

When he gets to his feet and offers me his hand, I ignore it and sit down across from him.

I can see the anxiety in his eyes, the glint of fear buried beneath false bravado. If I had to guess, he's in hot water with the pakhan, and I'm the only hope he's got left.

I order a scotch, neat, and allow the tension to hang between us. It's thick like the air before a storm. Maksim clears his throat, the sound grating on my last nerve.

"Let's cut to the chase," I snap.

He huffs out a chuckle. "I wasn't sure you'd show up."

"I wasn't sure either. But I'm here now, and I don't like when people waste my time."

"Then let's address the elephant in the room. Like I said over the phone, I was out of line last night. Your wife is an enchanting woman, and I got carried away."

"If you'd done that a year ago, you'd already be swimming with the fishes."

"I'm aware. And we're both aware that a year ago, you never would have accepted my invitation to Seven Lives in the first place."

I narrow my eyes at him over the rim of my glass.

He leans in closer, lowering his voice. "Why did you, Nero? Is it because you understand what I can do for you? We shouldn't let one tiny faux pas interfere with what might be a very mutually beneficial relationship."

A tiny faux pas? Fuck, is that how he'd feel about it if someone asked to fuck his wife? Disgust settles like a heavy weight inside my gut. "Spell it out for me, will you?"

"You have information that would be valuable to the pakhan. He would reward you generously for it."

"Huh. Yesterday, you thought I should pay *you* a very high price for the privilege of divulging that information to your boss, but now you're saying you'll reward *me*?"

Maksim raises his hands in a placating gesture. "Do you want me to admit it? You called my bluff. It happens in poker, and it happens in life as well."

I can tell it physically hurts him to have to prostrate himself before me.

I'm enjoying every fucking second of it.

"What makes you think that I'd betray my side?"

Maksim leans back in his chair, a calculating look in his eyes. "You've been stripped of your title and given to a boss who hates your guts. You're putting on a brave face—I'll give you that—but this can't be the life you want for yourself. The way I see it, you can either do what's right for you and Blake, or you can do what's right for them, the men who turned their backs on you. Seems like a no-brainer to me."

Maksim's words hang in the air, mingling with the faint scent of expensive cologne and the distant clinking of glasses from the bar.

I let the silence stretch, making it seem as if I'm taking my time to think it over. "And what exactly will your pakhan do for me if I help him win this war?"

"If you tell me where Messero and Ferraro store their weapons, I will bring that information to the pakhan and credit you as the source. After he kills them, he'll give you a place in the Bratva. A place worthy of a guy like you."

"I don't need him to kill Rafaele and Gino for me. One day, I'll do it myself."

Maksim clicks his tongue. "Don't be foolish. You know going after them solo means certain death. You seem to like your wife quite a bit. You really want to throw away your chance at spending a few more decades with her by your side? The pakhan has the manpower to destroy them for good. New York will never be the same."

I throw my arm over the back of the chair and give him an assessing look. "Your side has been slow to make any serious progress. The way I see it, the Bratva is flailing."

"We've got the manpower. The pakhan just needs something to help turn the tide in his favor. Your information could be it."

"Last night, you said you'd win with or without my help."

Maksim's facade cracks for a moment, a flicker of frustration crossing his features before he schools his expression into neutrality once more. "We will. But the pakhan's getting impatient. He's eager for this to be over. If we can take control of forty or fifty percent of their arms, they won't have enough to fight us back. Not to mention the psychological hit a move like that would make. They'd start looking for rats in their ranks. That's bad for morale."

It's true. The Bratva getting their hands on those weapons would be a big hit to the Italian side, and it might be the only thing that could help the pakhan at this point. They're losing, whether or not Maksim wants to admit that to me.

That means I've got all the leverage I could possibly want.

"Why should I trust you? How do I know you won't use the information I give you and take all the credit?"

Maksim sips his wine, his gaze not quite meeting mine. "I understand your concern, Nero. But you have my word. I'll make sure the pakhan knows exactly where the intel came from. You'll be rewarded handsomely, I promise."

I laugh. It's just too funny. Who the fuck does he take me for?

"No."

Desperation bleeds into Maksim's eyes. "No?"

"I'm not telling *you* shit. I don't trust you, and after last night, I don't think you can fucking blame me for that. The only person I'll divulge the locations of the warehouses to is the pakhan himself. Face-to-face."

"Impossible. The pakhan doesn't entertain visitors."

I stand up, glaring down at the damned vermin. "That's not my fucking problem. If he wants the information, he'll roll out the red carpet and invite me over. And if he doesn't, then I guess he doesn't want to win this war badly enough."

I take one last sip of my scotch, letting it burn a hole in my throat before dropping the glass onto the table with a satisfying clang. Maksim glares back at me, the gears turning in his head.

"You've got my number." I throw a few bills on the table. "Call me if you change your mind."

As I walk out of the dimly lit bar, the cold winter air hits my face, and I take a deep breath.

Maksim's going to have to put in some work to convince the pakhan to let me speak to him directly, but that's his business.

Now that I've made my move, I've got a far more important thing on my mind, namely my wife.

I'm not going to waste the progress we made last night. I feel energized and optimistic and *alive*.

I've got no idea how Maksim coming on to her led to us finally reconciling, but it feels like nothing short of a miracle. Having her in my arms again felt like the homecoming I've been waiting for my whole life, and I think she felt it too.

But as soon as Maksim called, her mood shifted to something darker. I can't blame her. A part of me was relieved when we thought it was all over and we could retire the act we've been putting on with Maksim. It's just that we're so damn close now... It would be a shame if all the work we've already done goes to waste.

I've got him exactly where I want him. All I have to do now is wait.

But I'm not going to sit around while Blake spins more stories in her head about how she has to change to fit into this world.

She doesn't have to do anything.

She just needs to take a breath, relax, and allow herself to be happy.

And I'm going to help her do exactly that.

CHAPTER 28

NERO

The next morning, I've got our bags packed before Blake wakes up. Last night, I called Alessio and asked for a few days off work, which the bastard gave me after some grumbling. If Maksim contacts me, we'll have to drive back, but I have a feeling it's going to take him some time to work up the courage to talk to the pakhan.

Around ten, I walk into Blake's room and take a seat on the edge of her bed.

She looks peaceful. Free from worry. The way she should look when she's awake. I smooth her hair away from her forehead and tuck it behind her ear.

"Hey, baby. Time to get out of bed."

A few moments go by before she stirs and blinks sleepily at me.

"Wake up, Sunshine."

She scrunches her nose, looking so fucking adorable I want to take a bite out of her. "Why?"

"We're going out of town. We talked about it, remember?"

She slides up against the headboard and yawns. "That was before Maksim called."

"Well, we're not gonna just sit around twiddling our thumbs while we wait for him to grow a pair and talk to the pakhan. Who knows how long that'll take."

Blake stretches her arms above her head, and the sheet puddles around her waist, giving me a view of her silky tank top. I distinctly remember peeling it off her at one point last night. She must have woken up and put it back on.

"Where do you want to go?"

"I have a place on the coast in Westhampton. I haven't been there in two years, but hopefully, it's still standing. I want to show it to you." It'll be cold, but being near water always makes me feel better. I hope it'll make her feel better too. I hope it will make her see how our days don't have to be filled with political drama and carefully constructed lies.

We can simply be us.

I press a kiss to the tip of her nose. "Just for two days. There's a beach there. Long and sandy. We can light a fire, make mulled wine, and read. You'll love it."

I should have known that "read" is the magic word. Her eyes light up. "That sounds nice."

I cup her face with my palms. "Then get your fine ass out of bed and get dressed."

For once, there's only light traffic leaving the city, so it takes us just under two hours to get to the seafront property on Dune Road.

"Rafe and I would come here in the summer for a few weekends each year," I tell her as we get out of the car. "He liked to get away when he had something on his mind that he couldn't figure out. It's a good place to think."

The air swirls with the distinct scent of salt and sand as we walk toward the weathered wooden porch.

I had a cleaning crew to come by before we arrived, and when I crack open the door, I see they did a great job. The place looks pristine.

Inside, the entryway is bathed in natural sunlight streaming through large windows that offer a panoramic view of the shimmering Atlantic.

That view is why I bought this house. The first time I saw it, it tugged on something deep inside me.

I didn't renovate the place after I bought it five years ago—it was never a priority given how little use it got—so it bears the taste of the previous owner, who had a thing for whites and pastel hues.

Maybe Blake would like to change some things in here. The thought of her putting her own personal touch on the space spreads warmth through my chest.

Fuck. I want to build a life with her. I want everything that's mine to be hers too.

I lead Blake farther inside. The soothing sound of waves crashing against the shore fills the open living space. A plush, white sofa faces the ocean. I've always found it easy to lose myself in the horizon.

I glance sideways at her. "What do you think?"

"It's beautiful."

There's a hint of a smile on her face that makes me relax a little. I hadn't even realized I was nervous to see her reaction.

We drift toward the wide deck that extends from the living area, and the wooden planks creak under our feet. The deck overlooks a stretch of pristine beach. I lean on the railing, taking in the expansive view. The beach is quiet and serene, dotted occasionally with walkers and playful dogs.

Blake leans on the railing beside me. "This is a world away from New York. It's so peaceful."

"Yeah. Perfect for an introvert like you."

She arches a brow. "You think I'm an introvert?"

"Aren't you? Back in Darkwater Hollow, your favorite hobby was to sit at home and read."

"No need to call me out like that."

"Just stating facts."

She huffs a laugh. "You're definitely an extrovert. You always light up around other people."

"I'm not going to argue with that. I don't like to be alone."

"Have you always been that way?"

"I think so." I can't remember ever being comfortable being alone. If Rafe didn't send Sandro with me to Darkwater Hollow, I wouldn't have lasted a week.

Shit. Is that why he did it? Did he somehow understand that I really fucking needed someone with me to have a chance at making it?

An ache appears inside my chest. I miss that *stronzo*.

I miss Sandro even more.

"Rafe's an introvert too. I guess I'm drawn to you people."

Blake crosses her feet at the ankles. "You said you'd come here together?"

I chuckle. "Yeah. He's really not big on the sand, though. He refused to walk up to the water. We'd sit out here on the deck and watch the waves while smoking cigars."

"Do you miss working with him?"

"I do. We spent a decade working side by side, and during that time, he was my closest friend. We were a good team."

I don't want to let my sudden nostalgia sour the mood, so I slide my arm around Blake and lead her back inside. "Let's unpack and grab a snack. I want to take you on a walk."

We put our supplies away in the kitchen and then venture out to stroll along the shore.

Blake yelps when a frothy wave races across the sand and reaches the tips of her sneakers. The water is painfully cold, and the air isn't much better.

Good thing I brought a blanket with me, because even in her thick hoodie, Blake's teeth start chattering.

I wrap the blanket around her and tuck her under my arm. "Do you want to go back?"

"No, this is nice." There's a wistful expression on her face, like she's somewhere far away.

"Tell me what you're thinking."

"My mom. She always wanted to see the ocean. There were so many things she said she wanted to do, but it was hard to do them with two small kids and little money, and when we got older, she got sick." The wind whips her golden hair around her face. "Sometimes at night, I'd sit by her side and think about the life she never lived. An alternate reality in which she never met my dad. Never had us. Where she could live only for herself."

"You think she regretted it? Getting with your dad?"

"God, no. If I were in her position, I'd be full of regrets, but she had a way of..." Blake sighs. "She ignored people's faults and saw silver linings."

"Hmm. You didn't like that."

"No, I didn't."

I bite on the inside of my cheek. This is why Blake is the way she is, isn't it? Why she's quick to slap labels on people—good or bad. She's rebelling against her mom's perspective on life.

She looks up at me as we walk on the sand. "Were you close with your mom?"

"I was. When I was kid, it always felt like it was me and her against my dad. We were a team."

"You're talking about your biological father?"

"Yeah." I sniff. "He treated her with resentment, and he was always annoyed with me. I'd do something kids just do sometimes—spill a drink, make a mess, break a toy—and he'd get so angry. I could tell he didn't like me, even if I didn't know why. And as I got older, I just started getting sick of being punished over nothing, so I decided I might as well earn it, you know?"

Blake nods. "Yeah, I get it."

"I'd steal change out of his pocket so that I could buy pizza at the cafeteria at school. Every time he caught me, it was like I'd committed murder. He'd beat my ass raw. By that point, I'd realized what he was scared of all along. He was terrified I was going to end up like my grandpa and ruin his reputation."

"Your mom's dad? The guy who was in the mob?"

"That's the one."

"That sounds really hard, Nero," she says in a quiet voice as we pass by a man walking his golden retriever.

I shrug. "It was, but it made me who I am. I have no idea who I'd be without that childhood."

"Is he still around?"

"Nah. Died two years back. I went to his funeral and all, but by that point, he was a stranger to me. My real dad was my stepdad. I already told you about him."

Blake gives me a sad smile. "He gave you the love and respect you always deserved."

I suppose he did. My biological father's death meant nothing to me, but I won't ever forget the day I got the call about my stepdad and my mom being killed.

I wish I'd been there that day. Maybe I could have saved them. I'd nightmares for months after, imagining I was in that restaurant with them, my back to the window the gunmen shot through. I'd always wake up just as the bullets hit.

We start walking back to the house, and Blake tugs the blanket tighter around herself. "The day I quit my job, Brett told me my mom helped my dad rob people on the side of the road." Her throat bobs on a hard swallow. "I told him he was a liar, but I think he was telling the truth."

I clench my jaw.

I haven't forgotten about that utter waste of space. Brett will get what's coming to him. But there's no rush.

He can live for now, glancing over his shoulder every time he sees a tall guy like me. When he thinks I've forgotten about him, when he believes the danger has passed, *that's* when I'll strike.

He will pay for everything he did.

"He wanted to upset you," I tell her.

"Yeah. But it doesn't change the facts. My mom wasn't perfect. I never deluded myself into thinking that she was. I used to wish she was stronger, and that she'd tell my dad to stay away from us instead of welcoming him into our home whenever he felt like coming around. But I never thought she'd do something like that."

The pain in her voice hits me right in the chest. "You don't know what she was going through at the time. Maybe your dad didn't leave her much of a choice."

"Maybe. But why would she never tell me about that? I feel betrayed, I guess. Growing up, I had so many people lie to me. She lied to me for a few weeks after she got her diagnosis, and when I learned the truth, I felt betrayed about that too, but this feels different. Somehow, it feels worse."

"I think in both instances, she was trying to protect you. Or maybe she was ashamed. She didn't want her daughter to be even more disappointed in her. How would you have reacted if she'd told you?"

We scale the steps of the deck, and Blake turns to me. The tip of her nose is pink from the cold, and her eyes seem sad. "I don't know. I probably would've gotten upset. From an early age, all I wanted was to have a normal family. To be like the rest of the kids in my class."

I lean down and give her a kiss. "Normal is boring, Sunshine. There's nothing boring about you."

Her lips twitch, but the sadness in her gaze lingers. I wish I knew how to make it disappear. I'll keep trying until I do.

"Is that how you felt when you first got to Darkwater Hollow?" she asks softly. "Bored?"

"I felt a lot of things. Boredom was one of them. Until I met you, that is."

"Would you ever do it again?"

"Walk away from this life?"

She nods. "Yeah."

I place my hand on the railing and look out toward the ocean. There are so many layers to that question.

"No one walks away from this because they want to. You either die, or you get forced out the way I was." I let out a breath. "I learned many lessons in Darkwater Hollow and one of them is that this is who I am. There's no getting away from it. No matter where I am or what my name is, this life will always find a way to pull me back in."

Blake bites down on her bottom lip, looking uneasy.

I wonder if she's still holding out hope that there's a way out of this for both of us eventually.

There isn't. This is our life, and there's no point in fighting it.

I take her hand in mine and pull her toward the house. "Let's head in."

CHAPTER 29

BLAKE

The sunset is windy but gorgeous, and Nero and I watch it from the deck, his arm wrapped securely around my shoulders.

The sound of the ocean waves crashing against the shore calms me. I'm sure that was Nero's intention when he brought me here. He doesn't know the secret I'm hiding, but I think he can sense there's something bothering me.

A heavy breath travels through my chest.

I can see a future with him, so why do I still need to have an escape plan? And is it really so bad that I do have one?

Getting that passport from Vita isn't the same as using it.

You still don't trust him. Not fully.

No, it's not that.

It's that I don't trust myself. Nero says I don't need to change, but I've already started to.

I'm not the girl he met in Darkwater Hollow anymore. And the woman I'm becoming? I'm not quite sure who she is or what she's capable of, and that scares the crap out of me.

A year from now, will I still be able to recognize myself? Or will I lose myself, the way my mom lost herself at the altar of her love for my father?

She never had a backup plan or a way out.

But I can. Just in case.

By the time we head inside to cook some dinner, the guilt is still there, but I've managed to pack it up in a thick cardboard box and shove it deep inside the attic of my mind.

Nero pulls out some beef, tomatoes, onions, and garlic, and we start prepping for the sauce we're making for the rigatoni sitting on the counter.

It almost feels like we're back in Darkwater Hollow.

We stand side by side as we chop the veggies, and I'm transported right to the moment months ago when he kissed me in my kitchen.

A smile pulls on my lips. My body lit up like a switchboard before I came to my senses and put an end to it. "Do you remember our first kiss?"

He bumps me with his hip. "With utter clarity. The shell-shocked look you had on your face is seared into my memory," he says with a laugh. "I thought you were just playing hard to get, until you declared that you were moving out."

I snort a laugh. "I couldn't believe your audacity."

"Don't lie. A part of you enjoyed it."

I elbow him in the ribs. "Maybe a very small part."

He grunts in mock pain and shoots me a grin that lights up his whole face.

My breath catches. He's so damn handsome.

I put my knife down and get on my tiptoes to kiss him. Just because I want to. Just because he's impossible to resist.

He leans down and kisses me back, sliding his tongue inside my mouth. Heat rises through my chest. By the time I tear myself away from him, I'm breathless.

I press a palm against the counter. "All right, I have to ask. What the hell were you thinking starting that fire?"

His brows arch in surprise. "We can joke about it now?"

I sigh. "I think it's been long enough. I can handle it."

He bites down on the corner of his mouth. "You were leaving. I needed to make you stay. But truth is, it was a major fuckup on my part."

"Well, yeah."

"I mean, I didn't intend for it to demolish your entire living room. I didn't realize it would spread like wildfire through your books. And when you told me you didn't have home insurance, I went into a full-blown panic. That's how that whole fake-dating idea came to me. I needed some way to explain why I'd fix everything without making it obvious I was doing it out of guilt."

I give my head a shake. "You're ridiculous." He set my house on fire to keep me close to him. What kind of a lunatic does that?

This is the first time that thought doesn't fill me with rage.

On the contrary. It's just... I mean, it's kind of...funny? And sweet?

My eyes snap wide. My God, am I for real?

Dumping the tomatoes into the pot, I walk over to the fridge and pour myself a glass of water.

Did I just make an excuse for what Nero did? It's one thing to forgive him, but to empathize with why he did it?

What's next? Will I be justifying murder?

It hits me then. I already am.

Nero is a killer—that is a *fact*—but that's not how I see him. That label feels like no more than a footnote on his personality. Irrelevant in the grand scheme of things.

A shiver runs through me. Who is this woman indeed?

After dinner, we make some mulled wine and go outside to sit by the firepit. The crackling flames lick at the night sky as I take a few sips.

I notice Nero brought a book with him—*The Divine Comedy*. I flipped through it myself a few days ago but found it largely incomprehensible.

"Did you bring that from home?"

He nods. "I saw you looking at it. It's one of my favorites."

Heat blankets my cheeks. "Is this where I admit I had a very hard time with it?"

He chuckles. "It's not just you. Took me years to really understand it. I've read multiple translations along with the original Italian. Can I read some to you?"

"Sure."

He opens it to the page that's earmarked and begins to read, pausing to explain the confusing parts.

Dante and his guide, Virgil, enter the outer ring of the seventh circle of hell, where the sinners who committed violence against others are punished. This area is a boiling river of blood. Murderers, tyrants, and others who were violent toward other humans are submerged in the river to varying depths, determined by the severity of what they did and how they sinned. Centaurs patrol the riverbanks, shooting arrows at any of the damned who try to escape their punishment.

It's a gruesome image.

I wonder why Nero's studied this book so much. It's the story of Dante's redemption, and maybe that's what draws Nero to it. Dante wanted to be redeemed, but Nero's embraced the darkness that inhabits him. He's accepted it as part of who he is.

Does he imagine himself as one of the sinners that stand in that river, boiling in thick blood with no way out?

That image chills me. If that's what he thinks is waiting for him, and yet he still keeps living the life he's chosen, he is far braver than me.

I admire the way he accepts the consequences of his decisions, refusing to hide from them, no matter how harsh they may be. That's exactly what he did when he chose to return to New York with me, isn't it?

He closes the book and tosses it on the chair beside the bench we're sitting on. "That's enough for tonight. Did I put you to sleep?"

"How could you? That was riveting. And somewhat disturbing."

"I can't tell if you're being a smart-ass or just a genuine nerd."

"Hey, there's a nerd here, but it's certainly not me. I'm not the one explaining *The Divine Comedy* to their unsuspecting spouse." I take a sip of my mulled wine and shoot him a sideways look. "Does anyone else know how well-read you are?"

It's hard to tell with the fire going, but I swear that he blushes. "If you're asking if I've attempted to explain *The Divine Comedy* to anyone before you, the answer would be no."

"Are there book clubs in the mob? Maybe you should start one."

"Fuck, just the thought of that..." He snorts. "Can you imagine me telling Alessio I'd like for us to meet once a week to discuss *Romeo & Juliet*?"

I bite down on my grin. "Throw him right into the deep end, huh? How about starting with something easier, like *Anne of Green Gables*?"

His chest vibrates with laughter. "That's fucking perfect. Did I ever tell you I think he wants to live on a farm? He has a farm in the Sims game he plays."

"Oh my God, Nero, what if he just needs some inspiration to go for it? Give that man the damn book!" I'm *crying*.

Nero puts his mug down on the ground and hides his face inside his hands, his whole body shaking. I've never seen him laugh this hard.

It takes both of us a good few minutes to calm down and be able to look at each other without going into another fit.

His dark eyes twinkling, he pulls me onto his lap, making me straddle his thighs. "All right, that's enough. I didn't bring you here so that you could bully me over my reading habits."

I wrap my arms around his neck and give him a crooked smile. "Why did you bring me here then?"

He wraps his hand around the back of my neck and crushes his lips to mine.

Everything feels so good in the moment. The heat from the fire, the heat from his mouth, and the way my body melts effortlessly into him.

His tongue lashes against my own for a long while. He's eager but unrushed, as if he knows he's exactly where he's meant to be. He slides his hands under my layers of clothing and wraps them around my bare ribcage, his fingertips teasing the underside of my breasts.

Tingles rush over my whole body. How is it that one light touch from him is enough to take me from zero to one hundred? Maybe it's the way he never tries to force pleasure. He takes his time and coaxes it out. He knows exactly how to read each quiver, gasp, and moan I make. Sometimes it feels like he can even read my mind. And that makes me wonder if he can sense the things I'm still hiding from him.

Grabbing his massive shoulders, I kiss him harder, pulling myself back to the present. I don't want to be anywhere else but here in this moment right now.

He moves his hands higher and cups my breasts. He sucks in a harsh breath through his nose and makes a small groan in the back of his throat. The sound is so sexy, and I scoot close to press our hips together, searching for the friction my pussy craves.

He's hard as a rock. The jeans we're both wearing are highly annoying barriers, but they don't stop me from grinding up against the ridge of his cock as best I can.

Nero makes a frustrated noise and pulls his hands out of my shirt. He undoes the button and the fly of my jeans and tries to shove his hand inside, but the angle I'm sitting at doesn't allow him much access.

"Fuck," he grunts. "How much do you like these jeans?"

"Hmm?" I blink dazedly at him. "Why?"

There's a hard tug and a sharp tearing noise.

"*Oh*. A lot actually."

"I'll buy you a new pair." He grins and slides his hand inside my panties. "There you are."

My lungs empty out as he teases his fingers over my slit. "You could have just brought us inside, you know."

"And miss the view of you coming apart for me beneath all these stars?" He looks up.

I follow his line of sight. He's right. The sky is full of twinkling lights. All those worlds and galaxies are witnessing what this man does to me without any judgment.

A shaky breath leaves my chest as his touch grows firmer. He dips his fingers inside me, and then pulls them out, and moves them to massage my clit.

I'm buzzing so hard that it won't take long. Each swipe gets me closer and closer to that blissful edge. I thread my fingers through his hair and stare into his eyes while he works my body into a frenzy.

The fire burning behind me is reflected in his gaze. "You're so damn gorgeous," he murmurs. "I love how wet you get for me."

My head lolls to the side as he applies more pressure and makes me mewl. When he slides his fingers back inside me, I'm so worked up that I start fucking them as if they're his cock.

Lust darkens his eyes. "Do you need something else, baby? Something bigger for that hungry pussy?"

"Yes," I whine, beyond shame.

I reach between us, undo his jeans, and slide my hand inside his boxers. My palm curls around his silky shaft, but I can't quite get him out.

"Hold on tight," he commands as he lifts his hips off the bench with me still sitting on him and uses his free hand to shove his jeans over his ass.

"Didn't want me to try and rip yours?"

"I would have loved to see you try," he says in a low voice as he pulls his cock out.

Watching his tatted hand wrapped around his shaft is so erotic it makes my mouth water. He rips my jeans farther down the seam, completely exposing my drenched panties.

And then he rips those as well.

A grin. "Hop on."

I scramble up his thighs, line us up, and then sink onto him. The second he's fully sheathed, a full body shiver goes through me from the delicious stretch. I clutch his shirt and roll my hips, searching for the angle that's going to get me there.

His hands grab my ass. "How's that?" he asks, his voice strained.

"Good," I pant, my pussy fluttering, my mind spinning. "So good."

He starts fucking me from below, meeting my thrusts with his own. His groans intermingle with my moans in the cold night air, making me wonder for a moment if the neighbors might hear us.

But then he changes his angle just so, and I decide I don't care. Nothing that feels this perfect could be wrong.

He speeds up his thrusts, leaning his head back while keeping his hooded gaze on me. "*Fuck*, baby. You're making me lose my mind."

I dig my fingers into his neck, searching for something to keep me tethered to Earth as I come undone. My eyes squeeze shut against the onslaught of pleasure that crashes through me.

Nero grunts and thrusts into me two more times, his hands digging into my thighs as he spills inside me.

When I manage to open my eyes again, I catch him staring at me, his chest rising and falling with harsh breaths. He tugs me against him and presses his lips against the shell of my ear. His hands travel over my back, rubbing it in soothing motions.

Something in the air shifts.

I think he wants to say it again. Those three magic words.

Will I say them back? Can I?

My teeth dig into my bottom lip. There's something inside me that's so tangled up that I can't figure it out. The moment I say those words, there will be no coming back from them. My transformation will be complete, and I'll become someone new.

A woman who loves a killer. A woman who's willingly married to a killer.

Can I accept that I'm her?

The silence lingers. It lingers as Nero pulls out of me and carries me inside the house. It lingers as he undresses me, cleans me up, and gets in bed with me.

I tuck myself against his chest and revel in his warmth.

I'll figure it out. I just need a bit more time.

Nero's phone rings. Whatever name he reads on the screen makes his brow furrow. He picks up. "Hello?"

I sit up, holding the duvet against my chest. Is it Maksim? Do we need to rush back to New York?

The thought of Nero meeting the pakhan sends a chill down my spine. He'll be walking into enemy territory. What if the pakhan does something to him the moment he gets the information he wants?

Panic claws my insides as a realization dawns on me. It'll be Nero's life on the line again. Did I even think about that when I encouraged him to go through with this? Or was I only thinking of myself?

Nero runs his fingers through his hair. "When?" A beat passes. "We're two hours outside of the city." He glances at me. "Tomorrow? Yeah, we can make it, I'm just not sure... Let me talk to her. Okay. Thanks." He hangs up and tosses the phone onto the nightstand.

"Who was that?"

"Cleo."

I let out a relieved breath. "I thought it was Maksim."

He scratches his chin. "They're hosting a thing for Sandro tomorrow."

"A wake?"

"More like a celebration of life, I guess. They want to remember him with the guys. Cleo asked if we want to come, but I wasn't sure you'd be—"

"I want to." Of course I do. Sandro saved my life. "Where is it?"

"Back in New York." Nero sighs.

"Won't Maksim find out we went to Rafe's?"

"It's not at his house. They rented out Sandro's favorite bar for it. Even if Maksim is watching us, no one will think twice about me attending a party in honor of the man who was forced out with me. There will be plenty of people there."

I reach over and squeeze Nero's hand. "Then let's go."

CHAPTER 30

NERO

Blake and I head out a few hours after breakfast the next morning.

On the drive, Blake asks me to tell her more about Sandro. Who he was in New York and what kind of work he did. What he was known for. What friends he had.

I surprise myself with the near encyclopedic knowledge I have on the kid. I guess we talked a lot in those first few months in Darkwater Hollow. We learned a lot about each other.

"How did you meet him in the first place?" Blake asks after a good hour of me telling her all sorts of stories about him.

"Rafe and I found Sandro driving in an illegal street race when he was just a fourteen-year-old kid." I chuckle. "He was driving one of the shittiest-looking cars, and he still won. The guy who came in second place was running his mouth that night, saying he was going to make sure Sandro never showed his face there again. Before that could go anywhere, I just grabbed Sandro and told him I had a job for him. One where he wouldn't get killed for driving well, and where he could earn enough in a few years to get whatever car he wanted. He just grinned and said, *"Sign me up, boss."*

"He would've followed you anywhere after that, huh?"

I take in a deep breath, my emotions swelling. "I didn't expect him to agree to leave with me. Not that Rafe asked, to be honest, but Sandro didn't make a big deal out of it. He got on board and drove me all the way to Missouri, and he was fucking cheerful through it all."

Blake sniffles. When I glance over, she's wiping under her eyes.

"We don't need to keep talking about him if you don't want to," I say softly.

"No, I'm glad we are. I feel like in the midst of everything that happened right after he died, I haven't had a chance to process his death." She gives me a watery smile, and it just fucking kills me. "I hope he ended up somewhere nice."

I swallow past the ball in my throat and turn back to face the road. "Yeah. Me too."

The party is happening at a bar called San Marco. I drive past the front door and the neon sign that hangs above it and go around to park at the back.

The place's got a Venetian theme. Blake and I enter through the back door and walk down a hallway that's been done up to resemble a canal. The tiles on the floor are the color of water, and on the walls, there are gondolas painted against the backdrop of Venetian homes.

It's kitschy and fun and unpretentious. Sandro preferred places like this to the glitzy restaurants he often drove Rafe and me to.

When we step into the main room, heads turn in our direction. First just one, then two, then the rest follow. It takes a few seconds, but all the conversations soon quiet.

My grip on Blake's hand tightens as I stare at the faces of the men who used to call me boss.

A few meet my gaze head-on and even grin, but others look down at their feet, like they're scared to see what's become of me. Funny. I still look the same—at least, I think I do—but sometimes, the way we're perceived has nothing to do with our appearance.

There's subtext swirling through the air.

A fallen god walks among us.

The crowd parts for Rafe. He walks up to me with measured steps, Cleo a few paces behind him. The silence is nearly absolute, broken only by the shuffling of feet against the worn tile floors. Rafe stops in front of me. His expression gives nothing away, but his eyes speak to me, just the way they always have.

Right now, they're saying, *I wish things were different.*

I shrug, a small movement only he'll notice. *It is what it is.*

He offers me his hand. "Glad you made it."

Our handshake pops the tension in the room. The people here know they've got to follow the don's lead, so the chatter starts up again, and the waiter who's been standing frozen since Blake and I walked in starts to refill people's glasses with red wine.

Cleo comes up to give me a tight hug before turning to Blake and doing the same to her. When she pulls away, she scans Blake's face, looking a bit worried. "Can I get you a drink?"

Blake's eyes find mine. I give her a small nod. Cleo's probably still feeling bad about how she greeted Blake the first time they met, and she wants to smooth things over.

They move toward the bar while Rafe comes up to stand beside me, his eyes tracking Blake and his wife.

"Did you pick this place because Sandro used to like it, or because your wife's finally managed to knock off a zero from your net worth?" I ask.

"She dropped that tactic to annoy me after I told her all it does is motivate me to make more money for her to spend."

I chuckle. "Well-played."

A waiter carrying a platter of hors d'oeuvres passes by the women. Cleo turns animatedly, pointing at something on the platter while speaking to Blake. I watch as the redhead grabs a napkin and loads it up with fried cheese balls. My lips quirk up.

"How's it going with your wife?" Rafe asks. "She doesn't seem to hate you anymore."

"Yeah, we've made progress. I just want her to be happy here."

"Is she?"

I mull it over for a moment. "Honestly? I don't know." The short time we spent at the shore was great, but I'm convinced there's still something weighing her down. I've just got no idea what.

"You've been back here for weeks, and you're telling me you still haven't won her over? That's not the Nero De Luca I remember. You never had any problems making women happy."

"She's different. Complex. I never quite have her all figured out."

Rafe palms my shoulder. "Let's sit."

We move toward a quiet corner of the room and take a seat at one of the empty tables. The wooden chair squeaks beneath my weight.

Another waiter appears with a bottle of red and fills our glasses. When he leaves, I heave a sigh.

"So did you have to get Gino's permission to have me here?"

A shadow passes over Rafe's expression. "We talked."

"Did he give you the full update on me?" I ask, wondering if Gino's finally brought Rafe in on his plan to kill the pakhan.

"He didn't say much."

Apparently not.

"How's he been treating you? He said you're working with Alessio."

I shrug. "Alessio's not that bad. Completely fucking crazy and a pain in the ass, but I think I like him. He's the kind of guy you definitely want on your side in a bar fight."

Rafe takes a slug of his wine. "You been getting friendly with Cosimo too?"

I glance at him. "You sound a bit jealous."

Rafe gives me a dark look, but I know I'm right. He misses me too. Maybe after I help get the Bratva out of our city, we'll finally be able to hang out like we used to.

That nostalgic feeling from last night sweeps right through my chest again.

I clear my throat. "To answer your fucking question, of course not. God, that guy is such a self-important prick. Send Fabi my condolences. I can't believe your angel of a sister is going to be married to that uptight fuck in just a few months."

"He knows better than to treat her with anything other than respect," Rafe says gruffly. "And your perception of him is skewed. You've always had something against him."

"Not always. Just after that time he stole my fucking wine. Do you remember that? A whole crate I personally ordered from that producer in Tuscany."

Rafe smirks. "Oh yeah."

"It was sitting there, waiting for me at Velluto, and he saw it in the cellar and demanded Tanner sell it to him. That kind of move shows a man's character. That guy's got *none*."

"I remember you making Sandro drive you over to Ferraro's at midnight so that you could confront Cosimo," Rafe says with a low chuckle.

"And the prick wouldn't even come down to talk to me." I lean back in my chair. "You know, I think Sandro actually brought me here afterward so that I could have a glass and calm down. There are plenty of guys who would've just wanted to get rid of their fuming boss as soon as they could, but Sandro was never scared of my anger."

Rafe nods, his gaze anchored on his glass. "He wasn't scared of much."

My chest grows tight. No, he wasn't. He wasn't even scared of death, because there's no way he would have thought to give Blake his car keys if he'd been consumed by fear.

"I killed the guys who got him, but it doesn't feel like enough."

Rafe's expression darkens. "Last week, we caught two Iron Raptors sniffing around one of our warehouses in Albany."

"For real? Jesus. I can't believe they'd be stupid enough to cross into our territory."

"We gave them a firm warning. Told them you were one of ours, and that moving on you would mean moving on both the Messeros and the Ferraros."

"I doubt Gino would lift a finger if it came down to it."

"Yeah, well, given he and I will be family soon, he won't have a choice."

"You think they're something we should be concerned about?"

"No. I doubt we'll see them around here again, but I'd be careful when traveling. Unless you want me to make contact with their president and see if we can come to an understanding. But given how many of their guys you killed..." He grimaces. "It won't be straightforward."

I rub my palm over my chin. "Yeah, I know." If Rafe pulled it off though, it would mean Blake could leave the state. She could go see her friend in California. Maybe that's what she needs.

What if she likes it so much there that she decides to never come back?

I twist the stem of my wineglass. "Have you ever felt wrong for doing what we do?"

Rafe shrugs. "I think wrong and right are arbitrary human constructs. What we do is survive. If we stop, we die. That's always been clear to me."

"Me too." But I've never had anyone push me to question it the way Blake has. And there's a nagging fear at the back of my mind that she still thinks she won't be able to thrive in this world. Like she's somehow not enough. Is that the reason for the doubt I sometimes see flicker in her eyes?

Pulling her into this thing with Maksim set the wrong precedent. It made her think she needs to be an active player in the game. That just isn't the case. Rafe would have never let Cleo get involved in something like this, so what the hell was I thinking?

My jaw clenches. I need to be better at protecting her from the darkest parts of this life. They're mine to navigate, not hers.

The crowd swells with some latecomers, drawing my attention to it.

Rafe stands up. "That should be everyone." He glances at me. "Care to say a few words?"

I clear my throat and get to my feet. "Yeah."

There's a small stage set up in the corner where a live band usually plays. Today, there's just a mic on a stand there.

I get up on the stage. It's hard to gather my thoughts, so I close my eyes.

There are so many things I could say. So many stories I could tell.

He was only twenty-two. What kind of a life could he have lived if he'd had more time?

Someone taps their fork against a glass. A few seconds pass before the room grows quiet.

I look out at the people gathered. His coworkers. His friends. His family. Not by blood, but by something more meaningful. Their own choices.

"Sandro was a good kid. Sorry—man. He'd always get mad at me for calling him a kid. All of you knew him as Rafe's driver, but I got to know him as someone else. Sam Wilkins. Entrepreneur. Construction expert. A pain in the ass, on occasion."

There are a few chuckles at that.

"And a very dear friend." I pause, sliding my gaze over the listening crowd. "You all knew Sandro, but I want to tell you a bit about Sam. You know what happened to us. Sandro got the short end of the stick and was told to get out of here with me. The guy didn't even fucking blink. It's not like we were leaving for a day or two, it was meant to be forever. I know I'm good company, but I'm not *that* good."

Laughs break out among the crowd.

"Anyway, we get to this place called Darkwater Hollow." I scratch the side of my mouth with my thumb. "I honestly had no fucking idea what we were going to do there. I was upset and angry and just lost."

I find Blake. She's standing beside Cleo, and judging by her expression, I can tell my words have caught her off guard.

She has no idea how dark things were in the beginning. Only Sandro did.

"It was Sandro's idea to buy a small construction business. While I was still internally kicking and screaming about being forced into this new life, Sandro didn't waste any time on that. He was a practical guy. He got to *work*, and he was so damn smart. We turned that business around in a few months, and from the outside, it may have seemed like I was leading the charge, but that's not true. It was all him. He grew into his own. He became a man. And he became someone I looked up to."

Someone in the crowd sniffs.

"When we first left, I had this idea in my head that I'd have to be responsible for him, but I was wrong. He didn't need me. I was the one who needed him, especially in those early days. Whenever I got too quiet, too deep inside my head, Sandro would pull me out. Crack a bad joke. Make a comment about a shitty driver. Babble on about a viral video he'd seen. It annoyed me back then. Like, why the hell couldn't he just let me think in peace? But now I see what he was doing. He could tell I was having a rough go at it, and instead of leaving me to my own devices, he cared enough to try to give me a hand."

Fuck. I'd do anything to have him walk through the door right now with that boyish grin on his face.

I take a sip of my drink, buying myself a few moments to pull it together.

"I know this is supposed to be a celebration of his life, and we'll celebrate right after I stop making you all cry, but there's one more thing I've got to say." I clear my throat. "In these parts, we don't throw around the label 'hero' very often. We know who we are, and we know what we do. But I want to make an exception for Sandro, because..." My throat is so damn tight.

Blake stares at me from across the room as silent tears run down her cheeks. I'm not sure I'd be able to get through this if she weren't here.

I lick my lips. "Sandro used his last moments to save my wife's life. And I'll always be grateful to him for that."

Faces turn toward Blake. There isn't a single dry eye in the room.

Cleo puts a comforting hand on her back. Blake's lips wobble a bit as she gives me a sad smile.

I lift my glass. "To Sandro, and to Sam."

"To Sandro, and to Sam," the crowd responds.

And we drink.

CHAPTER 31

NERO

Rubbing a towel over my wet hair, I wander through the penthouse, looking for my wife. I find her in the living room reading on the couch with a blanket draped over her lap. I just finished up my post-workout shower, and I'm ready to spend another day with her. It's my last day off before I have to get back to work and deal with Alessio's brand of crazy.

I walk over to where she's sitting and bend down to plant a kiss on the crown of her head. She tilts her head to look up at me, offering a soft smile.

Something flutters inside my chest. God, I'm like a fucking schoolboy searching for clues my crush is also crushing on me.

She's given herself to me physically, but I don't just want her body. I want all of her to be mine, without any hesitations, doubts, or fears. And I won't give up until I get that.

For a moment, I'm tempted to call Cleo and ask her if Blake gave her any clues about how she's really feeling about me, but I doubt Cleo would tell me. Besides, I want Blake to have friends she can trust here, so I decide to keep my nose out of their business.

"Want to go for a walk in Central Park?"

She glances toward the window. "It's raining."

"Barely. Don't tell me you're scared of a little drizzle."

She shakes her head and puts her book down. "Okay, but we have to stop by the coffee shop downstairs. I want a vanilla matcha latte."

"A vanilla matcha latte? Since when do you like those?"

"Since I tried one a week ago and my life was changed forever." She tosses the blanket off and gets to her feet. That oversized T-shirt that she's wearing as a dress looks familiar...

One of mine.

Fucking adorable.

"I'm going to go change," she says. When she passes by me, I get the urge to pull her to me and kiss her until she's breathless, but she seems excited about this latte.

I suppose I can wait.

We're putting on our shoes when the phone that's connected to the concierge desk rings.

I grab it off the cradle. It's probably a package. "Hello?"

"Mr. De Luca, you have a visitor."

"Who is it?"

"Mr. Garin and his wife," Alec says.

I frown. What the fuck? They've shown up uninvited?

"Did they say why they're here?"

Blake lifts her head at my tone. Leaving the laces on her sneakers alone, she stands up, her brow furrowed.

"No, sir. Should I ask?"

Is there a chance Maksim's here to take me to the pakhan? My pulse picks up speed. It's possible.

It's *very* possible. No warning. No time to prepare. Seems about right.

Why the fuck would he bring Ekaterina, though?

"It's just the two of them?"

"Yes."

I assess the risk. Two things could be going on here. Either he wants to negotiate a bit more, or he's here to say the pakhan's agreed to a meeting.

I've got to let them up.

"Okay, send them in." I hang up the phone. "Maksim and Ekaterina are here."

Blake's eyes widen. "What do we do?"

"Go grab my gun from the office and bring it to me," I tell her as I pull out my cell phone. I doubt I'll need the gun. Maksim wouldn't show up with his wife if he was here to try to kill me, but I'm not taking any chances. "I've got to call Gino."

Unease slips into Blake's expression, but she nods and jogs toward the office.

I dial Gino, counting each second he doesn't pick up his goddamn phone.

Fuck. C'mon.

Finally, it connects. "Maksim is here at my condo with his wife. I don't know why he's brought her with him, but I think this could be it."

"Good. Don't forget to wear the right shoes."

I glance down at the Chelsea boots I was about to put on. Gino's tech guy inserted a GPS chip into the heel so that they can track where Maksim takes me since he'll probably take my phone and toss a bag over my head. Once Gino has the pakhan's location, his men will be able to stage an attack.

"Make sure there's someone downstairs while I'm gone. I want Blake protected in case anything goes wrong on my end and Maksim's guys retaliate."

"They won't be able to break into the penthouse from the outside, Nero. She's safe."

"If they get past building security, they could reach our floor." I don't want anyone coming up here, banging on the front door, scaring Blake witless. "Send a car."

"All right. I'll send backup just in case. They'll be there in fifteen."

"Good."

The bell rings.

"They're here," I say.

"We'll be watching everything closely."

"I've got to go. I'll call or text as soon as I can."

"Good luck."

We hang up.

On the other side of my front door, I find the Garins dressed in their Sunday best.

Maksim smiles. I smile. None of our smiles reach our eyes. "Come on in," I say calmly, as if this is all perfectly fucking normal. "To what do I owe the pleasure?"

"We've got something to discuss." Maksim's gaze stays trained on me as he steps inside. Ekaterina files in after him. Judging by the scowl on her face, she isn't thrilled to be here. I don't understand why he brought her if he's taking me to the pakhan. Why would he want her to accompany us?

This doesn't smell right.

"Mind if we sit down?" Maksim asks.

"Follow me."

I lead them to the living room sofa just as Blake enters from the other side of the room. She's put on a bigger hoodie, probably to better hide the gun she should have somewhere on her.

Our eyes connect. Maybe I should have told her to stay in her room until we leave, but it's too late for that. I've just got to get Maksim and Ekaterina out of here as quickly as I can.

"Should I make some coffee?" Blake asks.

Maksim gives her a tight smile. "Not right now. Why don't we all have a seat?"

My hackles rise at him acting like he fucking owns the place, but I keep my mouth shut.

Blake comes to sit at my side, and I pull her close to my chest before I slide my hand under her hoodie and grab the gun she's got tucked in the waistband at her back. Carefully, I tuck it behind my own.

"The pakhan agreed to a meeting."

Adrenaline floods my veins. They bought our story. It worked.

Maksim takes out a silver cigarette case from his breast pocket. "Mind if I smoke?"

I want to snarl at him that, yes, I fucking mind, but I hold myself back. I'll have a chance to give him everything he deserves soon enough. "Go ahead. When does he want to meet?"

He slips a cigarette between his lips and digs into his pocket for a lighter. "Right now."

"We shouldn't keep him waiting then."

He lights the cigarette and takes a few drags like he has all the time in the world. Beside him, Ekaterina is perched on the sofa, strangely quiet but alert.

"Do you know the gentleman who lives in the penthouse below yours?" Maksim asks.

What the fuck is he going on about now? "No."

"Mr. Benoit. He's an art collector. Made his money by making a few very smart bets a couple of decades ago." Maksim blows out and smirks at me through the smoke. "You had no idea you've been having breakfast above a Monet all these years?"

"I could've been shitting above a Picasso for all I care. I fail to see the relevance of any of this."

Maksim's grin widens. "Mr. Benoit is sixty-two years old. He's kept in decent enough shape all these years, but nothing could be done about his vision, I'm afraid. He's gone completely blind. Imagine the tragedy of owning all that fantastic art and not being able to enjoy it."

"Maksim," I grind out, my patience waning.

"You sure you haven't seen him? He always wears these enormous dark sunglasses and a newsboy cap. I met him just after the four of us bumped into each other at that gala. I negotiated the sale of his collection to the pakhan. When I told him last week that we'd increase our offer by ten percent if he helped us out with something, he was happy to oblige."

I listen to him with growing apprehension, my hand tightening on Blake's hip.

Maksim leans forward. "Mr. Benoit and the pakhan are just about the same height and build. Mr. Benoit left his penthouse to get breakfast yesterday morning, but it was the pakhan who came back disguised as him."

My mouth goes dry. Blake's completely frozen beside me.

Maksim isn't here to take me to the head of the Boston Bratva.

He brought him to *me*.

"Why go through all this trouble?" I ask even though I already know the answer. The pakhan knows he's being hunted, and so he came up with a plan to get to me completely undetected.

Scenarios of what could happen next whir through my mind at the speed of fucking light. This is bad. Gino has no idea what's happening, and if the Russians have gone to these lengths to catch me off guard, they're far more cautious than we anticipated. With their boss here, they must have a perimeter set up around the penthouse, and there's a good chance they will spot the backup Gino's sending.

I'm going to be exposed.

Fuck!

Maksim finishes his cigarette and puts it out against one of my marble coasters. "I told you he doesn't take visitors. No exceptions. You should be honored he left the safe house for you. He wants to hear what you have to say. As long as you give him exactly what you told me you can, you'll be generously rewarded, just as we discussed."

I need to message Gino to tell him to call his guys back. But how? I can't whip out my phone in front of Maksim. Gino's men are going to be here any minute, and even if they somehow get close to the building undetected by the Russians the pakhan has likely stationed outside, Gino's going to eventually want to know why Maksim and I aren't coming out. What if he sends someone up to check on me while the pakhan is here?

It'll be a bloodbath.

I turn my head to look at Blake for the first time since Maksim started talking. She's staring at Ekaterina, her face a blank mask, but there's a drop of sweat rolling down her temple.

I need to get her out of here.

My gaze snaps back to Maksim. "The wives don't need to be here for this."

He leans back on the sofa and pops his ankle on his knee. "On the contrary. The pakhan himself requested their presence to ensure we conduct ourselves in a civilized manner. You don't need to worry. They're just insurance, that's all."

Ekaterina purses her lips and glances out the window. She's silent because she's nervous too. The pakhan is a paranoid fuck, and given his history with Maksim, he probably doesn't trust Maksim completely either.

"Blake, dear, go ahead and make us that coffee now, if you don't mind," Maksim says, taking out his phone.

Jesus, fuck. I want to scream in frustration, but I shove all of my rage down so that I can stay clearheaded.

My every move and word counts right now. I need to do everything I can to keep Blake safe.

Blake stands up and moves to the kitchen. I watch her walk away and try to think of a way to contact Gino to tell him to call his guys back. If she had her phone on her, maybe she could sneak a text to Gino. She has his number.

"Go help her, Katya," Maksim says to Ekaterina, who reluctantly gets to her feet, leaving her purse behind on the sofa, and follows my wife.

Son of a bitch. There goes that idea. Ekaterina will be watching Blake while Maksim watches me.

My heart pounds against my ribcage like a ritual drum. There's got to be something I can do.

"Nero?"

My gaze snaps to Maksim. He slides his phone back inside his jacket and looks at me.

"The pakhan's ready. If you're armed, this would be the time to hand me your weapons."

What would happen if I refuse? I could kill Maksim and Ekaterina and call Gino. The pakhan won't be able to get past the biometric lock and the steel front door if I don't let him inside. Once he realizes we've tried to play him, he'll flee the building. There's even a chance Gino will be able to grab him or track him to wherever he goes.

A sound from the foyer reaches my ears. It sounds like the front door opening.

No. That can't be.

Maksim smirks. "I was afraid you might get cold feet."

A thin layer of sweat breaks out over my skin.

"So I made sure to get your fingerprints from every glass you've ever left around me. That came in handy with your fancy lock."

Steady footsteps sound from down the hall, the sound echoing inside my head. Horror drips into my bloodstream.

"Your weapons, Nero," Maksim croons. "If I were you, I'd hurry."

I'm out of options. The only thing I can do is play along and pray Gino won't interfere before we wrap up this spectacle.

I slide my gun across the coffee table toward Maksim just as Yaroslav Andreyevich Sokolov, the pakhan of the Boston Bratva, walks into my living room.

CHAPTER 32

BLAKE

Ekaterina's hands tremble as she places the coffee mugs on the tray. "Your husband better know what he's doing," she mutters under her breath. "You don't want to see how the pakhan reacts when he's disappointed."

My gaze locks on the gray-haired man who just entered the living room flanked by four armed men. Even from twenty feet away, the dark, hollow pits of his eyes are unmistakable. There's something utterly soulless about them.

My pulse quickens. It's a steady thrum in my throat. The only thing keeping me grounded is how composed Nero remains. If he's feeling any stress, he hides it well, even as one of the guards pats him down.

Nero expected Maksim to take him to the pakhan, not bring him here unannounced. What does this mean for the plan he and Gino Ferraro put together? It's likely out the window now, and we're left improvising.

I have no idea what I can do to help ensure we survive this meeting.

But I must stay calm. Freezing up like I did in Maksim's office isn't an option. Not when both our lives are on the line.

"Nero De Luca," the pakhan rasps in a voice ruined by cigarettes and age. "We finally meet."

"Welcome," Nero says gruffly, shaking the man's hand. "Please, have a seat."

I focus on the task at hand, taking a small jar of sugar from the cupboard and placing it on the tray. It's easier to stay calm if I keep busy. "Does he take his coffee with milk?" I ask Ekaterina.

She crosses her arms, her eyes cold as they follow my movements. "No. He takes it black."

Across the room, the pakhan's lips curl into a half smile. "I always thought Messero was a smart man," he says to Nero. "Yet what he's done with you appears to be a gross miscalculation. By all accounts, you were a good consigliere. What happened that night?"

Nero shrugs. "Rafaele panicked. I had no idea the Ferraros were coming, so I mistook them for the enemy."

"Rafaele isn't one to fall prey to his emotions. He's a stoic man."

"His wife was in danger. Surely you're aware how important she is to him?"

The pakhan laughs, and the harsh sound echoes through the room. "I'm well aware of his weak spots. He protects them well."

"It's ready," Ekaterina says to me, nodding at the coffee pot. Her anxiety is palpable, practically vibrating off her. "Come on. Bring it to him."

"Why are you so scared of him if you're on the same side?" I ask quietly.

Her eyes flash with a mix of fear and frustration. "Same side or not, he doesn't suffer fools. I told Maks to wait a little longer before going to him with this idea, but Maks is impatient. If he's wrong about this, my hide is on the line along with his. Now, no more questions, hurry up."

Pity stirs in my chest at her barely suppressed terror. I study Maksim, who's sitting to the right of the pakhan, a self-satisfied smirk playing on his lips. She's right to be worried. Her husband *is* making a mistake.

Or at least he was, until he turned the tables on us.

The whole point of this plot was to give Gino a chance to kill the Russian leader, but he has no idea the pakhan is here.

The phone in my back pocket vibrates and my heart skips a beat. Could it be Gino?

I can't pick up the call in front of Ekaterina.

I place the coffee pot on the tray, trying to think of a way to sneak away for just a few seconds. The phone keeps vibrating.

"What are you waiting for?" Ekaterina hisses. "Go."

An idea appears. It's a gamble, but worth trying.

I pick up the tray and carry it over to where the men are sitting.

"Rafaele will regret putting his wife over your friendship," the pakhan says. "I will make sure of that. And Gino Ferraro will pay for how he's mistreated you."

Nero nods. "I appreciate that. I hope this can be the beginning of a fruitful partnership." His eyes flick to me as I set the tray on the coffee table. For a brief moment, I see a flash of desperation in his gaze before he blinks it away. "Thank you."

"No problem." The phone stops vibrating.

"Is this your wife?" the pakhan asks.

I offer the older man a polite smile. "Yes. I'm Blake De Luca."

His dark, terrifying eyes assess me as I pour the coffee into five cups. "How kind of you to make refreshments. If you don't mind, one of the guards will need to check you for weapons."

A growl escapes Nero. "No one touches my wife. She's not armed."

The pakhan's smile is cold. "I'm sure that's true, but I've always liked the phrase trust but verify. Why don't you remove your sweater so we can see if you've got anything tucked away?"

I glance at Nero, waiting for his nod of approval before I pull my hoodie over my head and toss it on the sofa. My heart pounds in my chest. What if they take my phone?

But the pakhan seems satisfied. He glances past me. "Katya, I didn't notice you over there. Have a seat, child. You too, Blake. Everything is fine."

My lungs expand with relief as I lower down beside Nero.

"This is a big moment for your husband, isn't it?" the pakhan continues. "One you might tell your kids about one day. It's not often that we consider allowing an Italian to come to our side, but for someone as legendary as your husband, an exception must be made." He smirks, folding his hands over his belly. "Nero, you wanted to talk in person. I presume it's because you want my personal assurance that I will take care of Messero and Ferraro. You have it. I give you my word, man-to-man. There won't be any deals made. They will die at my hand."

Nero nods. "I appreciate it."

"It will be my pleasure. And when it comes to your position... Well, we can discuss those specifics later." He makes a dismissive wave. "Let's not get bogged down with administrative details. I reward those who prove their value to me very well."

Nero shifts in his seat. "I've heard you are a generous man."

"Then speak, Mr. De Luca," the pakhan says, a note of impatience in his tone. "Say what you have to say."

The phone starts vibrating again just as I lift the coffee cup to my lips. I shift slightly on the sofa, trying to muffle the sound.

I can't hold this awkward position too long, so I decide to just go for it.

Tilting the cup too far, I let the hot coffee spill all over me.

"Ouch!" I jump to my feet.

Suddenly, four guns are pointed at me, and Nero lunges in front of me. "Do not point those at my wife," he snaps at the guards.

"I'm so sorry. I'm a klutz," I mutter.

The pakhan raises a hand. "Stand down, gentlemen. It's just an accident."

Coffee drips from my clothes onto the cream rug. "Can I go clean up?"

Maksim's eyes narrow as he studies me. "Go ahead, child. Artem will accompany you."

One of the guards steps forward.

"Like hell he will." Nero's fists clench, the tendons in his neck taut. "I don't want them alone."

The pakhan sighs. "This is getting tiresome, De Luca."

"Katya, you go," Maksim orders. "Surely you won't have a problem with that, Nero?"

Damn it.

Ekaterina tucks her purse under her arm and follows me out of the room. I can feel her eyes boring into my back with every step I take toward my bedroom.

In the closet, she props herself against the doorjamb and watches as I peel off my soaked shirt. Her lips curl, but her eyes stay unsmiling. "You've done well for yourself, haven't you? A waitress from Missouri, now living in a gorgeous penthouse in Manhattan with your handsome husband. Your mother must be proud."

I toss the shirt into the laundry bin. "My mother's dead."

"Hmm. Lucky you."

"Lucky?"

"The fewer people you care about, the better. Trust me."

My blood turns icy cold. "Why's that?"

"Because one wrong move by your husband today, and they would all be dead," she says so very confidently that I want to wring her neck.

This bitch.

"He's brave for talking to the pakhan the way he has. For standing up for you. But he's overdoing it, and it'll cost him. The pakhan doesn't like men who are too sentimental about their families. It creates too many liabilities."

A hole opens up inside my stomach. Is she hinting that the pakhan might kill Nero once he's no longer useful? I have no idea how Nero plans to get out of this, but his hands look like they're tied. He might be telling the pakhan the locations of those warehouses right this second. And once he gives all of them up, there are six armed men here who could take him out.

Oh God.

Acid surges up my throat. Ekaterina might just be trying to get into my head with her words, but I can't take that risk.

I pull on a clean shirt and brush past her, heading toward the bathroom.

"Where are you going?" she snaps.

"I need to pee. Are you going to watch me do that too?"

Before she can respond, I shut the bathroom door and lock it.

"You have one minute," she calls out. "I'm timing it."

I'm already turning on the tap and dialing Gino's number.

"Hello?"

"The pakhan is here," I whisper urgently.

A harsh intake of breath. "That explains the watch cars my guys just called me about. How many with him?"

"Four, plus Maksim and Ekaterina. They're just talking for now, but I don't know what he'll do once Nero gives him the information."

There's a long pause, and I can almost hear the seconds counting down in my head. "Are you there?"

"I'm thinking," Gino says gruffly. "Did Nero let them in?"

"They got his fingerprints for the biometric lock."

"Are yours programmed in as well?"

"Yes." Nero had them added a few weeks ago.

"Can you find a way to open the door for us?"

Knock. Knock. Knock. "Fifteen seconds!" Ekaterina's voice is muffled by the door.

I could get to the front door from here without passing the living room, but I'll have to get past Ekaterina first.

"I can try," I whisper. "How long until you get here?"

"Two minutes. My men are just outside the building. If you get there before they do, just get out of there. Leave the front door cracked open and get into the elevator."

What is he talking about? "I'm not leaving Nero."

"Blake—"

"No. I'm not leaving him here alone."

321

Gino swears. "Fine. When you get the door open, go to the farthest bathroom, lock the door, and lie down in the tub. Don't let anyone in unless it's Nero."

"Five seconds," Ekaterina snaps. "If you're not out here by then, I'm calling the guards!"

Shit. "I'm going." I hang up, slide the phone back into my pocket, and turn off the tap. "Coming!"

What the hell do I do? How do I get away from her? I need to knock her out somehow.

Oh God, can I?

There's no time to hesitate. I have to do it if I want to make sure Nero and I get out of this alive.

I grab a metal nail file from the counter and slip it into my pocket, my mind racing. Then I rush to the door.

We lock eyes, the tension between us thick enough to cut.

"I have to pee too," she says, her voice tight.

I blink at her. "Okay."

"Wait. Right. Here," she orders through gritted teeth. "Inside the bathroom."

Her heels click on the marble floor as she steps into the separate toilet area behind the door made of frosted glass.

I scan the bathroom, searching for something that doesn't involve stabbing her with a tiny piece of metal.

Maybe I could knock her out with a perfume bottle?

I grab a heavy glass one from the counter and hide it behind my back just as she reemerges.

She narrows her eyes, suspicious. She'll see me coming in the mirror. How do I do this?

I could turn off the lights and take advantage of her confusion. But what if I miss?

I have to take the risk.

As she washes her hands at the sink, I flick off the light and charge at her, doing my best to aim for the spot where her head connects with her neck. Vita told me that's the best place to strike during one of our lessons.

She yelps, but the bottle in my hand connects with something solid, and the sound dies in her throat. My free hand fumbles to find her, and I bring the bottle down two more times, aiming for the back of her head.

A heavy weight collapses against me, pulling me down to the ground. I try to catch myself, but I end up falling on my elbow. The pain is sharp, and I have to bite down on the inside of my cheek to stop from crying out. The taste of blood fills my mouth as I wriggle out from under Ekaterina's limp body and turn the light back on.

She lies sprawled on the floor, her eyes closed, a thin trail of blood seeping from the back of her head. She's out cold, but I know it won't last long. I have to move. Now.

Keeping as quiet as possible, I hurry to the front door, straining to catch any sounds from the living room. The conversation is still ongoing—Maksim's bark of a laugh echoes through the hall.

Ten steps. Five. Here.

I hover my thumb above the biometric lock, nerves stretched so taut I feel like I might snap. I need to time this perfectly. The lock's beep and click will be loud enough to draw attention if they hear it.

Maksim says something in Russian, and then a burst of laughter erupts from the room. I press my thumb to the sensor, holding my breath.

The lock beeps softly, and I hear the faint click as it disengages. I pull the door open just an inch, praying the noise was masked by the laughter and conversation.

Gino's men are already waiting outside.

The leader presses his finger to his lips and silently signals for me to step out of the way.

For a brief moment, I'm torn between following Gino's instructions and staying close to Nero. I know that if he sees me, he'll get distracted, and he needs to stay focused on protecting himself.

So I run.

The moment I reach my bedroom and slam the door shut behind me, the first shots ring out.

Fear grips me, freezing me in place as my emotions threaten to overwhelm me. Somehow, I pull myself back to reality. I grab the gun Vita gave me all those weeks ago from its hiding spot in the nightstand, tuck it into my waistband, and rush into the bathroom. I close the door behind me and wedge a chair under the handle.

Just then, Ekaterina begins to stir.

Damn it.

I watch her as she blinks against the harsh overhead light, her hands instinctively moving to her head. She's sluggish, disoriented. When she pulls her fingers back and sees the blood, she moans. "What did you do to me?"

More gunshots echo through the apartment.

"You'd better stay down," I warn, my voice tense.

Her bloodshot eyes narrow as they lock onto mine. Slowly, she pushes herself off the floor, wobbling unsteadily on her feet. "I'm going to throw up."

She gags, spinning toward the sink and dry heaving over it.

The gunfire outside seems to be getting closer. I hear someone shout. Panic flares inside me.

"We need to get into the tub," I urge.

She's still heaving, her breaths coming in ragged gasps. It's like she's having a panic attack.

And then, in an instant, she grabs her purse from the counter and pulls out a small gun.

Time slows.

"You bitch," she snarls, advancing on me, her eyes wild with fury.

I pull the gun from my waistband, trying to hold it steady. "Don't come any closer."

She takes another step forward, defiance etched on her face. "You won't shoot me. If you had it in you, you would've killed me while I was still passed out."

My body buzzes with adrenaline. "Put it down, Ekaterina."

"What did you do?" she spits, a tear slipping down her cheek. "Are you trying to get my husband killed?"

"Stay back!" I shout, desperation clawing at my throat. "Let them sort it out. They won't do anything to you."

She shoots.

The gunshot is deafening, a sudden, violent crack that echoes off the bathroom walls. Pain explodes through my abdomen, searing and intense.

I gasp, the burning sensation spreading like wildfire. My hand flies to the site of the impact. Warm, sticky wetness gushes over my fingers—blood.

Oh God.

I've never felt my heartbeat so acutely. Each throb amplifies the pain now blazing through my core.

A realization hits me hard.

If I don't act, I will die here.

My gaze lifts from the blood soaking my abdomen to Ekaterina. I can see in her eyes that she intends to finish the job.

And just like that, my breathless panic transforms into fury.

She shot me. She wants me dead. Does she really think I'm so weak that I'll just let her finish me off?

A force stirs awake inside me. A force that screams for me to do what's necessary. To do what's *just*.

The trigger beneath my index finger feels like it's burning as Ekaterina raises her gun again.

I squeeze it.

And then I squeeze it again. And again.

I empty the entire clip into Ekaterina until she collapses to the ground.

The room spins. I do my best to lower myself gently to the tiles, but I end up crashing once I'm halfway down.

My vision dims. Faint voices reach my ears, though I can't make out who they belong to.

And then everything goes black.

CHAPTER 33

NERO

I'm caught in a storm of chaos and gunfire.

One minute, I'm jotting down the addresses of the warehouses while Maksim and the pakhan talk about something in Russian, and the next, Gino Ferraro's men are storming my living room.

I snatch my gun off the coffee table and hurl myself over the back of the sofa.

"You motherfucker!" the pakhan shouts. "Kill him, Maks!"

A body crashes into me.

Maksim.

I roll, kicking out with my leg and connecting with Maksim's chest. He stumbles backward, then lunges again, throwing a punch, but I block it and counter with one of my own.

Maksim falls to the ground. Blood drips out of his nose and murder burns in his furious eyes. He scrambles behind an armchair, his gun cocked and ready.

I press my back against the wall, peeking out around the corner.

Gino's men have taken down two of the guards, but the remaining two are holed up behind the kitchen island with the pakhan.

Gino's guys can handle it. I need to finish off Maksim and get to Blake.

She must have found a way to let the Ferraro men inside. Smart girl.

A mix of pride and anger churns in my gut. I'm proud that she pulled it off, angry that she took such a risk.

That wasn't her job. The whole time the pakhan was talking, I was thinking about how to get her far from here. Turns out, she had a plan of her own. Spilling the coffee on herself was a brilliant idea.

I thought maybe without her in the room, I could try to attack the pakhan, but I didn't want to risk failing to kill them all. If I'd gotten myself killed, Blake would've been left alone.

They wouldn't have spared her.

Hold on. Where the fuck is Ekaterina?

I scan the room, but in the chaos and smoke, it's hard to make anything out. A bullet grazes my arm—a reminder that I've taken my eyes off Maksim for too long. The adrenaline coursing through me dulls the pain.

I aim and fire, but the bastard dodges just in time.

I need to end this. Now.

Crouching low, I weave through the furniture, closing in on Maksim.

I tackle him to the ground, making him drop his gun, but the fucker swings a hard punch at me, and his fist connects with my jaw. The impact forces me off him.

By the time I'm back on my feet, he's armed once again, but I don't give him the chance to aim. I grab his wrist and twist, forcing the gun skyward.

"You cocksucker," he spits, saliva spraying from his mouth.

I smile.

He pulls the trigger and fires into the ceiling. I twist his wrist harder until it snaps and the gun falls into my hand.

I don't hesitate. The next bullet rips through his kneecap, and he collapses with a scream that pierces the air.

"Fuck! Stop! I can help you!"

I shoot his other kneecap.

"Let me talk to Gino," he wheezes, desperation seeping into his voice. "I have information he'll want."

I crouch down, gripping his chin. "I don't give a fuck what Gino wants."

Fear washes over Maksim's face.

"You signed your death warrant the moment you made a move on my wife," I whisper. If I had more time, I'd play with him a little, but I need to check on Blake.

The next bullet pierces his heart.

He slumps to the ground, eyes wide and lifeless.

Good fucking riddance.

"Nero! You all right?"

I whip around to see Alessio charging into the living room, a machine gun in hand.

My eyes widen. I like his style. "I'm fine!"

He points it at the kitchen island and unloads a full clip, covering one of the Ferraro guys as he runs around the other side to get a clean shot at the cowering pakhan.

And then, just as suddenly as it began, it stops. The silence that follows is almost as jarring as the gunfire.

My ears are ringing, my shirt's drenched in sweat and blood, and the room is a wreck, but I'm still here.

I've got to find Blake.

I race through the penthouse, throwing open every door I pass until I reach her bedroom. It's locked.

"Blake!"

Silence.

I start ramming my good arm into the door, putting all my weight behind it.

"Blake! It's me!"

Why isn't she answering? Maybe she's panicking. *Damn it.* I've got to get to her.

On the next hit, the door bursts open. I scan the empty room in a frenzy before my eyes lock on the bathroom door. It's locked too.

"Blake! Sunshine, open up!"

I yank out my gun and aim it at the handle, but a split second before pulling the trigger, I hesitate. What if she's just on the other side?

Fuck, I can't risk it. The gun goes back behind my belt, and I throw myself at the door again and again, but the fucker's tougher than the last one.

"Move," a voice grunts behind me. Alessio barrels past, ramming his shoulder into the door with force.

"Together," I growl. "Three, two, one."

Our combined weight slams into the door. It crashes open with a splintering crack. The momentum propels me inside, and I stumble past the bodies on the floor.

One of them is Ekaterina. And the other...

My breath catches. The world around me narrows to a pinpoint.

No.

No.

I collapse to my knees beside Blake's lifeless form.

Blood. There's so much blood.

"Fuck. Fuck!" I tear off my shirt and press it hard against the wound in her abdomen. The fabric is soaked through instantly.

Alessio appears across from me, his hand reaching out—

"DON'T TOUCH HER!" I roar.

His gray eyes lock onto mine. "I'm going to check her pulse. Keep the pressure on the wound."

I'm trembling, my breath coming in harsh, uneven gasps. How did it come to this? How did I let this happen? My mind is racing, spiraling with guilt and helplessness. I should have been here. I should have protected her like I swore to her I would.

Alessio's fingers press against her neck, his expression unreadable as he waits for something—anything.

"Her pulse is there, but it's weak. We need to get her help now." He digs inside his jacket for his phone, and his voice is clipped as he makes the call. "We need the medical team here, immediately."

I can't tear my eyes away from Blake. She's so still, so pale. I can feel her slipping away, and no matter how hard I press against the wound, the blood keeps coming, seeping through my fingers like sand slipping through an hourglass.

I'm the one who dragged her into this. I failed her. She needed me, and I wasn't here.

Alessio barks more orders into the phone, but his voice fades into the background. All I can hear is the pounding of my own heart, the echo of my failure, and the shallow, fragile breaths coming from the woman I love.

"NERO, YOU NEED TO CALM DOWN," Alessio snaps, pulling me away from the wide-eyed medic, who doesn't waste a second before bolting down the hall. "They're going to kick you out if you keep harassing everyone who comes out that door."

"It's been two hours."

Two hours of not knowing if Blake is alive or dead. Two hours of replaying everything that happened, trying to pinpoint where I went wrong.

I can't stand this. I'm going to go insane.

"They're still operating on her—"

I shove Alessio against the nearest wall, pressing my forearm against his neck. "I need to see her. I need to know she's alive."

His jaw clenches, but he doesn't push back. Just stares at me with an emotion I didn't think he had the capacity to feel—pity.

I let go of him. "Gino never should have sent his team in."

Alessio lowers his voice. "If he hadn't, the pakhan might've killed you the moment he got what he wanted. That's why we were prepared to move on him as soon as you arrived at his location in the original plan. But then it all went sideways. If Blake hadn't called us, you might be dead right now."

"Do you think I—"

"And then they would have killed her too."

I squeeze my fists tightly. He's right, but I still want to argue and scream.

I've never felt so out of control, so beyond patience and reason.

"I know you want to blame someone, but sometimes, shit just happens. You know that as well as I do."

Blake shot Ekaterina eight times. The cleanup crew told Alessio it looked like Ekaterina had been hit on the back of the head too, meaning she and Blake fought.

How scared was my beautiful wife in that moment? How scared and how fucking brave?

She's stronger than she realizes, but she should never have been in a situation where she had to be that strong.

"Sit down." Alessio puts his hand on my shoulder.

I've got to give it to the guy. He's got balls to be touching me when I'm like this.

I shrug him off and pace to the other side of the waiting area, closer to the doors where nurses and doctors filter in and out. Above the doors is a clock.

The minutes tick by. I watch the hands move and try to remember to keep breathing.

Please be okay.

A doctor comes out and walks toward us.

I meet him halfway. "I'm Nero De Luca. Blake De Luca's husband. Do you have any news?"

The doctor—a dark-haired woman about my age—gives me a sympathetic smile. "Hello, Mr. De Luca. She's out of surgery, but she's in critical condition. We're doing every-thing we can to stabilize her right now. The bullet nicked a major blood vessel in her abdomen. She lost a lot of blood. We've repaired the damage and are now restoring her blood volume through transfusions. The next twenty-four hours will be crucial," she says gently, as if trying to cushion the blow of her words.

My chest tightens at the news, but a flicker of hope ignites inside me. She's alive. There's still a chance she'll make it through this.

"Can I see her?"

The doctor nods. "Yes, but only for a few minutes. She's still unconscious. Follow me."

My heart pounds as I trail behind the doctor through a maze of corridors. We finally reach a room with a glass window, and I see Blake lying on the hospital bed, hooked up to machines and tubes.

My lungs still. She's so horribly pale against the stark-white sheets.

The doctor opens the door and says something, but her words don't register. My legs feel like lead as I approach Blake, each step heavy with dread.

Hand trembling, I reach out to touch her. Her skin is cold, but the faint rise and fall of her chest tells me she's still breathing.

"I'll be back in five minutes," the doctor says, excusing herself from the room.

I pull up a chair beside the bed and take Blake's hand in mine, pressing it gently to my lips. "You're going to be okay, Sunshine. You can get through this. I know you can."

She doesn't react. Not even a twitch.

My vision blurs.

This is all your fault.

Memories of our time together flood my mind, each one more vivid than the last. I see her the day I moved in—her hands on her hips as she chastised me for leaving my trash on the front lawn. Her eyes were bright with that mix of exasperation and anger she always had when I pushed her buttons. Fuck, how those eyes got under my skin.

I remember the lazy afternoons in Darkwater Hollow, the sunlight filtering through the window as we sat on the sofa, her head resting on my shoulder as we watched movies and talked about nothing. There was peace in those moments, a sense of rightness that I'd never known before. She had a way of making the world feel softer, like it wasn't such a harsh place after all.

And then there was Christmas, just weeks ago. I can still see the way her eyes widened when she opened the envelope, the one that held the lease to her bookshop. I knew I'd nailed her present when she started tearing up. The way she'd looked at me then, awed and so fucking happy, made my heart swell with a love so deep it hurt.

But then the other memories surface, the ones that cut deep. I remember every tear she shed because of me, because of this life I dragged her into. All the times she told me she wanted to leave. All the times I refused to even consider it because of my stubborn conviction that she'd be safe with me. That she'd eventually embrace all of this.

Did I blind myself to the possibility that maybe—just maybe —she'd have been safer and happier without me? That all my promises of protection were nothing more than hollow words in a world where there are no guarantees?

A world she didn't choose. A world I dragged her into, kicking and screaming.

And now here she is, fighting for her life in a hospital bed.

She will never be truly safe with me.

It's one thing to choose this life with your eyes wide open, the way my mom did, deciding that the man she loved was worth the risk.

But Blake didn't choose this.

Her words ring in my ears. *"Sometimes, I wake up in the morning and feel like I'm drowning. I have no agency, no autonomy. You forced me to marry you. You forced me into this world, and even after weeks of trying to make it here, I still don't know how to."*

How could I have done this to her, the person I love most?

I don't know. But I do know that I can't do it anymore.

If she makes it through this, I have to let her go.

CHAPTER 34

BLAKE

When I wake up, everything hurts.

"Blake?"

It sounds like Nero, but that can't be him. He couldn't have gotten rid of the pakhan's men that fast.

My fingers twitch, searching for the gun that must have slipped from my grasp when I fell. Instead, they curl around soft fabric.

Where am I?

My eyes crack open, and the light is blinding. I groan. Something nearby is beeping.

I blink until the brightness dulls enough for me to see.

Nero's face comes into focus.

"Fuck," he breathes, his voice ragged. "Thank fucking God."

He presses his lips to my forehead, my brows, my cheeks. His hands wrap around mine, warm and comforting. "You have no idea how worried I was about you."

I look past him, confused. What is this place? The walls are stark white, bare except for a clock ticking above the door, but there are flowers lined up on the windowsill. Beside me, a machine beeps rhythmically, and there's a tube taped to my arm.

A hospital.

I swallow. My throat is dry and raw. Flashes of a memory hit me. Flashes of the last time I woke up in a place like this. The motorbike accident was years ago, but I still remember the aftermath clearly. The pulsating pain at the back of my head. The cast on my leg itching like crazy. My mom crying by my bedside while my father told her to shut up and stop making a scene.

"Sunshine, how do you feel?" Nero's thumb brushes gently over the top of my hand.

"How did I get here?" Mentally, I'm still in that bathroom, the floor spinning beneath my feet, Ekaterina pointing her gun at me.

Pain.

Then red, so much red.

I look down at myself, but I can't see my abdomen under the hospital gown and the blanket over me.

I try to sit up.

Oof. Big mistake.

Nero springs to his feet, his hands on my shoulders. "Careful, baby."

I breathe through the sharp pain, my eyes flicking to the monitors beside me. Numbers and graphs pulse on the screens, but they're just cryptic symbols to me. I wish I knew what they meant.

"How long has it been?" I ask, my voice coming out a whisper.

"Two days."

Two days. It feels like just seconds ago that I was holding that gun, my finger on the trigger.

"Is the pakhan dead?"

"Yes."

"Then you're a Ferraro capo."

"I am." There's no happiness in his tone. Not even relief at having gotten his promotion. Is it because he's worried about me? Or is it something else?

I register the bandage on his arm. "You were hurt?"

"It's nothing. Just a graze that'll heal in no time." He gives me a soft smile. "You saved both of our lives."

"What about Ekaterina?"

Nero's jaw hardens. "She's gone."

Gone. As in dead. As in...I killed her.

I *killed* someone.

The realization hits like a punch to the gut, followed by a wave of nausea so strong I groan.

"I'll call the doctor," Nero says.

Those moments in the bathroom replay in my mind like a nightmare. I bite on the inside of my mouth and taste copper. Oh God. What have I done?

I'm a killer. I took someone's life.

It doesn't feel real. It doesn't feel like something I'm capable of, but the truth is there. Undeniable and cold.

I pulled the trigger.

There's no coming back from this. I'll never be the same. How can I be? I've done the unthinkable.

The door bursts open, revealing a man in scrubs. "Hello, Blake," the doctor says. "How are you feeling?"

I press my hand to my lips. "Like I'm about to be sick."

"That's normal after anesthesia," the doctor explains, moving to check the monitors. "You might feel nauseous, dizzy, and disoriented for a few days until your body adjusts."

It's not the anesthesia. It's the fact that I've done something I never thought I was capable of, and amidst the shock, confusion, and fear, there's one emotion that's missing.

Guilt.

"Are you in pain?"

I blink and force myself to answer his question. "My abdomen is."

"I'll adjust your pain medication." He reaches for the IV line and carefully turns a dial. "We had to remove a bullet. By the time you arrived, you'd lost more than a liter and a half of blood."

"When can she go home?" Nero asks, his voice tense.

"I'd like to keep her here for another five days at least, as we need to monitor her for any potential infections. In addition, I want to make sure she doesn't bleed more."

Five days? After the motorcycle accident, they discharged me the next day. Probably because we didn't have insurance, and my father wasn't keen on paying for my care out of pocket.

Tears well up unexpectedly. If he knew what I'd done to survive... I have a sick feeling he'd be proud.

The last thing I ever wanted was to behave in ways that would make my piece-of-shit father proud.

The doctor leaves.

Nero takes my hand again and says something about me not needing to worry about anything. That I'm safe. That I'll be out of here soon.

But his words don't bring any comfort. I keep my eyes squeezed shut, my mouth sealed tight, until darkness drags me back under.

NERO DOESN'T SLEEP. For the next few days, whenever I wake up, he's there, keeping an eye on me from a chair placed beside my bed.

He makes sure I have everything I need, feeds me the food the nurses bring, and overreacts to every comment I make about something hurting.

When I need to use the bathroom, he's there, walking me to the toilet with a carefully placed arm around my waist. I cling to him, weaker than ever. The room I'm in isn't large, but it seems to magically expand in size when I'm trying to get to the other side.

The care with which he's treating me stirs up unpleasant, shameful feelings. I don't deserve his compassion. I don't deserve *anyone's* compassion. I was right to be scared of what being in this world could do to me, but I had no idea what kind of monster truly lurked within.

Cleo and Rafaele come by to see me. Rafaele wishes me a quick recovery in a few short words, his voice low and gruff. He stands at the foot of the bed, hands in his pockets, and watches the monitors as if he's silently assessing my condition and verifying if the doctors are right.

Cleo is the opposite. She rushes over to my bedside, hugs me, and then proceeds to ask me a million questions about how I'm doing. Unlike her husband, she pays no attention to the monitors, but she comes up with a long list of things I "absolutely need" for my recovery—a weighted eye mask, lavender-scented pillow spray, and something called a "healing crystal" that she swears by. But despite her slightly ridiculous suggestions, I'm warmed by her genuine concern.

When the men leave the room to get some coffee, she pulls up a chair, sits down, and clasps my hand. "I've been there, you know? My own father held me at gunpoint. Only I didn't manage to save myself like you did. I had to wait for

Nero and Rafe to come to my rescue." She exhales, her gaze distant. "It took me a long time to get over it."

Of course. I've heard the story from Nero's point of view, but I never thought about what it was like for Cleo.

"How did you feel in the aftermath?"

"Angry. And I felt guilty for everything—for being dumb enough to jump into my dad's car, for not fighting his men harder, for being the reason Nero and Sandro got sent away." She blinks at me, her eyes the color of bright emeralds. "And honestly, I can't say that I've stopped feeling guilty, even after all this time."

My face falls, and I look down at my lap.

I feel guilty for what happened to Sandro. I feel guilty for lying to Nero. But I don't feel guilty for killing Ekaterina.

I wish I did.

Because my lack of guilt seems so much worse. It makes me feel sick, messed up, broken. What is wrong with me?

In the days following Cleo and Rafe's visit, Nero doesn't bring up the night I got shot at all, as if he knows talking about it might make me spiral. During the hours I'm awake, he reads to me. Sometimes we play cards, and he lets me win.

There's a delivery one afternoon. An extravagant bouquet of peonies, roses, and lilies of the valley.

Nero brings it to me so that I can smell the flowers. "From Vita. There's a card. She and Gino wanted to visit, but I told them no. I didn't want them to disturb you."

I fish out the small sealed envelope. "You didn't read it?"

"It's for you."

I tear it open and pull out the card. On the front is a painting of flowers, just like the ones in the bouquet, with the words "Get Better Soon" written in cursive. Inside, there's a simple message above a phone number. "Thank you. Remember to call me if you need anything."

Tears prick the backs of my eyes.

Well, here it is. I finally got what I wanted. My favor. My all-important escape plan, should I ever need it.

I should be happy, right?

But I'm not.

Because now I feel even more trapped—trapped being a version of myself I don't recognize.

"ALL OF THE damage in the living room has been repaired," Nero says as he unlocks the front door of the penthouse when we finally leave the hospital a few days later.

I sigh from where I'm sitting in a wheelchair. Despite telling Nero it is completely unnecessary, he insisted on wheeling me in from the car to the elevator.

He's treating me like I'm still fragile, but I've been doing a lot better in the last two days. I'm down to taking only a few Tylenol to manage the pain.

My body is healing, but my soul feels like it's adrift.

He wheels me in, guiding me all the way through the pent-house, and stops in front of my bedroom door. "I got the bathroom completely redone. I don't want anything in there

346

to trigger bad memories of that night, but if it's still too much, let me know."

I blink in surprise. I thought he'd take me to his room. Before this, I was planning to move in there with him, but I just hadn't gotten around to it. "Why don't we go to your room?"

A flicker of emotion crosses his face—something I can't quite read. "We can if you want."

I frown. That's not the enthusiastic response I'd anticipated. He hasn't tried to kiss me since I woke up after the surgery. On the forehead and cheeks, yes, but never on the lips. There've been times I've caught him looking at my mouth, but he's held back.

Why?

Our eyes connect. His are filled with unease, as if he's wrestling with something deep inside.

"No, this is fine," I say, trying to mask the disappointment creeping in.

He nods and leads me into the room, helping me climb up on the bed and then pulling the blanket over me. His movements are gentle, but there's something distant in them, a hesitance that wasn't there before.

I want to ask him what's going on. I want to hear what he thinks about everything that happened. But I'm too afraid to hear his answer, so I keep my questions to myself.

My sleep that night is restless. Whenever I wake up, I find Nero on the other side of the bed, lying on his side. Sometimes his eyes are open, watching me. Other times, they're closed, and his brow is furrowed in his sleep.

I dream of gunshots, men shouting, and cold metal beneath my hands.

When I wake up, the sun's risen, and Nero's gone.

The doctor arrives sometime later, checking on me under Nero's supervision, and he tells me the wound's healing exceptionally well. An older woman brings me my meals. Nero's hired her to be our chef.

By midday, I'm tired of marinating inside my sheets. I throw the covers off, get to my feet, and walk out of the room.

Nero comes around the corner, his eyes widening when he realizes I'm on my feet.

"Blake, slow down."

"You heard the doctor. I'm fine. It barely even hurts anymore." I hike the edge of my pajama top up to show him the wound. It doesn't look pretty, but the skin has begun to heal. "I can't keep lying here all day anymore."

I walk past him into the living room. It looks completely different with the new furniture—two new leather couches, a darker rug, and a glass coffee table. Everything is neat and pristine, as if trying to erase any trace of what happened here.

I pour myself a glass of water in the kitchen, where the countertop and cabinetry have all been replaced. Nero follows me, his gaze flickering with unease. There's obviously something weighing on him.

How much longer am I going to skirt the topic? I blow out a breath. "Nero, what's going on? I can tell something's bothering you."

He presses his palms against the counter, his gaze locked on mine from across the island. The tension in his shoulders tightens, like he's bracing himself for something. "I wanted to wait until you're better."

"Wait for what? I'm better. Just tell me."

He hesitates, his jaw working for a moment. Finally, he exhales. "All right. I'll be right back." He leaves the room and comes back a minute later with a brown envelope in his hand.

He hands it to me. "This is for you."

I open it and dump the contents onto the island.

A passport clatters out from among the documents.

My surroundings dim as I focus on the small booklet. "What is this?"

"A new identity," he says softly. "So you can start over fresh. If you want."

I pick up the passport, my heart lodging in my throat. How did he know this was what I was after? Did he talk to Vita? I never told her exactly what favor I'd ask for, but maybe he guessed.

"You want me to leave?"

"Of course I don't," he says, his words raw and laced with pain. "But I'm giving you a choice. I never should have taken that from you in the first place, but I had to in order to keep you safe then. Now that we've resolved the situation with the Ferraros, I won't hold you here against your will."

"What about the Iron Raptors? Won't they come for me if I leave?"

"I talked to Rafe. He got in contact with their president, and they've negotiated a deal. They're no longer a threat."

I blink through the sudden tears in my eyes. "Why the change of heart? You were so adamant before that I belonged here with you."

"When I found you bleeding out, I knew I couldn't force you to be here anymore. My mother was shot because of my stepdad, but I never blamed him for her death. My mom knew the life she committed to living and the consequences that came with it. She accepted them because she loved him. And you..." He trails off.

My hands begin to shake. *I love you too. As much as someone can love a person when they despise themselves.*

"You never made that commitment," he whispers. "Not willingly. I forced you into it, and I kept telling myself it would all work out fine because I wanted you here with me. But seeing you fighting for your life made me realize I love you more than my own selfish desire to keep you with me. If what you want is a life far away from the darkness that comes with me, I won't stand in your way."

Inside me, something shatters. He's letting me leave. I went to all these lengths to get my own way out, thinking he'd never have the capacity to do this.

And he's proven me wrong.

Nero takes a step forward. "That's what you've always wanted, right? A choice?"

It was. It should be. But the celebratory fireworks I expected to feel right about now are nowhere to be found. Instead, my chest vibrates with a dull ache.

"If you decide to go, I'll help you get anywhere you want to go. And you'll have enough money that you'll never have to work again." His voice breaks, and he turns away from me, his shoulders slumping.

I stare at his back. My hands itch to glide under his shirt, to pull him close and press my cheek against his warmth.

But I can't do that.

I love him, but it's not him I'm running from. I'm running from the person I've become living in his world.

So I say the words, knowing I can never take them back. "I'll leave tomorrow."

CHAPTER 35

NERO

I pace outside Blake's bedroom while the doctor's in there checking to make sure she's clear to travel. Deep down, I'm clinging to the slim hope he'll say she should wait a few more days. Not because I plan to try and change her mind, but because I want to hold on to every last second I can get with her.

There's a gaping hole in my chest where my heart used to be. Who knew doing the right thing could feel so unbearably wrong?

Gino called a few days ago with an update. The Bratva is in disarray with the pakhan dead. Some have already fled town, while the rest are scrambling to select their next leader. The Ferraros are taking advantage of the chaos to pick off everyone who might want the position. Soon, there won't be any candidates left, and the Bratva will retreat.

Gino also told me to report for duty as capo today. I didn't say a word in response. What was there to say? Blake nearly died getting me that title. If anyone deserves my gratitude, it's her—not Gino Ferraro, who risked nothing for this so-called victory.

The doctor comes out of Blake's room, his leather satchel in one hand. "All good. She's doing great. I told her that since she's flying private, she should make sure to move around the cabin when she can."

I'm torn between wanting to hug him and wanting to slit his throat. Blake's going to be fine. That's what matters most. But the selfish bastard in me rages.

She's really getting on a flight today.

"I'm sending a nurse with her too, just in case," I say.

He smiles reassuringly. "She'll be fine. Nero. But I appreciate the precautions you're taking."

"Thanks." My voice barely works as I force the word out.

He pats me on the back and leaves.

Blake's zipping up her suitcase when I walk into her bedroom. She doesn't look my way.

My gaze lingers on her golden hair. "I'll call the car. They should be here in fifteen."

She nods, keeping her back to me. "Thanks."

There's a hurricane inside my chest, and any second now, it'll swallow me whole.

"You sure you don't want me to come with you to the airport?"

Her movements still, and she takes a shuddering breath. "I'm sure."

I leave her room. Minutes crawl by. I'm barely holding it together on the living room sofa, waiting for her to come out with her stuff. I can't do anything but sit here and attempt to breathe. Even glancing at my phone feels like too much.

And then she's here, dressed in a pair of jeans and a zip-up sweater. "Could you grab my bag? The doctor told me not to lift anything heavy for a while."

"Of course," I manage to choke out.

I bring the suitcase to the foyer, and we stand by the front door and stare at each other for a few long, painful moments.

I keep hoping she won't do it. That at the last second, she'll change her mind and stay.

Don't go. Please don't go. Choose me. I know I'm not perfect, but I will spend the rest of my days loving you better than anyone else ever can. I'll make all of the darkness that comes with me worth it. I promise.

Her lips part and tremble. Can she hear my thoughts? Can she see them written all over my face?

I don't get to keep her against her will, but if she *chooses* to stay, if she *chooses* to be with—

Her gaze drops to the floor. Without another word, she opens the front door, wheels her suitcase out, and slips away.

My lungs seize as I take in a painful breath.

She's gone.

I stand there staring at the door for what feels like an eternity, knowing this moment will forever be imprinted in my memory.

The moment I lost everything.

Eventually, my feet carry me into her bedroom. Standing here, it's so easy to imagine she's coming right back.

The books she read over the last few days are still sitting on the nightstand. Her extra blanket is folded neatly at the foot of the bed. There's an empty mug from the tea she had this morning on the dresser.

Get out of here.

I can't.

It's awful and heart-wrenching, but some part of me craves the torture. It craves the dull ache at the back of my throat, the tightness behind my eyes, and the way I can't breathe when I remember her being here just moments ago.

I rewind the last few months, looking for all the places I went wrong. It's not hard to find them. So many mistakes made, so many lies told.

I had thought we could make it despite all of it. That our connection was strong enough to withstand the weight of everything else. Maybe that's the problem with never having loved anyone before her—I made love into something mythical, something that can conquer all.

But maybe love is simpler than that. Maybe it's just doing the right thing for the other person, even if it tears you apart.

CHAPTER 36

BLAKE

"Where are you flying to, Mrs. De Luca?"

I muster up a smile for the driver, who's probably been watching me dab at my tears with my sleeve for the last thirty minutes. "San Francisco."

"Beautiful city. You're visiting family?"

"A friend." With the Iron Raptors no longer a threat, I called Del last night and asked if I could stay with her for a bit.

"I hope you enjoy it. We're just five minutes away from the airport."

I wrap my arms around myself.

Yesterday, when I made my decision to leave, I thought it would bring some comfort, but I barely slept all night. I kept waiting for a gut feeling to hit, for something to reassure me that I'm doing the right thing.

It never came.

The car glides through the airport gates, and the private terminal comes into view. I should be relieved that by the end of today, I'll be sitting in Del's living room. Instead, there's a gnawing sense of loss deep inside my belly.

I couldn't stomach saying goodbye to Nero without crumbling. So I said nothing. I just left.

It's been less than forty minutes, and I already miss him. I miss his touch. I miss his smell. I miss the way his skin feels beneath my hands. The whispered endearments. The kisses against my hair. The way his hands feel enveloping mine. I miss the burn of his scruff against my thighs. The silkiness of his hair as I run it through my fingers.

Most of all, I miss his eyes. The way they can say so much without him saying a word.

I did the right thing. So why doesn't any part of it feel good?

The driver stops at the entrance, and I force myself to move, to get out of the car, to walk into the terminal. I barely register the sleek private waiting area or the woman who greets me with a polite smile and offers me a coffee.

I choke out, "No, thank you," and then sit down in the farthest chair in the corner, hoping she won't try to start a conversation.

This is for the best.

That's what I keep telling myself, but it's not working. The truth is, I don't want to go. I don't want to leave Nero, even though I know staying means losing more of who I used to be. Who I've always thought I should be. The person I've become in his world is someone I hardly recognize—a person who can kill without guilt, who can justify the unthinkable.

But I love him.

God, do I love him.

And maybe that's why I have to go—because the love I have for him is too big, too consuming, and it's turning me into someone I don't want to be.

A soft chime echoes through the waiting area, and a woman in a uniform appears in the doorway. "Mrs. De Luca, we're ready to board."

I nod. The motion feels mechanical, like I'm watching someone else move my head. I wipe my clammy palms against my jeans and get to my feet.

The woman leads me through the terminal, the sound of our footsteps muffled by the thick carpet. We reach the door that opens out to the tarmac where the private jet is waiting. The stairs have been lowered, and there's a lone figure standing at the bottom, ready to escort me up.

We step outside.

This is it.

All I have to do is walk up those stairs, and I'll be free. Free from the life that's twisted me into something unrecogniz-able. Free from the love that's somehow both the best thing and the worst thing that's happened to me.

But my feet won't move.

I bite down on my lips to stop them from quivering and stand there, staring at the steps.

It's like my body is rebelling against my mind.

Go. Just go. You've made your choice, and now you have to live with it.

"Blake!"

The sound of my name jolts me from my thoughts.

"Blake, wait!"

It's Cleo. She's running toward me, her red hair whipping around her face. My eyes widen. Why is she here? Did Nero send her? If he's decided he won't let me leave after all, why didn't he come himself?

And why does the thought of him forcing me to stay fill me with so much damn relief?

Cleo comes to a stop before me and bends over, pressing her palms against her knees. "Fuck, Gem's right. I'm out of shape," she pants. "Give me a second."

"What are you doing here?" My voice trembles, caught somewhere between relief and confusion.

She tilts her head up, looking at me from under her thick lashes. "Rafe told me you're leaving on his plane. And I just..." She takes a few short breaths. "I kept thinking about our conversation at the hospital, about how I told you I still felt guilty about all the crap that went down when I got taken by my dad, and I just got this idea in my head that maybe I scared you. You had this freaked-out look on your face. I didn't mean that I think you'll never feel better about what happened, or something crazy like that. I mean, I am totally fine! I say stupid, thoughtless things *all* the time. I didn't mean to make you want to run away."

A nearly hysterical laugh bubbles out of me. "Cleo, the problem isn't what I'm feeling. It's what I'm *not* feeling. I *don't* feel guilty for shooting Ekaterina. Not even a little bit." My voice chokes. "I don't know who I am anymore. I don't know who I've become."

Cleo's gaze softens. She takes a step closer, her eyes searching mine. "That's what's bugging you?"

"I'm all twisted up," I whimper. "My dad was a criminal too. He was a terrible person. I spent all my life trying to prove to everyone in my town that I wasn't anything like him. That I was good. That I had integrity. And within weeks of being here, I've become a killer. I'm not even sorry that I killed Ekaterina."

Cleo reaches out and gently cups my face with both hands, her thumbs brushing away my tears. "I get it. You're scared, and that's okay. But don't think for a second that what you did means you're some kind of monster. You did what you had to do to survive."

"I'm scared of who I'm becoming." The words barely make it past the lump in my throat. "I want to be with Nero, but I'm terrified of what being with him is turning me into."

She sighs. "Come with me. Let's sit down and talk this through. No pressure, no expectations. Just two girls having a conversation."

I hesitate, my gaze shifting back to the stairs of the plane.

"It'll still be here after we talk if you decide you still want to go," Cleo says. "I promise. He's our guy, so he's on our clock."

Talking to someone sounds...nice. But I don't know Cleo all that well. Can I trust her?

Screw it. I've got nothing to lose.

So I nod. "Okay."

We walk back to the terminal in silence, the wind tugging at our hair and clothes. Inside, Cleo leads me to a small café I hadn't noticed before and finds us a table close to the window.

"Let's get some food," Cleo suggests. Her voice is light, but there's an undertone of concern. "I always think better on a full stomach."

I manage a small smile. "That sounds nice."

She orders for both of us—club sandwiches, chips, and two glasses of Coke. When the food arrives, she nudges one of the plates toward me, her emerald eyes urging me to take a bite.

I pick up the sandwich and nibble at the corner. It's bland and unappealing, but it's something to focus on other than the storm of emotions inside me.

"So," Cleo begins, her tone gentle, "why don't you tell me exactly what's on your mind?"

I put the sandwich down. "I feel like I've lost myself in this dark, ruthless world."

Cleo nods, her expression thoughtful. "I get that. Believe me, I do."

"Do you? Doesn't it just feel normal to you? You grew up in it."

"And I hated every second of it. My parents were awful, just like your dad. I decided from an early age I wanted *nothing* to do with this life. I swore I'd never marry a mobster, and that I'd find a way to leave this world and all the things that go with it—the violence, the danger, the constant moral compromises."

My eyes widen with shock.

She smirks. "What? Nero never told you? The only reason I married Rafe was to help my sister, Gem. She was engaged to Rafe but fell in love with another guy. I walked down that aisle swearing to myself that I'd never have a real relationship with him. I was convinced that besides being smoking hot, he had no redeeming qualities."

I drag my Coke closer and take a sip. "How did you deal with it?"

Cleo's lips press together as she considers her words. "It wasn't easy. There were times I questioned everything—my choices, my morals, my sense of right and wrong. But what I realized is that it's not about shutting out the darkness completely. It's about finding a way to shine your light, even when the darkness is all around you."

I swallow hard, her words hitting close to home. "But what if I can't?"

She reaches across the table, takes my hand in hers, and squeezes it gently. "Why did you shoot Ekaterina?"

"Because she was about to kill me."

"And how did you get into that situation in the first place?"

"I...I guess I was alone in the bathroom with her because I had tried to find a way to get help. For Nero and I."

"So you did something really damn brave to help save the man you love. What's monstrous about that?"

362

I bite down on the corner of my mouth.

"Do you love Nero?"

"Yes," I answer softly.

"Why do you love him?"

A million reasons come to mind. "The way he takes total responsibility for his actions. I've never met anyone who does it to the same extent that he does. When he makes mistakes, he commits fully to fixing them. I admire that a lot about him."

Cleo stays silent, letting me continue.

"I love how loyal he is, and how far he's willing to go for the people he loves."

She smiles. "I know a bit about that."

"His love is intense, possessive, all-consuming. He doesn't hold anything back. And that can be overwhelming sometimes, but most of the time..."

"It just takes your breath away in the best kind of way?"

"Exactly."

Cleo's eyes sparkle with amusement. "If you were ever locked up in jail in a foreign country, and you had one phone call, who—"

"I'd call him." I don't even need to think about it.

"So you trust him with your life?"

"Yes. And he's just...fun." A smile tugs on my lips. "He has a sense of humor. He's so confident. And he's a great cook. And he's stupidly hot."

Cleo laughs. "That's a lot of good qualities for someone who's a killer."

"I don't think of him as one. When I look at him, that's not who I see."

"It sounds like you've accepted the darkness in him. You just haven't accepted the darkness within you."

My eyes widen. Accept the darkness within me? The very thought sends a shiver down my spine. "I'm not sure I can."

"There's darkness in all of us. You don't have to embrace it, but you do have to accept that it's part of you. It doesn't define you. It's just one piece of the puzzle." She takes a sip of her drink. "By the way, there are plenty of people not in the mob who do bad things."

She's right. People like Brett.

People like me.

"But where there's darkness, there's light. And just like you listed all the light you see in Nero, I'm sure he could tell you all the light he sees in you. He's probably the one who sees it better than anyone, because he needs it."

"What do you mean?"

"Sometimes, Rafe comes home with the heavy scent of cruelty and fear practically radiating off him. I don't delude myself by thinking he just pushes some papers around at a desk. But when he comes to me, no matter what kind of a day he's had, he's still my husband. My love. My best friend. And there's something beautiful in being that one person this powerful, terrifying man can just drop the mask and be himself with."

Tears well up again, but this time, they're not just tears of fear and despair. There's a swell of hope there too, a reminder of this great foundation of love, loyalty, and even integrity that Nero and I share.

Cleo's voice softens even more. "You don't have to do this alone, Blake. And you don't have to run away to protect yourself. You're stronger than you think."

I take a shaky breath, tightening my grip around Cleo's hand. "But what if staying means I lose the best parts of myself? What if I become someone even Nero won't recognize?"

She gives me a reassuring smile. "Nero fell in love with you because of who you are, not because of the things you've done. And he knows that the world he's brought you into has its own dangers. But he loves you, and he'll help you through it. You just have to give him the chance."

Can I?

The clouds outside part, and sunlight pours through the window, warming my skin. Something shifts inside me. The fear is still there, but it's no longer paralyzing. I don't have all the answers, but I know one thing for sure. I don't want to run away.

"Thank you," I whisper, squeezing her hand one last time before letting go.

Her eyes are filled with warmth. "Anytime. Now, let's finish our lunch and then figure out what you want to do next."

I pick up the sandwich and take a few more bites. What to do next...

Ah. Of course. "I want to go back to Nero, but I need to make a stop somewhere first," I say, glancing at Cleo. "Do you mind if I make a quick call?"

"Sure."

I dig inside my purse for my phone and the small "Get Well" card I kept, then dial the number written on it.

"Vita? It's Blake. I'd like to meet."

CHAPTER 37

NERO

Ring. Ring. Ring.

I'm sprawled out on Blake's bed like a giant fucking starfish, staring blankly at the ceiling.

My head throbs with a pounding rhythm. My chest aches. I've been lying here like this ever since she left, unable to get myself to do anything else.

Ring. Ring. Ring.

Whoever's calling can go straight into the fiery pits of hell. I hope they suffer as they burn.

Ring. Ring. Ring.

That's the phone connected to the concierge desk. *Alec, take a hint.* I'm not interested in visitors. Closed for appointments until next month. Scratch that, next year. It's fucking February, so yeah. Perfect.

Ring. Ring. Ring.

I'm going to fucking kill whoever this is.

I sit up. My body protests, every muscle feeling like it's been replaced with lead. I stomp over to the front door and snatch the phone off the cradle. "*What?*"

"Alessio Ferraro is here for you, sir."

"Tell him to fuck right off," I growl.

"Sir, please! I'm afraid I can't say that."

"Why not?"

"He's not taking no for an answer."

"What's the point of having security here? Where are they?"

"They're here. Cowering."

"Jesus, fuck," I mutter. "Okay. Whatever. Send him up."

I drag my palms over my face, exhaling a heavy breath before moving to unlock the door. A few moments later, the elevator dings and slides open.

A groan escapes me at the unwelcome sight of the man. He looks like the fucking grim reaper in his uniform of all black.

He steps out of the elevator. "You're three hours late for work."

"You know what? Fuck you. I really don't want to do this with you right now."

I try to swing the door shut, but he stops it with his foot. "You're a capo now. You've got people to boss around. Money to collect. Businesses to run."

"I said... Fuck. You."

368

I push at the door, but he pushes right back just as hard.

Ugh. Whatever. If he wants to come in and annoy me, he can go ahead.

I let him in and walk away, heading straight for the bar in the corner of the living room. I grab a glass decanter filled with whiskey and pour myself a glass.

Alessio watches silently as I splash in a large messy pour, then he lifts his eyes to mine.

We maintain eye contact as I down the entire thing.

"What's wrong with you?" he asks as I slam the glass down and move to refill it.

"Everything."

"Where's Blake?"

"Gone."

"Where did she go?"

"San Francisco. And she's not coming back."

"Why not?"

"Because we're over, Alessio. We're done. So fuck you, and fuck the Ferraros, and fuck being a capo. I don't give a fuck if you want to kill me. Go ahead and put me out of my misery, will you?" I don't care anymore. Not now that Blake's decided I'm not worth the trouble that comes with me.

I move to the sofa and sit down with my whiskey. Outside, the sun is peeking through the gray clouds as if it's just any other day. It doesn't give a fuck that my life is over. I pick up the remote that controls the blinds and bring them all the way down.

Alessio sits across from me. "As your old boss, I'm supposed to make sure you successfully transition to your new position."

I ignore him and take a big sip.

The whiskey doesn't even burn as it goes down my throat. A pleasant haze wraps around my mind, softening the harsh edges of reality. I put the glass down and close my eyes, hoping to sink into that haze, but instead, I see Blake standing by the front door, looking at me with those haunting blue eyes, right before she walks out.

Letting her go was the right thing to do. I had to let her choose, to let her decide what kind of a life she wants for herself. It was probably the most selfless act of my entire miserable existence.

But it feels like I let my heart walk out the door with her, leaving nothing but a broken husk inside my chest.

I hear Alessio get to his feet and walk away.

Asshole. He's threatened to kill me on more than one occasion, but when I actually want him to do it, he fucking leaves.

Pressing the heels of my palms against my forehead, I let out a groan.

I thought I knew heartbreak, but this feels even worse than the agony I felt when I drove Blake from Missouri to Vegas and then to New York. She wanted nothing to do with me then, but at least she was with me. Her hurt and anger dimmed my world, but it didn't drain it of color the way her absence does now. Everything feels gray, empty.

"Drink this." Something clanks against the coffee table.

I crack one eye open. Alessio brought me water.

"Did you spike it with arsenic?"

"You have a morbid sense of humor."

"I thought you of all people might appreciate it." I gulp half the glass down. Maybe if I drink it, he'll finally leave.

"Do you have someone I can call? Someone who could...fix this?"

"It's unfixable."

Alessio sighs. "I'll have to talk to Dad about it. He won't be happy you didn't show up on day one."

"I don't—"

"Give a fuck. I know." He rubs his palm over his head, looking befuddled. "This is why I don't have friends. People are too complicated."

"You seem to know how to crack 'em well."

"They're only simple when their life is at stake. Everyone just wants to survive."

"Not me."

"Hence the confusion," he mutters.

I finish the water, put the glass back down, and curl up on the sofa. I don't want to talk anymore. I don't want to think anymore. I just want darkness to claim me so that I don't feel anything.

Just when I'm about to cross over the line into unconsciousness, I feel someone drape a blanket over me.

"GET UP."

Something nudges against my leg. I ignore it.

"Nero, get up."

"Mmm, leave me alone." I lift my leg onto whatever surface I'm currently lying on and turn on my side, away from the person making all that noise.

It works. I'm left alone. Slowly, I'm pulled back into the dark—

WHOOSH.

Cold! Oh fuck, that's cold!

I sit up with a gasp. "What the fuck!"

A lot of things register quickly. I'm on the sofa, my shirt is drenched, and there's someone standing over me, but it's too fucking bright to see who it is.

I raise my hand, shielding my eyes. "Rafe?"

"How long have you been lying here like this?" Rafe demands, sounding annoyed.

I groan again. Why would he open the blinds? I'm disoriented, dizzy, thirsty, and my retinas feel like they've been burned.

"I don't know. What time is it?" I pluck at my wet T-shirt.

"Six p.m."

Which means it's only been four hours since Blake left. It feels like I've been out for far longer than that.

My gaze meets Rafe's. "Why are you here?"

"Alessio called me. I was in a meeting in Albany. Drove here as soon as I could."

"You didn't need to do that. I'm fine."

Rafe rolls his eyes. "You smell like you bathed in whiskey."

"I think I slept it off. Mostly."

"I'm taking you to the park. You need to be taken for a walk and aired out."

"I'm not a fucking puppy," I mutter.

His gaze narrows. "What's that?"

Ugh. That's his don't-give-me-that-shit voice. He's not gonna leave until I do as he says.

"Never mind." I push off the sofa and get to my feet. That's a mistake. Everything wobbles until Rafe grabs my elbow and steadies me.

He sighs. "I should have come here as soon as you said you needed the plane for Blake. Why did you let her go?"

I extract my elbow from his grip. "Because it was the right thing to do. There's nothing more lethal than a woman who makes you want to do the right thing, is there?"

The hard lines of his expression soften. "C'mon. Go put on a new shirt, and let's go. You can wax philosophical once we're outside."

We take a taxi to Central Park. The place is crowded with tourists, dog walkers, and old men hunched over chessboards. We grab coffee from a truck and amble down a winding path.

"I never brought Blake here," I tell Rafe. "Tried to once—the day we got the pakhan. Maksim showed up just as we were about to go, and that was that." Now I'm never going to get the chance to take that walk with her. My throat tightens.

"Tell me what happened this morning."

"She nearly died from that bullet wound, Rafe. I forced her into this marriage, into this world, and she nearly fucking died because of it. So I gave her the freedom to make her own choice." I exhale. "She chose to go back to a normal life over a life with me."

Rafe sips on his coffee. "Why?"

"Probably because she didn't want to end up like my mom. Killed while out for dinner."

"She was worried about her safety?"

"She didn't say that explicitly. She didn't say anything, really. She just said she was going to leave, and the next day—today—she was gone."

Rafe's expression remains unreadable as we continue walking, but I can tell he's thinking, analyzing. He's always been the calculated one, the one who plans ten steps ahead. That's why he's a don, and I'm just the capo drowning in whiskey and regret.

"You're an idiot," he finally says.

I snap my head to the side, glaring at him. "Excuse me?"

"You heard me. You're an idiot." He takes another sip. "Giving her the choice to stay was the right move, but letting her go without even fucking asking her to explain herself was foolish."

My anger spikes. "What right did I have to do that?"

Rafe stops walking and turns to face me, his eyes hard and unyielding. "You're not the only one hurting in the aftermath of the shit show that went down with the pakhan. Do you think your wife isn't going through stuff? You gave her a choice, sure. But did you ever consider that she might not want that choice? That she wasn't in any state to make a decision that big, that quickly?"

I frown, unsure how to respond.

"How did you behave around her after she got shot?" he presses.

"I was caring, concerned, maybe a bit overbearing." I swallow. "And...distant."

"Why?"

"Because I feel guilty!"

"And so you pushed her away," Rafe says, stepping closer. "You pushed her away prematurely in case she chose to leave. You probably thought it'd make your pain easier to handle—which is bullshit, by the way. Ask me how I fucking know." He scoffs. "When she needed you the most, you shut down and made her feel like she was alone in this world. Blake didn't need you to give her an out from this life. She needed you to be with her in it. To face it together."

I clench my jaw, the words hitting a nerve. Is it possible he's right? "I *was* there with her. I watched her fight for her life after she got a bullet in her belly. She never would've been shot if it weren't for me."

"We are all responsible for our own decisions, Nero. You told me she wanted to go through with Gino's plot. She knew the risks involved."

I shake my head. "Did she?"

"Don't be condescending. Of course she did. She's not an idiot. Whatever her motivations were, she thought it was worth it."

She wanted to help *me* so that I wouldn't be Alessio's lackey anymore. She wanted to get me out of a situation that a normal fucking man would never even find himself in.

We sit down on a bench. Ordinary people move past us—people whose daily lives aren't defined by life-or-death stakes.

I never wanted to be one of them.

Until now.

Something swift and silent tears through my chest. "I don't want to be a gangster anymore."

In my periphery, I see Rafe look at me.

My palms press against the bench, my fingers wrapping around its edge. "What the fuck is the point of this? Any of this? I always thought living this life would make me the right kind of man. A man who deserves respect. A man who can provide. Who can protect. But that's not true, is it? It was a fantasy I created for myself. I just didn't want to become like my father—stubbornly principled and useless."

"You're missing the point."

"Am I?"

"It's not about whether you're a mobster or not. Maybe the problem is you romanticized the lifestyle, and now that you love someone, you're finally realizing it's not all sunshine and rainbows. There are trade-offs. Ones I'm very familiar with."

Fuck. Is Rafe right? Have I romanticized this life up until now? Perhaps. And in doing so, maybe I dismissed Blake's fears instead of figuring out how we could tackle them together head-on. She was afraid being in this world would change her, and I kept telling her she was wrong...but was she?

Haven't I noticed the change in her? She became more cautious here in New York. And also more bold and more brave.

Instead of denying reality, I could have acknowledged it. And I could have reassured her that even though she was adapting to her circumstances, it wasn't something she had to fear. I could have told her that nothing would ever take her inherent goodness away. That if anything, her goodness shone even fucking brighter in the shadows.

But none of that would have saved her from getting shot. That happened because of me, because of who I am.

I glance at Rafe. "Pretty big trade-offs, don't you think? Let's just be honest about it for once. The people we love? They're never truly safe. There's always a target on our backs, which means there's a target on theirs."

"Would you throw yourself in front of a bullet to save Blake?"

"Of course. I wish I'd had the opportunity to do that when Ekaterina shot her."

"You think the average person has someone who's willing to do that for them? I know this life is hard, Nero, but don't be so fucking arrogant to think we've got it worse than everyone else. Sure, there's always a target on our backs, but we have armies to protect the ones we love. We move mountains to keep them safe."

I stay silent, absorbing his words.

"That man you've always wanted to be? A protector, a provider, a man who people respect? You are him, but not because you're a mobster. Not because of some fucking label. How many made guys do you know who aren't any of those things? You are that man because of your character and your actions. And I'm pretty fucking sure Blake can see that."

"Then why did she leave?"

"Maybe she just needs some time to process what happened. Maybe it's not over yet."

I huff a breath. "I don't need to torture myself with false hope."

"Have a little faith."

"You know I'm a fucking atheist."

Rafe tsks. "Your nonna would be disappointed. Did Blake leave with her wedding ring still on?"

I think back to this morning. "She did."

"Then maybe she's not as sure about what she wants as you think."

I pull my hand out of my pocket and look at my own gold wedding band. The one I put on myself at the jewelry store when I bought it along with Blake's diamond band.

I wish Blake had slid it on my finger. I wish she'd smiled at me while she did it. I wish she'd kissed me afterward and said she loves me.

Too bad wishing for things doesn't make them real.

CHAPTER 38

NERO

Rafe drops me off at home and tells me to call him if I need anything.

I check my phone. No missed calls since Alessio this morning. Not even an angry phone call from Gino. I wonder how he reacted when Alessio told him I didn't show up. Maybe he's cutting me some slack because my wife got shot during a mission he sent us on, but I'm not under any fucking illusions.

He'll expect me back on duty soon. Tomorrow, or the next day.

But not tonight.

With a groan, I sink into the sofa. I've drunk enough today, but the itch is still there. The whiskey bottle glares at me from across the room, daring me.

I try to resist. I really do. But after a few minutes, I give in and pour myself another glass. I take a long swig. I want the burn to chase away the edges of despair gnawing at my insides, but it doesn't work. The alcohol doesn't numb me the way it used to. The pain is still there, sharp and unyielding.

As I lift the glass to my lips again, Rafe's words echo in my mind.

"You pushed her away prematurely in case she chose to leave. You probably thought it'd make your pain easier to handle—which is bullshit, by the way."

I lower the glass and stare at the oscillating liquid. Was I really that fucking blind? Blake had been trying to tell me something, something I'd dismissed because I couldn't—or wouldn't—face it.

She'd been afraid of what she was becoming—afraid that loving me, being with me, was changing her into someone she didn't recognize. And instead of facing that fear with her, I let her face it alone.

The thought slices through me like a blade.

I grab the remote and turn on the stereo, desperate for anything to drown out my thoughts. A few taps on my phone, and *Dummy* by Portishead streams through the speakers. It's an album that always takes me places. I hope it'll take me far away from here, because if my thoughts keep spiraling, I'm going to go after Blake, and I can't do that.

I can't undo the decision she made for herself, no matter how much it fucking hurts.

My body melts into the sofa, and my eyes drift shut. I'm more tired than I realized, because soon, sleep tugs at me.

In my dream, I'm at a restaurant having a good meal with Rafe, Sandro, and some of the other guys. We're shooting the shit. The servers bring out the food, and it's decadent. Perfectly cooked steak, crispy potatoes, sautéed wild mushrooms… They keep placing side dishes until there's no space left on the table.

The food's good, but the conversation's better. We weave from one topic to the next, cracking jokes and busting each other's chops. I'm electric, in my element, among my people.

A lightness fills my chest. This is what I used to love so much. The feeling of brotherhood. Of belonging.

We're men who do bad things, but we also know how to be good to each other.

Light and dark. Yin and yang.

Suddenly, Rafe and the guys disappear in a swirl of smoke, and when the smoke dissipates, it's *her* I see.

Blake stands in front of the table, her body poured into a stunning midnight-blue dress.

"Glory Box" comes on, the first few soulful notes resonating through the restaurant.

I reach for the glass of whiskey I've got in front of me and lift it to my lips. "I hate my own mind sometimes."

She slides into the booth beside me. "Why's that?"

"It won't let me forget you, even in my dreams."

Her hands come up to my chest. "Your dreams?"

"*You're* a dream. A beautiful dream. But when I wake up, you'll be gone."

She steals the whiskey from my hand and presses her lips against the same spot mine just touched. "I'm not going anywhere."

I cup her jaw. She feels so damn real in my hands. "Goddamn it," I whisper. "Do you think I'm strong enough to withstand this? To have you here whenever I close my eyes? Taunting me with your beauty, your wit, your perfectly pink lips..."

She exhales a harsh breath.

I drop my hand and take my glass back from her. "I didn't think you were so cruel."

"Wake up."

I swing my head from side to side. "No."

"If I'm a dream, when you open your eyes, you won't see me anymore."

My chest heaves. She's right. All I have to do is open my eyes...and see that she's not really here...

I huff a defeated chuckle. "Never mind, then. There is no peace for me, not here, and not there. If I have to choose my purgatory, I may as well stay in the one that has you in it."

The music stops.

My eyes snap open. "Hey—"

The living room comes into focus. I'm still on the sofa.

And Blake—the real Blake—is sitting beside me.

My heart skips a beat.

"Sunshine," I breathe. "You came back."

She smiles, her eyes glistening. "I did. I couldn't get on that plane. I couldn't leave you."

I blink. And she's still here. Warm and real. "Why?"

She climbs onto my lap and wraps her arms around my neck. "Because I realized something. A truth I've been fighting against ever since I was a kid. I've spent my life putting people into two boxes—good or bad—and it wasn't until you that I realized people aren't that simple. No one is. Not even me."

I brush her golden hair away from her face. "That's true, there's nothing simple about you. Trying to fit you into a box would be like trying to contain all the beauty of the universe inside a single glass jar."

Her teeth dig into her bottom lip. "Let me finish before you make me cry."

A smile tugs on my lips. "I'm sorry. I'll shut up."

She takes a deep breath. "I never told you this, but I forgave you for what happened in Darkwater Hollow a while ago. I've learned to trust you again. And I've fallen for you. Again."

For a moment, I just stare at her, unable to speak.

Fallen for me. Could that be true?

I swallow hard. "You know who I am..."

"Yes," she says, her fingertips brushing softly over my cheek. "I do. I see *all* of you—the light and the dark—and I love both."

My heart feels like it's about to break out of my chest.

"I realized it when you took me to your beach house. I spent so long judging you for who you were, but all that judgment just melted away there. All that was left was the man I love. The man who knows me better than I know myself. The man who'd do anything for me."

My throat tightens. "If you felt that way at the beach house, why did you leave?"

"Because I had to come to terms with my own darkness. My own sins." She sighs, her voice trembling slightly. "I was scared, Nero. So scared of losing myself completely. When I killed Ekaterina, I didn't feel guilty, and it felt like I lost my humanity. In the end, it wasn't your darkness I was fighting, it was my own. Somehow, it was easier for me to love you than to love myself."

I cradle the back of her head with my hand. "I understand now. And I'm sorry I didn't give you the space you needed to process all that. I dismissed your concerns, pretending you could stay the same when everything around you had changed. You were right. That's impossible. But, baby, while you change and grow based on your experiences here, I'll be right there by your side, supporting you through it all. You never have to feel ashamed or afraid to show me any new part of you. I love it all—the dark, the light, the gray."

A tear escapes and slides down her cheek. "I know."

I wipe the tear away, a grin tugging on my lips. "Pinch me, will you? I need to know this isn't an illusion. Men like me don't get everything they could possibly want, do they?"

She doesn't pinch me. Instead, she leans forward and presses her lips to mine.

Electricity surges through me, just like that very first time we kissed, back when we were both different people. I was Rowan, the man who'd lost himself, and she was Blake, the woman who would never fall for a criminal.

So much has changed.

But not this. Not our connection. It's something that defies reason and logic and just *is*.

I slide my fingers into her hair and deepen the kiss with a groan. She moves closer, digging her nails into my shoulders.

I'm instantly hard. Having my wife back in my arms is all it fucking takes.

She breaks the kiss and presses her forehead against mine, panting against my lips. "God, I missed you. Just a few hours, and I missed you like crazy."

"When you left, you took a piece of me with you," I whisper. "The most vital one."

"I know. And now I'm here to give it back." She folds her hands over my heart.

A cocktail of emotions shoots up through my veins.

Exhilaration. Desire. *Love*.

She pulls back, meets my gaze, and gives me a breathless smile. "I love you, Nero."

Fuck.

I can't take it anymore. I need to feel all of her, to have her close, closer than this, closer than words can bring us.

In one swift movement, I stand up, gripping her by her thighs. She makes a surprised gasp, her arms clinging to my shoulders, her eyes locked on mine.

"I need to be inside of you," I whisper against her lips as I carry her through the penthouse to my bedroom.

The bedroom where my wife belongs.

We fall onto the bed.

My mouth crashes onto hers, the kiss fueled by the need to make her feel every bit of desire that's raging inside me.

Her hands roam over my back, my hair, pulling me closer, urging me on. I press my body against hers, savoring every curve, every inch of the woman who's made me whole again.

I pull away just enough to peel off her clothes, revealing inch after inch of flawless pale skin.

When she's completely bare on the bed, her hair fanned out on the sheets, I lift her leg and press a kiss to the inside of her ankle.

A blush spreads across her cheeks. "What happened to needing to be inside me?"

"I got distracted by the view," I murmur, trailing my lips up her calf. "I've never seen anything as beautiful as my wife spread out naked on my bed."

She grins. "You mean our bed, right?"

"Not until we christen it." I put her foot down flat against the mattress and place the next kiss against her inner thigh. Goosebumps ripple over her skin. "So for now, you're in my territory, and I get to do whatever I want with you." I place a kiss right against her slit and drag my tongue through her folds.

Her taste—exquisite. Her moans—pure bliss. But fuck, it's the way she clutches my hair when her orgasm sweeps over, the way she rubs her cunt against my face that makes me nearly lose it.

I shove my jeans off and move up her body, hovering over her as she catches her breath. Her expression is dazed but determined as she flips onto her belly, pushes herself up, and hikes up her ass.

The sight of her makes me groan.

"Inside, now," she demands, but I'm already on my knees behind her, spreading her thighs and running my fingers over her slick core.

The moment I thrust into her, my mind goes blank. There's nothing but us—just me, her, and this perfect moment. Slowly, I pull out, savoring the way she arches her back and pushes her ass up even more, as if inviting me back in.

"I can't believe I get to do this for the rest of my life," I mutter, entranced as I thrust back in.

She tosses her hair over her shoulder, glancing back at me with hooded eyes. "Same."

A grin tugs at my lips. *Mine.* She's all mine.

I reach for that hair—my obsession—and coil it around my fist, making her arch just a little more. "Hold on, baby."

The second her hands wrap around the top edge of the mattress, I give her my all.

I pound into her, hard and fast, my balls slapping against her clit, her moans getting louder and louder. The ten-thousand-dollar bedframe, supposedly unbreakable, makes a worrying creak.

Fuck it. If it breaks, we keep going.

I feel her pussy start to spasm around me. "Oh God, Nero. So. Good."

I release her hair, gripping her thighs as my own orgasm rushes through me—a wild, consuming force. My eyes squeeze shut, and I let out a low groan as my cum spills out of my cock in harsh spurts.

I nearly collapse on top of her but catch myself just before I crush her small form into the mattress, rolling us over instead. We lie there panting and trembling. It's perfect.

After a long moment, she moves to tuck herself under my arm, fitting perfectly against my side.

She lays her hand flat against my chest. "I have to tell you something."

I trace her spine with my knuckle. "Yeah?"

"I've been hiding something from you for a while."

The tense note in her voice cuts through my blissful haze. "Okay. What is it?"

She exhales a heavy breath. "When I met with Vita for lunch that one time before we agreed to Gino's plan, I asked for something in exchange for convincing you to do it. A favor. She said I could ask for anything. Initially, I was going to ask her to help me leave you."

My lungs empty out.

"It tore me up lying to you," she says softly. "I made it seem like the only reason I wanted to go through with this mission was to help you, but really, I had my own selfish motive."

That's what it was... The guilty look I noticed in her eyes when we were at the beach house.

"Will you forgive me?"

I press a kiss against her head. "There's nothing to forgive."

The tension that slipped into her body eases. "Well, she still owed me that favor. Before I came here, I went to see her." She lifts her head off his chest and meets my gaze. "I asked her to get Gino to let you go so you can be Rafaele's consigliere again."

What?

The air seems to leave the room all at once. I stare at her, dumbfounded. "Baby, that's—"

"It's done."

"No way." Impossible. Gino would never.

A grin tugs on her lips. "It's done. It's happening."

"How?" I choke out.

"Can't you tell Vita's got Gino wrapped around her little finger? Took a few hours of them talking, but she made it happen. You're back."

I sit up, turn to face her on the bed, and cup her cheeks. That world that seemed so gray just before she came back is fucking technicolor now.

"I love you so fucking much, Sunshine." There is nothing, absolutely nothing in the world, I won't do for her.

And when she smiles at me with that twinkle in her eyes, I know she knows it too.

EPILOGUE

NERO

KT Bar & Grille in Hazard, Kentucky, isn't the kind of place you'd bring a date.

The floors are sticky, and the smell of stale beer hangs in the air. A neon sign buzzes softly in the corner, casting a sickly green light that barely reaches the rest of the room. There's a jukebox in the corner, but it's silent, and the only sound is the low murmur of the few patrons scattered around the bar.

It's the sort of place that feels forgotten, tucked away from the rest of the world. It's the sort of place where people go when they don't want to be found.

"Another one?"

I nod, sliding my empty glass toward the bartender. He refills it with Angel's Envy and passes it back.

"You been to these parts before?"

"Not really," I say from beneath my cap. "Drove through once or twice."

"What brings you to Kentucky?"

"Just visiting a friend."

A friend who's running late. I check my watch and sip my drink. Patience has never been my strong suit.

The door to the outside opens, letting in a gust of wind. I listen to the sound of the newcomer's footsteps—heavy, evenly spaced.

Is it him?

The man takes a stool two seats down from mine at the bar.

"Hey, Brett. The usual?" the bartender asks.

I smile to myself.

"Yeah, thanks."

The bartender pours him a frothy pint and sets it on the counter. "Here you go. Will you gents be good here on your own for ten minutes? I gotta take my break, and Sally called out."

"Go ahead," Brett says, already pulling out his phone.

The moment the bartender disappears in the back, I slap a twenty-dollar bill onto the bar and stand up.

Honestly, I didn't think Brett would fucking skip town after he heard what I did to those Iron Raptors, but that's exactly what the coward did. He handed his bar back to his daddy and left the state. He probably figured the Raptors might come after him after his meddling in my business got their guys killed. But it looks like they've forgotten about him.

I've got a much longer memory.

I approach him quietly, taking in his hunched posture and the way he's glued to his phone. The guy's so wrapped up swiping through his online dating app that he doesn't notice when I stop right behind him. I lean in, my voice low.

"She can do better."

He freezes, his fingers hovering over the picture of a grinning brunette. Slowly, he looks up. The color drains from his face, and fear floods his expression.

A slow grin spreads over my face. Oh, I'm going to enjoy this.

"What the—"

"You knew I'd find you eventually," I interrupt, keeping my voice casual. "But we can talk about that outside. You and me need to have a little chat."

He swallows hard, glancing around the nearly empty bar as if searching for an escape route. The bartender's already in the back, and the other patrons are too busy nursing their drinks and not giving a fuck about a pretty boy who's not from around these parts.

When he doesn't move, I decide to help him out. I'm a nice guy like that. Grabbing the collar of his jacket, I yank him off the stool and onto his feet.

He makes a pitiful yelp.

"Let's go, Brett. You've kept me waiting long enough."

He stumbles as I steer him toward the exit. He tries to resist, but it's pointless. When we reach the door, he makes an attempt to wrench free. He probably thinks he can make a run for it, but I tighten my hold and shove him outside.

The chilly night air wraps around us. The street is quiet, the distant hum of traffic the only sound. A guy and a woman are smoking at the other end of the building.

Brett eyes them desperately.

I smirk. "They look like smart people, don't they? Smart enough not to interfere."

"Listen, man, I didn't—"

I shove him against the brick wall, cutting him off mid-sentence. "I lied. There's nothing left to talk about at all."

His eyes grow wide. "Please, just tell me what you want."

A car pulls up behind us, the trunk popping open.

I lean in. "I've already got it all."

With that, I grab him by the collar, toss him into the waiting trunk, and slam it shut.

5 hours later

"Well, that was fun. Thanks for making the time, guys."

"When you said you wanted a bachelor party the night before your wedding, I didn't think you had this in mind," Rafe drawls, leaning against a wall of our makeshift torture room.

Alessio did a fucking excellent job getting it set up. It's pretty much a replica of his "palace," but a bit cozier and more intimate.

When I invited him to join Rafe and I, he looked flattered. When I told him my plan, I swear, I'd never seen him so excited.

He glances at Rafe from where he's packing up his tools. "I wish I could convince Cosimo to do something like this. Instead, he's got Romolo planning his bachelor trip to Sicily. Rom always gets too many girls and not enough real entertainment."

Rafe narrows his eyes. "Your brother's marrying my sister. Tell him if he gives her chlamydia, I'll cut off his dick, sauté it, and force-feed it to him for breakfast."

Alessio smirks. "I'll relay the message."

I chuckle. These two are something else.

With the Bratva pushed out of the city, the Messeros and the Ferraros are the undisputed rulers of New York, but that doesn't mean the joining of the families has been smooth sailing.

We're still all learning how to work together without wanting to break each other's necks, but we'll get there eventually.

I clap my hands together. "Alright, enough chitchat. We've got to get our guest of honor all packed up and tossed into a river."

For all the tough-guy posturing Brett did back in Darkwater Hollow, he broke swiftly and easily.

But we didn't rush it. We took our time making him pay. I wanted him to feel ten times the fear and terror that Sunshine felt when she was taken by the Raptors.

I wanted him to hurt.

And he did.

Alessio slaps his hand against my shoulder. "Rafe and I have a crew coming to handle it. We figured you did enough cleanup for a lifetime during your few weeks with me."

"Seriously? Fuck, you guys are spoiling me."

Rafe's lips quirk into a rare smile. "That's what friends are for. Now, let's get out of here."

As we step out into the night, the cool air hits my face, and I take a deep breath. The stars twinkle in the clear Kentucky sky, and I feel like everything is exactly where it's supposed to be.

"Gentlemen," Rafe says, brushing off his hands, "I'd say this was a productive evening."

I run my fingers through my hair. "Yeah. Just the kind of send-off I was hoping for."

This was the last loose end I needed to tie up before the wedding.

I'm about to marry the woman I love. Again. And nothing—not even the ghosts of the past—will stand in my way.

BLAKE

The next morning

"Your groom is late," Del announces, glancing up from my phone with a teasing smile. "Or should I say husband? Wait, does he revert back to groom for the day? This is all very confusing."

"It is," Cleo chimes in from her spot on the sofa in the bridal suite. "My oldest sister had a similar situation with her husband. They eloped first, then threw a big wedding later for everyone else."

"Is that like a mob thing? Getting married twice?"

I wince as I fix a pin in my hair. "Del."

She shoots me a sheepish grin. "Sorry, am I not supposed to say that? Still figuring out the etiquette."

"Trust me, the etiquette has been drilled into me since birth, and I still don't follow it," Cleo says with a flick of her hand. "But the two-wedding thing is weird, isn't it? I guess a surprising amount of people don't get it quite right the first time."

Del nods thoughtfully, her gaze drifting back to the phone. "Makes sense. Oh, Nero's texting again... Wow, he's really sorry. He's promising to make it up to you tonight by— Damn, girl, he's got a mouth on him."

I snatch the phone out of her hand. "That's the last time I let you keep an eye on my messages."

Del laughs. "He was just getting to the good part."

I shake my head and glance at myself in the mirror. My heart races as I take it all in. The dress fits like a dream, the fabric cascading down my body like it was custom-made for me.

Oh that's right—it *was*. Because apparently, when you're getting married in front of the New York Cosa Nostra, no expense is spared.

I slide my hands over the luxurious fabric, excitement fluttering in my stomach.

My first wedding was rushed and chaotic. This time, everything is planned, perfect, and deliberate.

But it's not the stunning reception hall, the dinner menu, or even the dress that has me smiling like a fool.

It's the fact that I'm getting to rewrite the story of how I married the man I love.

Cleo stands. "We should get going. They're a half hour away. I'll go get the driver."

"Okay, we'll be right there," I say back.

She tosses me a smile over her shoulder as she steps out of the room.

Over the past few months, Cleo's become more than just a friend—she's become a confidante, someone I can count on. We've even started a tradition of a weekly happy hour, which usually end with us wandering into boutiques and making questionable purchases.

At first, I hesitated to spend Nero's money. But after he insisted—several times—that I wasn't spending enough and even threatened to start shopping for me if I didn't loosen up, I finally relaxed.

Of all the things I've bought, though, my favorite has been the little touches for the beach house. Nero and I escape there whenever we can, and with summer approaching, I can't wait to spend even more time there with him.

Del steps up beside me, placing her empty champagne flute on the vanity. "Ready to go?"

I exhale, trying to calm the butterflies in my stomach. "I think so."

Her eyes meet mine in the mirror, and they're suddenly filled with tears. "I can't believe my best friend is about to walk down the aisle."

"Oh, don't cry," I say, standing up and handing her a tissue.

Del's lips wobble as she takes it and dabs at her eyes. "After everything you two have been through, seeing you here, happy and glowing... It's beautiful. I'm so damn happy for you."

I wrap my arms around her, emotions thickening inside my throat. "I'm so glad you're here with me."

She squeezes me tightly. "If he ever stops making you deliriously happy, I'll kill him myself."

A sob that's more laughter than tears escapes me. "Deal."

She drags her palm over my back. "You're sure, right?"

"More sure than I've ever been about anything." My certainty burns brightly inside my chest. Everything in me says *this man is it*.

Del nods, wiping at her cheek. "Then let's go and get you married."

NERO

I drag my palms over my lips. "I can't believe I'm late for my own wedding."

It's almost noon and we've just landed at JFK.

The plan was to zip it back to New York in Rafe's private jet and be back by three a.m., but the fucking weather kept us grounded until the sun began to rise.

"We'll make it," Rafe says. "I already called your planner, and she said they built in a buffer and can start fifteen minutes late. Tiny's here waiting for us with your suit."

As soon as we get down the steps, we fucking gun it to the Escalade parked on the tarmac.

I change into my suit as we speed down the road toward the church in Westchester where Blake and I are having our wedding. Rafe helps me with my bow tie. Alessio procures a comb from somewhere so I can tame my hair.

"How do I look?" I ask, smoothing my palms over my tuxedo jacket.

"Like a happy bastard who's ready to walk down the aisle," Rafe says.

I grin. "Fuck yeah, I am."

It's been two months since Blake chose me. Two months of pure fucking bliss.

The day after she came back, we took that walk through Central Park, and that's when the idea to give her the wedding she truly deserves struck me.

We'd get married in a beautiful church, surrounded by our family and friends, and she'd finally have the chance to be the beautiful bride she was meant to be.

A week later, while we were browsing through a bookshop in our neighborhood—a place she's fallen in love with—I brought up the subject. The way her face lit up when I suggested it told me everything I needed to know.

And today, we're finally going to make it happen.

I can't wait to paint right over those memories from the Vegas chapel and create something far more meaningful and pure.

I also can't fucking wait to see her reaction when I tell her I bought that bookshop for her.

I catch sight of her just as we pull up outside of the church. We've agreed to walk in together, hand in hand, despite tradition. It's a symbol of the fact that we're committed to facing everything life throws at us—the good and the bad—together.

She's standing there, radiant in her wedding dress, the white fabric flowing around her like she's floating.

She looks like a fucking angel.

Damn it, there's something in my throat.

I step out of the car and jog toward her, my heart racing inside my chest. "Baby, I'm sorry! Got held up."

When I get to her, she smacks me lightly with her bouquet, but she's smiling so hard that she's practically glowing with joy. "Am I going to have to drag *you* down the aisle this time?"

I cup her cheeks and press my lips to hers, and the world around us fades into a blur.

Everything is so right, so damn perfect.

I pull away and grin. "Wherever you go, I go, Sunshine. Always."

BLAKE

2 hours later

"A toast to Mr. and Mrs. De Luca!"

The room erupts in cheers, the sound echoing off the high ceilings of the grand reception hall. I'm nestled in Nero's arms, sitting on one of his thighs. He shamelessly dragged me there as soon as we sat down at our sweetheart table.

"Bacio! Bacio!" The chant starts softly and then builds in strength, the word passing from one guest to another.

I look up at Nero, my heart swelling with emotion. His dark eyes, filled with love and a hint of mischief, meet mine, and a slow smile spreads across his face.

"Bacio!" The chant grows louder.

He cups my face in his hands, his touch gentle yet possessive, as if reminding me that I'm his, and he's mine. Forever.

"Should we give them what they want?" he asks low enough so only I can hear.

"It would be rude to disappoint our guests, especially after we've kept them waiting," I tease.

When our lips meet, it's soft at first, a tender brush of skin that sends warmth flooding through me. But then he deepens the kiss, slipping his tongue inside my mouth, tugging on my bottom lip with his teeth.

The cheers around us intensify, but I barely register them.

How can I, when my husband—the most infamous consigliere in New York and the best man I've ever known—is kissing me like this, with raw abandon?

Pure joy bubbles up inside my chest.

I can't believe how far we've come—how far *I've* come.

When Nero first brought me to this city, I couldn't imagine how loving a man like him would force me to confront my own shadows.

But it's not just his darkness that I've embraced—it's my own as well.

I've chosen this life with him, fully aware of the risks and the dangers.

I've chosen to embrace his world, knowing that it's not always going to be easy or safe.

Because at the end of the day, I don't want easy or safe.

I just want *him*.

DELETED SCENE

Have you already read the deleted scene from When He Desires in which Rowan does a bit of not-so-innocent spying on his new neighbor?

If not, you can scan the QR code to get "The Voyeur":

JOIN GABRIELLE'S GALS

Talk about the Fallen God duet with other readers and get access to exclusive content in Gabrielle's reader group!

Made in the USA
Monee, IL
04 September 2024

65159348R00246